EVERY NOTE PLAYED

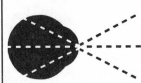

This Large Print Book carries the
Seal of Approval of N.A.V.H.

EVERY NOTE PLAYED

LISA GENOVA

WHEELER PUBLISHING
A part of Gale, a Cengage Company

Farmington Hills, Mich • San Francisco • New York • Waterville, Maine
Meriden, Conn • Mason, Ohio • Chicago

LIBRARY OF CONGRESS CIP DATA ON FILE.
CATALOGUING IN PUBLICATION FOR THIS BOOK
IS AVAILABLE FROM THE LIBRARY OF CONGRESS.

ISBN-13: 978-1-4328-4804-0 (hardcover)

Published in 2018 by arrangement with Scout Press, an imprint of Simon & Schuster, Inc.

Printed in the United States of America
1 2 3 4 5 6 7 22 21 20 19 18

For my parents

In loving memory of
Richard Glatzer
Kevin Gosnell
Chris Connors
Chris Engstrom

Why do you stay in prison when the door is so wide open?

— Rumi

PROLOGUE

Richard is playing the second movement of Schumann's Fantasie in C Major, op. 17, the final piece of his solo recital at the Adrienne Arsht Center in Miami. The concert hall is sold-out, yet the energy here doesn't feel full. This venue doesn't carry the prestige or intimidating pressure of Lincoln Center or the Royal Albert Hall. Maybe that's it. This recital is no big deal.

Without a conductor or orchestra behind him, all audience eyes are on him. He prefers this. He loves possessing their undivided attention, the adrenaline rush of being the star. Playing solo is his version of skydiving.

But this entire night, he's noticed that he's playing on top of the notes, not inside them. His thoughts are drifting elsewhere, to the steak dinner he's going to eat back at the hotel, to the self-conscious examination of his imperfect posture, criticizing the flatness of his performance, aware of himself instead of losing himself.

He's technically flawless. Not many pianists alive today could traverse this demandingly fast and complex section without error. He normally loves playing this piece, especially the bombastic chords of the second movement, its power and grandiosity. Yet, he's not emotionally connected to any of it.

He trusts that most, if not all, of the people in the audience aren't sophisticated enough to hear the difference. Hell, most people have probably never even heard Schumann's Fantasie in C Major, op. 17. It forever breaks his heart that millions listen to Justin Bieber all day long and will live and die without ever hearing Schumann or Liszt or Chopin.

Being married is more than wearing a ring comes to mind. Karina said this to him some years ago. Tonight, he's just wearing the ring. He's mailing it in, and he's not sure why. He'll get through this last piece and have another chance here tomorrow night before flying out to LA. Five more weeks of this tour. It'll be summer by the time he gets home. Good. He loves summer in Boston.

He plays the final phrasing of the third-movement adagio, and the notes are gentle, solemn, hopeful. He's often moved to tears at this point, a permeable conduit for this exquisite expression of tender vulnerability, but tonight he's unaffected. He doesn't feel hopeful.

He plays the final note, and the sound lingers on the stage before dissipating, floating away. A moment of quiet stillness hangs in the hall, and then the bubble is punctured by applause. Richard stands and faces the audience. He hinges at the waist, his fingers grazing the bottom of his tuxedo jacket, bowing. The people rise to their feet. The houselights are up a bit now, and he can see their faces, smiling, enthusiastic, appreciating him, in awe of him. He bows again.

He is loved by everyone.

And no one.

■ ■ ■ ■

ONE YEAR LATER

■ ■ ■ ■

CHAPTER ONE

If Karina had grown up fifteen kilometers down the road in either direction north or south, in Gliwice or Bytom instead of Zabrze, her whole life would be different. Even as a child, she never doubted this. Location matters in destiny as much as it does in real estate.

In Gliwice, it was every girl's birthright to take ballet. The ballet teacher there was Miss Gosia, a former celebrated prima ballerina for the Polish National Ballet prior to Russian martial law, and because of this, it was considered a perk to raise daughters in otherwise grim Gliwice, an unrivaled privilege that every young girl would have access to such an accomplished teacher. These girls grew up wearing leotards and buns and tulle-spun hopes of pirouetting their way out of Gliwice someday. Without knowing specifically what has become of the girls who grew up in Gliwice, she's sure that most, if not all, remain firmly anchored where they began and are now schoolteachers or miners' wives whose unrequited ballerina dreams have been passed on to their daughters, the next generation of Miss Gosia's students.

If Karina had grown up in Gliwice, she would most certainly not have become a ballerina. She has horrible feet, wide, clumsy flippers with virtually no arch, a sturdy frame cast on a long torso and short legs, a body built more for milking cows than for pas de bourrée. She would never have been Miss Gosia's star pupil. Karina's parents would have put an end to bartering valuable coal and eggs for ballet lessons long before pointe shoes. Had her life started in Gliwice, she'd still be in Gliwice.

The girls down the road in Bytom had no ballet lessons. The children in Bytom had the Catholic Church. The boys were groomed for the priesthood, the girls the convent. Karina might have become a nun had she grown up in Bytom. Her parents would've been so proud. Maybe her life would be content and honorable had she chosen God.

But her life was never really a choice. She grew up in Zabrze, and in Zabrze lived Mr. Borowitz, the town's piano teacher. He didn't have a prestigious pedigree like Miss Gosia's or a professional studio. Lessons were taught in his living room, which reeked of cat piss, yellowing books, and cigarettes. But Mr. Borowitz was a fine teacher. He was dedicated, stern but encouraging, and most important, he taught every one of his pupils to play Chopin. In Poland, Chopin is as revered as Pope John Paul II and God. Poland's Holy Trinity.

Karina wasn't born with the lithe body of a ballerina, but she was graced with the strong arms and long fingers of a pianist. She still remembers her first lesson with Mr. Borowitz. She was five. The glossy keys, the immediacy of pleasing sound, the story of the notes told by her fingers. She took to it instantly. Unlike most children, she never had to be ordered to practice. Quite the opposite, she had to be told to stop. *Stop playing, and do your homework. Stop playing, and set the dinner table. Stop playing, it's time for bed.* She couldn't resist playing. She still can't.

Ultimately, piano became her ticket out of oppressive Poland, to Curtis and America and everything after. *Everything* after. That single decision — to learn piano — set everything that was to follow in motion, the ball in her life's Rube Goldberg machine.

17

She wouldn't be here, right now, attending Hannah Chu's graduation party, had she never played piano.

She parks her Honda behind a Mercedes, the last in a conga line of cars along the side of the road at least three blocks from Hannah's house, assuming this is the closest she'll get. She checks the clock on the dash. She's a half hour late. Good. She'll make a brief appearance, offer her congratulations, and leave.

Her heels click against the street as she walks, a human metronome, and her thoughts continue in pace with this rhythm. Without piano, she would never have met Richard. What would her life be like had she never met him?

How many hours has she spent indulging in this fantasy? If added up, the hours would accumulate into days and weeks, possibly more. More time wasted. What could've been. What will never be.

Maybe she would've been satisfied had she never left her home country to pursue piano. She'd still be living with her parents, sleeping in her childhood bedroom. Or she'd be married to a boring man from Zabrze, a coal miner who earns a hard but respectable living, and she'd be a home-maker, raising their five children. Both

18

wretched scenarios appeal to her now for a commonality she hates to acknowledge: a lack of loneliness.

Or what if she had attended Eastman instead of Curtis? She almost did. That single, arbitrary choice. She would never have met Richard. She would never have taken a step back, assuming with the arrogant and immortal optimism of a twenty-five-year-old that she'd have another chance, that the Wheel of Fortune's spin would once again tick to a stop with its almighty arrow pointing directly at her. She'd waited years for another turn. Sometimes life gives you only one.

But then, if she'd never met Richard, their daughter, Grace, wouldn't be here. Karina imagines an alternative reality in which her only daughter was never conceived and catches herself enjoying the variation almost to the point of wishing for it. She scolds herself, ashamed for allowing such a horrible thought. She loves Grace more than anything else. But the truth is, having Grace was another critical, fork-in-the-road, Gliwice-versus-Bytom-versus-Zabrze moment. *Left* brought Grace and tied Karina to Richard, the rope tight around her neck like a leash or a noose, depending on the day, for the next seventeen years. *Right* was the path not chosen. Who knows where that might've led?

Regret shadows her every step, a dog at her heels, as she now follows the winding stone path into the Chu family's backyard. Hannah was accepted to Notre Dame, her first choice. Another piano student off to college. Hannah won't continue with piano there. Like most of Karina's students, Hannah took lessons because she wanted to add "plays piano" to her college application. The parents have the same motive, often exponentially more intense and unapologetic. So Hannah went through the motions, and their weekly half hour together was a soulless chore for both student and teacher.

A rare few of Karina's students authentically like playing, and a couple even have talent and potential, but none of them love it enough to pursue it. You have to love it. She can't blame them. These kids are all overscheduled, stressed-out, and too focused on getting into "the best" college to allow the nourishment passion needs to grow. A flower doesn't blossom from a seed without the persistent love of sun and water.

But Hannah isn't just one of Karina's piano students. Hannah was Grace's closest friend from the age of six through middle school. Playdates, sleepovers, Girl Scouts,

soccer, trips to the mall and the movies —
for most of Grace's childhood, Hannah was
like a younger sister. When Grace moved up
to the high school and Hannah remained in
middle school, the girls migrated naturally
into older and younger social circles. There
was never a falling-out. Instead, the friends
endured a passive drifting on calm currents
to separate but neighboring islands. They
visited from time to time.

Hannah's graduation milestone shouldn't
mean much to Karina, but it feels monumental, as if she's sustaining a bigger loss
than another matriculated piano student. It
trips the switch of memories from this time
last year, and it's the end of Grace's childhood all over again. Karina leaves her card
for Hannah on the gift table and sighs.

Even though Hannah's at the far end of
the expansive backyard, Karina spots her
straightaway, standing on the edge of the
diving board, laughing, a line of wet girls
and boys behind her, mostly boys in the
pool, cheering her name, goading her to do
something. Karina waits to see what it will
be. Hannah launches into the air and can-
nonballs into the water, splashing the
parents gathered near the pool. The parents
complain, wiping water from their arms and
faces, but they're smiling. It's a hot day,

and the momentary spray probably felt refreshing. Karina notices Hannah's mom, Pam, among them.

Now that Hannah is moving to Indiana, Karina assumes she won't see Pam at all anymore. They stopped their Thursday-night wine dates some time ago, not long after Grace started high school. Over the past couple of years, their friendship dwindled to the handful of unfulfilling moments before or after Hannah's weekly piano lesson. Tasked with shuttling her three kids to and from a dizzying schedule of extracurricular activities all over town, Pam was often too rushed to even come inside and waited for Hannah in her running car. Karina waved to her from the front door every Tuesday at 5:30 as Pam pulled away.

Karina almost didn't come today. She feels self-conscious about showing up alone. Naturally introverted, she'd been extremely private about her marriage and even more shut-in about her divorce. Assuming Richard didn't air their dirty laundry either, and that's a safe bet, no one knows the details. So the gossip mill scripted the drama it wasn't supplied. Someone has to be right, and someone has to be wrong. Based on the hushed stares, vanished chitchat, and pulled plastic smiles, Karina knows how she's been cast.

The women in particular sympathize with him. Of course they do. They paint him as a sainted celebrity. He deserves to be with someone more elegant, someone who appreciates how extraordinary he is, someone more his equal. They assume she's jealous of his accomplishments, resentful of his acclaim, bitter about his fame. She's nothing but a rinky-dink suburban piano teacher instructing disinterested sixteen-year-olds on how to play Chopin. She clearly doesn't have the self-esteem to be the wife of such a great man.

They don't know. They don't know a damn thing.

Grace just finished her freshman year at the University of Chicago. Karina had anticipated that Grace would be home for the summer by now and would be at Hannah's party, but Grace decided to stay on campus through the summer, interning on a project with her math professor. Something about statistics. Karina's proud of her daughter for being selected for the internship and thinks it's a great opportunity, and yet, there's that pang in Karina's stomach, the familiar letdown. Grace could've chosen to come home, to spend the summer with her mother, but she didn't. Karina knows it's ridiculous to feel slighted, forsaken even, but her emotions sit on the throne of her intellect. This is how she's built, and like any castle, her foundational stones aren't easily rearranged.

Her divorce became absolute in September of Grace's senior year, and exactly one year later, Grace moved a thousand miles away. First Richard left. Then Grace. Karina wonders when she'll get used to the silence in her home, the emptiness, the memories that hang in each room as real as the artwork on the walls. She misses her daughter's voice chatting on the phone; her giggling girlfriends; her shoes in every room; her hair elastics, towels, and clothes on the floor; the lights left on. She misses her daughter.

She does not miss Richard. When he moved out, his absence felt more like a new presence than a subtraction. The sweet calm that took up residence after he left filled more space than his human form and colossal ego ever did. She did not miss him then or now.

But going to these kinds of family events alone, without a husband, tilts her off-balance as if she were one cheek atop a two-legged stool. So in that sense, she misses him. For the stability. She's forty-five and divorced. Single. In Poland, she'd be considered a disgrace. But she's been in America now for over half her life. Her situation is common in this secular culture and imposes no shame. Yet, she feels ashamed. You can take the girl out of Poland, but you can't take Poland out of the girl.

Not recognizing any of the other parents, she takes a deep breath and begins the long, awkward walk alone over to Pam. Karina spent an absurdly long time getting ready for this party. Which dress, which shoes, which earrings? She blew out her hair. She even got a manicure yesterday. For what? It's not as if she's trying to impress Hannah or Pam or any of the parents. And it's not as if there will be any single men here, not that she's looking for a man anyway.

She knows why. She'll be damned if anyone here looks at her and thinks, *Poor Karina. Her life's a mess, and she looks it, too.* The other reason is Richard. Pam and Scott Chu are his friends, too. Richard was probably invited. She could've asked Pam if Richard was on the guest list — not that it mattered, just to be forewarned — but she chickened out.

So there it is, the stomach-turning possibility that he might be here, and the even more putrid thought that he might show up with the latest skinny little twentysomething tart hanging on his arm and every self-important word. Karina rubs her lips together, making sure her lipstick hasn't clumped.

Her eyes poke around the yard. He's not standing with Pam and the cluster of parents by the pool house. Karina scans the pool, the grilling island, the lawn. She doesn't see him.

She arrives at the pool house and inserts herself into the circle of Pam and Scott and other parents. Their voices instantly drop, their eyes conspiring. Time pauses.

"Hey, what's going on?" Karina asks.

The circle looks to Pam.

"Um . . ." Pam hesitates. "We were just talking about Richard."

"Oh?" Karina waits, her heart bracing for something humiliating. No one says a word. "What about him?"

"He canceled his tour."

"Oh." This isn't earth-shattering news. He's canceled gigs and touring dates before. Once, he couldn't stand the conductor and refused to set foot onstage with him. Another time, Richard had to be replaced last minute because he got drunk at an airport bar and missed his flight. She wonders what reason he has this time. But Pam and Scott and the others stare at her with grave expressions, as if she should have something more compassionate to say on the subject.

Her stomach floods with emotion, her inner streets crowding fast as a fervent protest stands upon its soapbox in her center, outraged that she has to deal with this, that Pam especially can't be more sensitive to her. Richard's canceled tour isn't her concern. She divorced him. His life isn't her problem anymore.

"You really don't know?" asks Pam.

They all wait for her answer, lips shut, bodies still, an audience engrossed in watching a play.

"What? What, is he dying or something?"

A nervous half-laugh escapes her, and the sound finds no harmony. She searches the circle of parents for connection, even if the comment was slightly inappropriate, for someone to forgive her a bit of dark humor. But everyone either looks horrified or away. Everyone but Pam. Her eyes betray a reluctant nod.

"Karina, he has ALS."

CHAPTER TWO

Richard lies in bed awake, satisfied by a full night's sleep, his eyes alert and unblinking, staring vaguely at a curled slice of peeling paint on the vaulted ceiling directly above him. He can feel it coming, an invisible presence creeping, like ions charged and buzzing in the air before an approaching electrical storm, and all he can do is lie still and wait for it to pass through him.

He's in his own bedroom when he should be waking up in the Mandarin Oriental in New York City. He was supposed to play a solo recital at David Geffen Hall at Lincoln Center last night. He loves Lincoln Center. The almost-three-thousand-seat venue had been sold-out for months. If he were at the Mandarin, he'd be about ready to order breakfast. Possibly for two.

But he's not at the Mandarin in New York, and he's not in the company of a lovely woman. He's alone in his bed in his condo on Commonwealth Avenue in Boston. And even though he's hungry, he waits.

Trevor, his agent, sent out a press release canceling his tour, claiming tendinitis. Richard can't understand the point of publicizing this misleading information. They bite the bullet now or they bite the bullet later. Either way, the barrel of the gun stays firmly pointed at Richard's head. True, he first assumed he was dealing with tendinitis, a frustratingly inconvenient but common injury that would heal with rest and physical therapy. He'd been so frustrated with taking even a few weeks away from the piano, worried about what it would do to his playing. That was seven months and a lifetime ago. What he wouldn't give to have tendinitis.

It's possible his agent is still in denial. Richard is scheduled to play with the Chicago Symphony Orchestra in the fall. Trevor hasn't canceled this gig yet, just in case Richard is somehow better by then. Richard gets it. Even now, six months after his diagnosis, he still can't fully wrap his mind around what he has, what's going to happen. Many times in any given day, when he's reading or drinking a cup of coffee, he's symptom-free. He'll feel totally normal, and he'll either forget that the past several months have happened, or a confident rebellion rises.

The neurologist was wrong. It's a virus. A pinched nerve. Lyme disease. Tendinitis. A temporary problem, and now it's resolved. Nothing's wrong.

And then his right hand won't keep time when playing Rachmaninoff's Prelude in G-sharp Minor, chasing and not catching the tempo. Or he'll drop his half-full cup of coffee because it's too heavy. Or he doesn't have the strength to manage the fingernail clipper. He looks down at the grotesquely long fingernails of his left hand, the neatly trimmed nails of his right.

This is not a temporary problem.

He will not be playing in Chicago in the fall.

He's naked, has always slept in the nude. All those years next to Karina in her high-necked flannel pajamas and kneesocks. He tries to picture her naked but can only imagine the other women. This would normally arouse him, and he'd welcome the pleasant distraction of masturbation right now, but the dreadful anticipation of what's coming has him anxious, and his dick lies limp and still like the rest of him.

His body heat has created a cozy cocoon beneath the covers, a stark contrast to the uninviting temperature of his bedroom. He braces for the shocking sharpness of cold air against his skin as he whips the sheet and comforter off his body. He wants to see it when it comes.

His eyes scrutinize the length of his arms, each knuckle of each finger, especially the index and middle fingers of his right hand. He evaluates his chest and stomach for irregularities amid the rise and fall of his breathing. He drops his gaze to his legs, his toes; his senses heightened and ready, a hunter scanning for a flash of white fur.

He waits, his body a pot of water on the stove, the setting dialed to high. It's only a matter of time. A watched pot will eventually boil. Of course, he hopes it won't come. But also, perversely, he lies there welcoming it, its familiarity dancing through his body.

The first bubble breaks the surface, a pop in his left calf. It vibrates there for a few seconds, the opening act, then jumps to his right quadriceps, just above the knee. Then the pad at the base of his right thumb flickers. Over and over and over.

He can't bear to witness this one in particular, this spasm in his dominant thumb, yet he cannot look away. He silently pleads with it, this microscopic enemy within. By sheer coincidence, for he knows he possesses no power over its intentions, it leaves his hand, tunneling in the space between his skin and fascia like a mouse burrowing within the walls of a house, and invades his right biceps next. Then his bottom lip. These rapid, fluttering seizures ripple from one part of his body to another in rapid succession, a roiling boil.

Sometimes, the twitching lingers in one place. Yesterday, it got stuck in a quarter-size segment of his right triceps, contracting in intermittent, repetitive pulses for several hours. It set up shop there, obsessed there, fell in love and couldn't move on, and he panicked that it would never stop.

Yet he knows with absolute certainty that it will stop. At some point, the twitching in every single muscle group — in his arms, his legs, his mouth, his diaphragm — will stop forever, and so he should embrace the twitching. Be grateful for it. The twitching means his muscles are still there, still capable of responding.

For now.

His motor neurons are being poisoned by a cocktail of toxins, the recipe unknown to his doctor and every scientist on the planet, and his entire motor neuron system is in a death spiral. His neurons are dying, and the muscles they feed are literally starving for input. Every twitch is a muscle stammering, gasping, begging to be saved.

They can't be saved.

But they aren't dead yet. Like the fuel light in his car that alerts him when he's low on gas, these fasciculations are an early-warning system. As he lies naked and cold on his bed, he starts doing math. Assuming he has about two gallons left in the tank when his fuel light is triggered and that his BMW conservatively does twenty-two miles per gallon in the city, he could go forty-four more miles before running out of gas. He imagines this scenario. The last drop of gas used. The engine gears ground to a halt. Seized. The car stopped. Dead.

The right side of his bottom lip twitches. Without understanding the biology, he wonders how much muscle fuel remains in his body and wishes the twitching could be enumerated.

How many miles does he have left?

CHAPTER THREE

As Karina walks a little over five blocks to Commonwealth Avenue, she's barely aware of her surroundings — sparrows nibbling on crumbs of a dropped muffin beneath a park bench; a fierce dragon tattoo covering the bare chest of a skateboarder; the aggressive whir of the board's wheels as he whizzes by her; a young Asian couple strolling hip to hip, hand in hand; a breeze perfumed with cigarette smoke; a baby wailing in a stroller; a dog barking; the alternating choreography of cars and pedestrians at every intersection. Instead, her attention is held inward.

Her heart races faster than required for her walking pace, making her anxious. Or maybe, likely, she was anxious first, and her heart rate responded. She speeds up in an effort to synchronize her external action with her inner physiology, which only makes her feel as if she were rushing, late. She

checks her watch, which is utterly unnecessary. She can't be early or late when he
doesn't know she's coming.

She's worked up a sweat. Stopped at the
next corner, waiting for a WALK signal, she
pulls a tissue from her purse, reaches under
her shirt, and blots her armpits. She digs
around for another tissue but can't find one.
She wipes her forehead and nose with her
hands.

She arrives at Richard's address and stops
at the base of the stairs, looking up to the
fourth-floor windows. Behind her, the spires
of Trinity Church and the sheer vertical
glass of the John Hancock building rise
above the rooftops of the brownstones on
the other side of Comm Ave. He has a lovely
view.

This street in the Back Bay is especially
posh, housing Boston's Brahmins, cousins
to their neighbors on Beacon Hill. Richard
lives on the same block as many of Boston's
elegant and elite — the president of BioGO,
a Massachusetts General Hospital surgeon,
the fourth-generation owner of a two-
hundred-year-old art gallery on Newbury
Street. Richard makes decent money, excep-
tional for a pianist, but this address is way
out of his league, probably his version of a
midlife crisis, his shiny red Porsche. He

must be mortgaged to the hilt.

She hasn't seen him since Grace's high school graduation, over a year ago now. And she's never been here. Well, she's driven by twice before, both times at night, both times ostensibly to avoid traffic, purposefully rerouting from her preferred course home from downtown Boston, slowing to a crawl just long enough to avoid instigating honks from behind her, barely long enough to capture a quick blur of high ceilings and a nonspecific golden glow of a home inhabited.

She resents that Richard got to be the one to move out, to start over, fresh in a new place. Memories of him haunt her in every room of their once-shared home, the rare good as unsettling as the common bad. She replaced their mattress and their dinnerware. She removed their framed wedding picture from the living-room wall and hung a pretty mirror there instead. It doesn't matter. She's exactly where he left her, still living in their house, his energetic impression left behind like a red-wine stain on a white blouse. Even washed a thousand times, that brown spot is never coming out.

She could move, especially now that Grace has gone off to college. But where would she go? And do what? Her stubbornness, that impenetrable bedrock of her personality, refuses to give these questions actual consideration beyond calling them nonsense. So she stays put, frozen in the three-bedroom colonial museum of her devastated marriage.

Grace already had her license when Karina and Richard separated, so she was able to drive herself over to her father's "house." His bachelor pad. Karina walks up the stairs to the front door of his brownstone, and her mouth goes sour. At the top step, her stomach matches the taste in her mouth, and the word *sicken* grabs the microphone of her inner monologue. She feels sick. But she's not sick, she reminds herself. Richard is.

The sour in her stomach turns, fermenting. Why is she here? To say or do what? Offer pity, sympathy, help? To see how bad off he is with her own eyes, the same reason drivers rubberneck when passing the site of an accident — to get a good look at the wreckage before moving along?

What will he look like? She has no reference point other than Stephen Hawking. A hand puppet with no hand in the body, paralyzed, emaciated, unable to breathe without a machine, his limbs, torso, and head positioned in a wheelchair like a little girl's floppy, cotton-limbed rag doll, his voice computer generated. Is that what Richard will look like?

He might not even be home. Maybe he's in a hospital. She should've called first. Calling somehow seemed scarier than drumming up the nerve to show up at his front door unannounced. Part of her believes that she caused his illness, even though she knows that such thinking is narcissistically absurd. How many times has she wished him dead? Now he's dying, and she's a despicable, hellbound, horrible woman for ever wishing such a thing, and worse, for having derived sick pleasure from it.

She stands before the doorbell, torn between following through and turning around, passionate counterpoints creating a quagmire of indecision, pushing and pulling her from within. If she were the gambling kind, she'd put her money on leaving. She breaks through her inertia and rings the bell, surprising herself.

"Hello?" asks Richard's voice over the intercom speaker.

Karina's heart beats in her tight, acidic throat. "It's Karina."

She tucks her hair behind her ears and pulls at her bra strap, which is sticking uncomfortably to her sweaty body. She waits for him to buzz her in, but nothing happens. Opaque white curtains cover the windows in the door, making it impossible to see if anyone is coming. Then she hears footsteps. The door opens.

Richard says nothing. She waits for him to look stunned that she's here, but that doesn't happen. Instead his face is motionless but for his eyes, which hint at a smile, not exactly happy to see her, but satisfied, right about something, and her heart in her throat already knows that this visit was a disastrous idea. He continues to say nothing and she says nothing, and this nonverbal game of chicken probably takes up two seconds, but it stretches out in agonizing slow motion beyond the boundaries of space and time.

"I should've called."

"Come on in."

As she follows him up the three flights, she studies his footing, assured and steady and normal. His left hand slides along the banister, and although it never loses contact, the banister doesn't appear to be assisting him. It's not a handicapped railing. From behind, he looks perfectly healthy.

It was a rumor.

She is a fool.

Inside his condo, he leads her to the

kitchen, dark wood and black counters and stainless steel, modern and masculine. He offers her a seat on a stool at the island, overlooking the living room — his Steinway grand, a brown leather couch, the Oriental carpet from their den, a laptop computer on a desk by the window, a bookcase — sparse and tidy and singularly focused. Very Richard.

An army of at least two dozen bottles of wine stands at attention on the kitchen counter, an uncorked neck and a puddle of red at the bottom of a goblet in front of him. He loves wine, likes to fancy himself a connoisseur, but typically indulges in a special selection only after a performance or in celebration of an achievement or a holiday or at least with dinner. It's not even noon on a Wednesday.

"These were from the cellar. This 2000 Château Mouton Rothschild is exquisite." He pulls a glass from a cabinet. "Join me?"

"No, thanks."

"This" — he waves his hand back and forth in the air between them — "unexpected visit or whatever it is needs alcohol, don't you think?"

"Should you be drinking so much?"

He laughs. "I'm not tackling all of these

today. Tomorrow and tomorrow and tomorrow."

He grabs a beautiful black bottle with a
golden sheep embossed on it, already open,
and pours her a generous glass, ignoring
her answer. She sips, then smiles out of
obligation, unimpressed.

He laughs again. "You still have the dis-
criminating palette of a farm animal."

It's true. She can't discern the difference
between an expensive bottle of Mouton and
a jug of Gallo, nor does she care, and both
traits have always driven Richard mad. And
true to patronizing form, he's essentially
just called her a stupid pig. Karina clenches
her teeth, biting back the comment that will
leave her mouth if she opens it and the urge
to throw $100 worth of his precious wine in
his face.

He swirls, smells, sips, closes his eyes,
waits, swallows, and licks his lips. He opens
his eyes and mouth and looks at her as if
he's just had an orgasm or seen God.

"How can you not appreciate this? The
timing is perfect. Taste it again. Smell the
cherries?"

She tries another sip. It's okay. She doesn't
smell cherries. "I can't remember the last
time we shared a bottle of wine."

"Four years ago, November. I was just

41

home from Japan, wrecked from the flights. You made *golabki,* and we drank a bottle of Châteaux Margaux."

She stares at him, surprised and intrigued. She has no memory of this evening, so readily and fondly retrieved by Richard, and wonders if it simply wasn't significant enough to her to hold on to or if the memory faded, crowded out by too many other experiences that didn't jibe. Funny how the story of their lives can be an entirely different genre depending on the narrator.

They lock eyes. His look a bit older than she remembers. Or not older. Sadder. And his face looks more defined. Although he's always been thin, he's definitely lost weight. And he's grown a beard.

"I see you've stopped shaving."

"Trying something new. You like it?"

"No."

He grins and takes another sip of wine. He taps the rim of his glass with his finger and says nothing, and she can't figure out whether he's deciding which of her buttons to push or showing restraint. Restraint would be new.

"So you canceled your tour."

"How did you hear?"

"The *Globe* said it was tendinitis."

"So is that why you're here, to check on

my tendinitis?"

He's baiting her, asking her to spell it out, to say the three letters, and her apprehensive heart beats too fast again. She brings the goblet to her lips, avoiding his question and her answer, swallowing a mouthful of wine along with her real reason for being here.

"I used to think you sometimes canceled for the attention."

"Karina, I'm abandoning several thousand people over the next three weeks who were all planning on spending an entire evening paying attention to me. Canceling is the opposite of calling attention."

Again, they lock eyes, and the energy exchanged is somewhere between an intimate connection and a showdown.

"Of course, it did get your attention." He smiles.

He sticks his nose into his goblet and inhales, then drains the remaining gulp. He looks over the bottles on the counter and pulls a soldier from the back row. He fits the hood of the opener over the top of the neck and begins to twist, but he keeps losing his grip before making any progress. He lifts the opener off the bottle and examines the top, rubbing it with his finger. He wipes his hand on his pants, as if it had been wet.

"These hard-wax-capsule corks are a bitch

to open."

He repositions the opener and tries and tries, but his fingers keep slipping and have no command over the twisting mechanism. Without thinking much of it, she's about to offer to do it for him when he stops and hurls the bottle opener across the room. Karina ducks reflexively, even though she was never in danger from the object's trajectory.

"There it is," he accuses her. "That's what you came to see, yes?"

"I don't know. I didn't know."

"You happy now?"

"No."

"That's why you came here. To see me humiliated like this."

"No."

"I can't play anymore, not well enough, and I won't be able to ever again. That's why my tour was canceled, Karina. Is that what you wanted to hear?"

"No."

She stares into his eyes, and standing squarely in the windows of his rage is pure terror.

"Then why are you here?"

"I thought it was the right thing to do."

"Look at you, suddenly a model Catholic, concerned about right and wrong. With all due respect, my dear, you wouldn't know right from wrong if it fucked you up the ass."

She shakes her head, sickened by him, disgusted with herself for not knowing better. She stands. "I didn't come here to be abused by you."

"Oh, there you go, carting out that word. No one's abusing you. Stop using that word. You've brainwashed Grace. This is why she won't talk to me."

"Don't blame me for that. If she's not talking to you, maybe it's because you're a prick."

"Or maybe it's because her mother is a vindictive bitch."

Karina takes the bottle he couldn't open by the neck and smashes it against the edge of the counter. She drops the broken bottleneck and steps away from the expanding puddle of wine on the floor.

"That one smells like cherries," she says, her voice shaking.

"Leave. Right now."

"I'm sorry I ever came here."

She slams the door behind her and runs down the three flights as if she were being chased. She had such good intentions. How did that go so wrong?

How did it all go so wrong?

Rage and grief assault her from all sides, and her legs suddenly feel loosened and drained, powerless to continue. She sits on the top step of the front stoop, facing the beautiful view —. the joggers on Comm Ave., the pigeons in the park, the spires of Trinity Church, and the blue glass of the Hancock — not caring who sees or hears her, and sobs.

CHAPTER FOUR

Richard sits down at his piano for the first time in three weeks, since August 17, the day his right index finger gave up the fight, the last of his right-handed fingers to fall deaf to his wishes. He'd been testing it daily. On August 16, he could tap his right index finger ever so slightly. He clung to this accomplishment, pathetically celebrating this movement that required massive mental and physical effort and that looked more like a feeble tremor than a tap. He placed his entire life's hope on that finger, which eight months ago could dance across the keys of the most complex, athletic pieces without missing a beat, striking each note with just the right amount of force.

FORTISSIMO!

Diminuendo.

His index finger, every finger of his right hand, a finely calibrated instrument. If he made a single mistake while rehearsing, if one of his fingers lacked confidence, strength, or memory and stumbled, he'd stop instantly and start the piece over from the beginning. There was never room for error. No excuse for his fingers.

Eight months ago, his right hand held five of the finest fingers in the world. Today, his entire right arm and hand are paralyzed. Dead to him, as if they already belong to a corpse.

He picks up his lifeless hand with his left and places it on the keys, setting his right thumb onto middle C, pinkie on G. He feels the cool sleekness of the keys, and the touch is sensual, seductive. The keys want to be caressed, the relationship ready and available to him, but he can't respond, and this is suddenly the cruelest moment of his life.

He stares in horror at his dead hand on the beautiful keys. It's not simply that his hand is motionless that makes it appear dead. There's no curl to his fingers. His entire hand is too straight, too flat, devoid of tone, personality, possibility. It's atrophied, flaccid, impotent. It appears fake, like a Halloween costume, a Hollywood prop, a wax prosthetic. It can't belong to him.

The air in the room thickens, too solid to breathe, and he can't seem to remember how to inhale. A wave of panic slips through him. He places his left fingers on the keys, arm extended, wrist up, fingers curled, loving the keys they touch, and he inhales sharply. He heaves air through his lungs as if running for his life while his desperate eyes search the keys and his two hands for what to do. What the hell can he do?

He begins to play Brahms I, actual notes with only his left hand, the right-hand notes with his mind's ear. He played this fifty-minute concerto with the Boston Symphony Orchestra at Tanglewood last summer. Eighty-seven pages memorized and played as near to perfection as anyone ever has. Some nights the music is well played and applauded, and other nights, the music is transcendent. He lives for those transcendent nights.

That evening on the lawn, the entire orchestra was more than simply a cover band for Brahms. They were an open conduit, breathing life into the music, and he felt that ecstatic, energetic connection between his soul, the souls of the other musicians, the souls of the audience on the lawn, and the soul of the notes. He's never been able to adequately describe the equation or the experience of this alchemy. Using language to convey the magic of Brahms would be like using a wooden classroom ruler to measure the speed of light.

While playing solely with his left hand, he closes his eyes to lose sight of his immovable corpse hand, and this cut-and-paste, mind-body performance is satisfying to him for a bit. But then he's rocking his torso back and forth, an unshakable habit criticized by many of his teachers as being either distracting or indulgent, and accidently knocks his right hand off its position on the keys. His entire dead arm dangles from his shoulder like a dropped anchor, heavy and painful, likely dislocated again.

He uses it. The pain in Brahms I, the gravitas, the longing, the loss, the battle in the stormy first movement, like walking into war. The haunting solo played by his left hand. The lonely memory of the melody playing in his mind. The agony in his shoulder. The loss of his right hand.

He dares to wonder what part of himself he'll lose next. His gut and his mind agree.

Your other hand.

He wails aloud and strikes the keys harder with his left hand while he still can. He loses the sound of the melody in his memory and can now hear only what is real, vibrations produced by hammers and felt and strings and vocal cords, and the absence of the right-handed notes feels like a death, a loss of true love, the bitter end of a relationship, a divorce.

It feels just like his divorce. He lifts his left hand high above the keys and hesitates, stopping the piece just before the crescendo. of the first movement, his heart pounding in his shoulder and in the sudden silence, the unfinished song, his interrupted life. He curls his left hand into a fist and pounds the keys as hard as he can as if in a street fight as he weeps, betrayed and heartbroken all over again.

CHAPTER FIVE

It's Family Weekend at the University of Chicago. Grace insisted that it wasn't necessary for Karina to come. Karina already knew what the campus looked like, Grace argued. They'd bought sweatshirts and T-shirts and bumper stickers and coffee mugs from the campus store last year. Karina sees Grace's dorm room and roommate and gets caught up every Sunday when Grace FaceTimes her. Karina thought Grace seemed a little too invested in her opposition to the visit, as if protecting her privacy or independence or some big secret. But Karina could not be dissuaded. The airfare was reasonable, and she was missing her daughter.

They're at Common Grounds, a homey hipster campus coffee shop, and the big secret is sitting next to Grace, one hand on his triple-shot latte, the other on Grace's thigh. Matt has overly styled brown hair, a shadow of a beard, and blue eyes that become amused whenever he talks. He's clearly crazy about Grace. And although she's trying to play it cool in front of her mother, Grace is crazy about him, too.

"So Grace says you're an amazing pianist," says Matt.

Karina holds her pumpkin-spice latte midway between her lips and the table, suddenly unsure of which way she was going with it. She's caught surprised, moved that Grace would describe her this way. Brag even. Richard is the amazing pianist, not her. Or maybe Matt simply has them confused. Or he's kissing up to his girlfriend's mother.

She sets her cup on the table. "No, that's her father. I'm just a piano teacher."

"She's amazing," says Grace, assertively correcting her mother. "But she gave up her career to stay home with me. This is why I'm never getting pregnant. I'm not wasting my education on raising some kid."

"Some bratty kid," says Matt, smiling.

Grace playfully shoves his arm, squeezing his biceps before letting go. Karina sips her latte and licks the foam from her lips as she watches them. They're definitely having sex.

Karina and Grace are close, but they don't discuss such things, a trait seemingly passed

53

down from Karina's mother, like her green eyes and proclivity for waking before dawn no matter how exhausted she was. Karina had exactly one conversation with her mother about sex. She was twelve and forgets the wording of what she asked, but she remembers her mother's response as she washed dishes at the sink, her back to Karina: "Sex is how babies are made. It's a sacred act between husbands and wives. Now go bring the towels in off the line." End of story, forever.

Karina got little more from the nuns and her friends. She remembers feeling horrified and embarrassed when Zofia told her that Natalia was giving boys blow jobs under the bleachers in the gymnasium, mostly because Karina wasn't quite sure what a blow job was and didn't have the courage to ask. Whatever it was, she knew for sure that Natalia was going to hell for it.

When Karina was sixteen, her boisterous and beautiful friend, Martyna, was sent away to live with an aunt. She returned nine months later, her disposition subdued, her eyes averting others, pointing to her shoes. Everyone in town gossiped about her. Martyna was damaged goods. No one would ever marry her now. Such a shame.

Karina had imagined the baby Martyna

left behind, a daughter or son she would never know, and the spinster's life ahead of her. Right then, she'd made a promise to herself. She would not end up ruined like Martyna or imprisoned like her mother, chained to the kitchen, cooking and cleaning day and night for decades, raising five children. Karina would not lose control of her life.

When Grace was a freshman in high school, they had "the talk." Karina was determined to make it more informative than the "wisdom" her mother had imparted to her and consciously didn't include any Catholic shame or misogynistic mythology. *No sex before marriage, no birth control — those aren't God's rules, honey. Those rules were made by men.* They were in the car, on their way to one of Grace's soccer games, more side by side than face-to-face, but a big improvement over Karina's mother's back side. Karina's speech included information about condoms and the pill, STDs and pregnancy, intimacy and love.

Sex isn't a sin. But you have to protect yourself. Birth control is the woman's responsibility. She winces now as the words play in her mind, just as she did when she said them aloud to Grace in the car, reliving the guilt. Using birth control isn't a sin. She did what she had to do.

Thou shalt not lie.

Lying is a sin.

If Grace remembered one thing from that conversation, Karina always hoped it was the admonition *Whatever you do, don't get pregnant.* She's sure she repeated it several times, and although she could only glance at the side of Grace's face while driving, Karina could sense Grace's embarrassment and eye rolling.

She looks at Grace straight on now, and her face is self-assured and radiant. She's in control of her life. Karina's glad to see the message was received, but she didn't mean *ever.* Did she somehow communicate that as well?

"Well, I am pretty awesome. So it was all worth it, right, Mom?"

"Yes, honey."

"Do you teach at a school?" asks Matt.

"No, at home. In my living room."

"Oh."

"Really, she's at least as good as my dad, but he gets all the glory."

"Have you talked with your father?" asks Karina.

"Not recently. Why?"

Karina hasn't heard anything about Richard since that horrible day in July when she went to see him. Although he couldn't open the wine bottle, she's still not convinced he really has ALS. He probably has something like carpal tunnel or tendinitis, injuries common to every pianist at some point, pesky but ultimately benign. If Richard really has ALS, he'd tell his only daughter, wouldn't he?

"I think he's supposed to play here in Chicago next month."

"I don't know anything about it." Grace shrugs her right shoulder. "Why are you still keeping track of where he's going to be? You need to get your own life, Mom."

Karina feels her cheeks flush. Grace's quick comment is too sharp, an insulting slap, and it feels cruel, especially in front of Matt, someone who doesn't know Karina's complicated history. But she believes Grace's insensitivity was unintentional and swallows the urge to defend herself. She and Grace have had many heart-to-hearts about this over the past year. Now that Grace is in college, Karina could move. She could live in New York or New Orleans or Paris. She could give up teaching and play again. She could reinvent her life. Or at least track down the one she abandoned. She could do anything. Or at least something.

"Where's *your* musical talent?" Matt asks Grace.

"I'm, like, the best karaoke singer ever."

"The best worst. You sure you weren't adopted?"

"I look just like her."

"Or maybe you were dropped on your head?"

"That would explain my taste in men."

This time Matt shoves Grace's arm, and Grace giggles. *Men,* not *boys.* When did her little girl become a young woman?

It occurs to her that Grace is the same age Karina was when she met Richard. They were in Sherman Leiper's Technique class together. She knew nothing about Richard except that he seemed awkward and intensely driven. She could feel him staring at her in class, too shy to talk, for almost an entire semester. Then one day, he did.

They were at a keg party at one of the dorms. Emboldened by beer, he introduced himself. One beer turned into many, catalyzing their attraction, but not until she heard him play piano did she fall for him. They were alone in a practice room, and he played Schumann's Fantasie in C Major, op. 17. He was so connected to the piece that he seemed to become unconscious of her presence. His playing was powerful yet gentle, assured, masterful. And the composition is so utterly romantic, still one of her favorites. By the time he played the final note, she was in love.

They had sex morning and night, more often than she brushed her teeth. She spent her days memorizing Bach and Mozart and her nights memorizing the shape of him, the first and last notes of every day played on each other's body. They were passionate, insatiable for piano and each other. Nothing else existed. She'd never been happier.

She knows this is her history, the early chapters in the biography of her life, yet she feels utterly disconnected from it. She remembers that first year with Richard, yet these memories, these snapshots of body parts tangled up in bedsheets, feel as if they must belong to someone else, a character in a book she read long ago.

The thought of Richard even kissing her now is revolting, that she ever desired him crazy, that they were married surreal. Yet it all happened.

She watches Grace listening to Matt, smiling, flirting, enamored, and wonders what their narrative will be. She hopes her daughter fares better in love and marriage than she did. *Don't repeat the mistakes I made.*

Could Karina have seen the red flags

through the thick haze of lust at twenty? Was there any way to predict all that would unfold? Possibly. Richard was always a bit of a narcissist, a fragile egomaniac, a selfish prick. She naïvely thought these were the character traits of any talented, ambitious man. The price of admission. She respected his dedication to piano and admired his confidence. Looking back, she can see that his dedication was desperation, his confidence was arrogance, that he was always a house of cards.

Still, in the beginning, their relationship was intoxicating and held the promise of a great love story. In the end, it was dog shit. *Till death do us part.* That's a man-made rule, too. An unreasonable one, she thinks. Everything begins and ends. Every day and night, every concerto, every relationship, every life. Everything ends eventually. She wishes she and Richard had ended better.

The playlist in the coffee shop, which had been a steady stream of pop songs — Ed Sheeran and Rihanna and Taylor Swift — switches abruptly to Thelonious Monk.

"Mom, listen. You used to play something like this when I was little. Remember?"

Karina stares at Grace with her mouth open, shocked. Grace had to have been three or four. "Yes. I can't believe you do."

"What kind of music do you play now?" asks Matt.

"Classical. Mostly Chopin, Mozart, Bach."

"Oh, nice."

"How come you don't play this?" asks Grace.

A million reasons.

"I don't know."

Grace looks up and away, at nothing in particular, and listens. The song is " 'Round Midnight," a late-night loungy ballad that makes Karina feel as if she should have her hands around a gin and tonic instead of a pumpkin-spice latte. She imagines the keys under her fingers as she plays along with her mind's ear, the motor plan unfolded like an old family recipe, still legible after so many years. She feels the notes vibrating in her heart, and she's swept up in an intense longing, approaching something close to sorrow. Regret. She listens to Monk playing jazz, and her heart fills with regret.

A smile enlivens Grace's face, and her eyes brighten. "I love it, don't you?"

Karina's cheeks flush pink again. She nods.

"I do."

CHAPTER SIX

In the languid, not-quite-conscious moments before Richard opens his eyes, newly
familiar black notes dance across crisp white
sheets of paper behind his lids. He hears
the sound of the notes as his mind sees
them, ascending arpeggios that call him like
a siren to his bench. He opens his eyes. A
ribbon of bright white light slices through
the midline of the drawn heavy drapes of
his bedroom. Another day.

He instructs the fingers of his left hand to
play scales on the fitted white sheet, his
morning ritual. His daily exam. He studies
this symphony of simple movement, the
sequential, rapid lift and drop of each finger
like a sewing-machine needle, the machin-
ery of tendons, knuckles, veins, and muscle,
no less miraculous and essential to him than
his beating heart.

Satisfied, he gets up, pees, and walks into
the kitchen to prepare breakfast, resisting

ar I.

d sits tall at his bench, places his
nd on his lap, and turns the sheet
ver, hiding the notes. He'll play it
e from memory. He positions his
on the keys and waits. He imagines
nce of several hundred in his living
e conductor and orchestra in his

ncerto begins immersed in dark-
reboding storm in the bass and
isters, the solemn contrabassoon,
ering drums. Richard's solo begins
minute and a half in. His hand
e scales, lifting everyone out of the
orm, evoking visions of shimmer-
ht. His left fingers have full com-
all eighty-eight keys, traversing
o heaven, the piece richly embod-
he hand.
centration is fiercely devoted to
, yet he isn't thinking. He's been
Ravel for nine hours a day, and
usic is pulsing inside him, the
every sharp and rest and stac-
ed in the muscles of his hand as
mind. He can't tell if his eyes are
is fingers or following them,
He's reached that magical part
e where he's no longer playing

the impatient pull of his Steinway for the moment. Sitting naked at the kitchen-island counter, he sips hot coffee through a straw while vaguely studying his feet. He commands his toes to wiggle. They comply. Bending his neck and curling his upper torso down, he stretches his lips to meet a powdered doughnut in his hand. His left shoulder has started to lock, limiting the vertical mobility of his arm. He tries not to dwell on the advancing paralysis that this new symptom likely predicts. Maybe the disease will stop there, in his left shoulder. He could live with that.

As he alternates between doughnut and coffee, he allows his thoughts to peer down the rabbit hole and imagines the impact if this disease doesn't stop there. He pans around the room, his field of view narrowed like a series of close-up shots in a horror movie — the cabinet knobs (most already out of reach), the coffeemaker, the sink, the refrigerator-door handle, the light switches, his phone, his computer. His piano. He'll have two paralyzed arms. No hands. He won't be able to feed himself, scratch his head, wipe his ass. He stares at his piano as he sucks up the last drops of coffee. Maybe the disease will stop in his shoulder.

Finished with coffee and doughnut, he

wants to lick clean the dusty white sugar covering his fingertips but instead wipes it onto the bare skin of his thigh. He'll continue brewing coffee throughout the day, but only for the invigorating aroma it diffuses throughout his home. More than a cup gives him the shakes.

Done with breakfast, he showers, bending over to shampoo his hair, in and out before the bathroom mirror fogs. He examines his furry face at the vanity. It's been almost two weeks since he last shaved. He can still adequately manage the job with his left hand, but he hasn't felt like bothering. Maybe he'll shave today.

Although he's right-handed, a life at the piano has made him essentially ambidextrous. He feels so lucky. He smiles. But his smile in the mirror is dressed in a beard he doesn't want, and he thinks of all the people in the world with two healthy, functional hands and clean-shaven faces who don't have ALS, and his mind mocks him for feeling fortunate. His smile is a betrayal of his grim reality, a Pollyanna fool's mission. *What do you have to smile about?* Shamed, he stops. His closed-lipped face is somber, serious, covered in black hair, a bit menacing, a much more appropriate portrayal of a forty-five-year-old man with a fatal neuro-

muscular disease. He beard.

He stands before hi by so many sleeves an ers not dressing at all bers what he's ready he goes in the compl direction. He pulls o

Socks and trousers able. Lace-up shoes his feet into patent- top half. His eyes f he hopelessly puzzl the waistcoat, the c hell with all that. jacket sleeve over buttons a single chested body wi Ready to perform

Being mathem sumed that playin would be at mos with two, but h For the past thr obsessed with M certo for the Le minute piece pl whole orchestr nally compose Wittgenstein,

World W
Richa
right ha
music o
this tim
left hand
an audie
room, th
kitchen.
The co
ness, a f
tenor reg
the thund
about a
climbs th
sinister st
ing sunlig
mand ove
from hell t
ied with o
His con
every note
practicing
now the m
memory o
cato encod
well as his
directing
witnessing.
of the curv

64

the music. The music is playing him.

He hears the whimsical cat-and-mouse game, the call-and-answer conversation between the music he's creating and his mind's rendition of the strings and horns. The song now ascends into hopeful possibility, each note and imagined marching drumbeat reaching toward triumphant ecstasy. Closer and faster without rushing, a crescendo that vibrates and steadily rises in his body like the expectation of certain orgasm, he plays along with the imagined massive orchestra, louder, closer, higher, finally ending all at once, like the dramatic climax of an epic film, in heroic victory.

And with that last resonating note, the victory is his. He looks to the darkened living room, the shades still drawn, adrenaline dancing through his heart as he receives the applause, the audience rising in a standing ovation. He turns to the kitchen to acknowledge the orchestra and thank the conductor. He stands and bows to the couch.

In the stark silence of his apartment, the experience of Ravel's concerto exciting his soul, he imagines taking this performance to a real venue with a real orchestra. He could do this. He could tour this piece as a guest with symphonies the world over. Of course he could. His career isn't over. His agent is going to love this.

He sits back at his bench, readying to play it again. He positions his left hand on the keys, but instead of hearing the orchestra begin in his mind's ear, he hears only the oppressive silence of his empty apartment and a voice in his head, an arrogant naysayer stealing his confidence, talking him out of this pathetic plan.

Richard lifts his left arm straight out in front of him. It begins to tremor just below shoulder height. He tries to will it higher, recruiting every muscle fiber he can conjure to the job, but his arm won't budge any farther. Exhausted, he lowers his hand back onto the piano keys.

Instead of beginning his solo, in opposition to the overbearing silence and the voice in his head, he plays a single note, D, with his pinkie. He holds the key and the foot pedal down, listening to the singular sound, bold and three-dimensional at first, then drifting, dispersing, fragile, decaying. He inhales. The smell of coffee lingers. He listens. The note is gone.

Every note played is a life and death.

Maybe the disease will stay in his shoulder. The voice in his head knows better and insists on another peek down the rabbit hole. No hands.

Richard leaves the piano. He retreats to his bedroom, undresses, and crawls back into bed. He does not call his agent. He lies on his back, staring at the ceiling, wishing he could stop time, hiding from his future, knowing without any doubt or hope that someday soon he won't simply be peeking down that rabbit hole.

He's going to live and die in there.

CHAPTER SEVEN

Alone in a cheerless examining room, Richard waits for Kathy DeVillo. It's the beginning of October, and this is the fourth time he's waited in a similarly impersonal room for her, the first instance almost a year ago. Kathy is the nurse-practitioner overseeing his medical care at the ALS clinic. *Care* is the term they use here, and Richard doesn't openly object, but care is not what's provided every three months when he comes for his appointment. The staff all mean well. He has no doubt of this. Kathy is nice and clearly cares about her job and him. But as an ALS care coordinator, her pockets contain little more than tongue depressors.

These clinic visits primarily amount to data collection, a chronicling of worsening symptoms indicative of disease progression. Every three months, the losses are noticeable, significant, and Kathy and others record these losses in various charts. Each clinic day is a Q&A series aimed at measuring what has gone from bad to worse. Kathy will offer some practical strategies for coping, some sympathetic nodding, and a preview of coming attractions: *You think this is bad, wait till you see what's next!* His neurologist might adjust the dosage of Rilutek. He might not.

It takes at least three hours to do all the measuring, and by the end of every clinic day, Richard's morale is battered and defeated. He swears he won't come back. What's the point? Given that he has only a limited number of hours left as an animated being on this planet, to squander any of them sitting still in this room with Kathy, or waiting for Kathy as the case may be, feels like an egregious injustice or at least utterly irresponsible. Yet, he comes. He does as he's told, which surprises him, as passive obedience isn't at all consistent with his character.

If he had to put his soon-to-be-paralyzed left finger on it, he'd admit that he dutifully comes to each clinic appointment because he still has hope. Maybe there will be a breakthrough, a new clinical trial drug, something to slow it down, a cure. It could happen. What were the odds that a boy raised to devote his time equally between football, tractors, and Bud Light in rural

"Live Free or Die" New Hampshire would grow up to be a world-renowned concert pianist? Probably the same as some scientist discovering the cure for ALS. It could happen. So he waits for Kathy.

She finally enters the room, pink faced and out of breath, as if she'd just jogged over from another wing of the hospital. She's wearing tortoiseshell glasses, a black knit sweater unbuttoned over an untucked white blouse, pants that are too short for her, and flat shoes fit for running the halls of the hospital, her look more librarian than nurse. She washes her hands while saying hello, then settles into the chair opposite Richard and reads his record of decline from three months ago, his new baseline, the treacherous edge from which he'll now cliff dive.

She looks up at him and raises her eyebrows. "Where's Maxine?"

"No longer together."

"Oh, I'm so sorry."

"That's okay."

With the exception of Maxine, Richard's relationships with women had about the same shelf life as a carton of milk. Most met him after a performance, at a VIP cocktail party or charity fund-raiser, starstruck and fascinated. They fell hard and fast, looking past his wedding band when he was married. In the beginning, they also tolerated his moodiness and the time he committed to the piano instead of them. They saw his passion for the music of Brahms, Chopin, and Liszt, the love and devotion he was capable of, and assumed the skills were transferable. To everyone's disappointment, he's never been able to love a woman the way he loves the piano. Not even Karina.

So, invariably, the women became frustrated, lonely, and dissatisfied with their lot as second fiddle. Third, if they realized they were in line behind his wife. At first they tried even harder. It never worked. He doesn't know why. Maybe human beings are capable of only so much passion. The pie has only so many pieces. For Richard, all but a sliver is devoted to piano. He loves women, appreciates them as much as any man, but ultimately they find themselves achingly hungry with him. And he refuses to feed them. His artistry for playing piano seduces them. His lack of artistry as a man is why they leave.

Steeped in denial, he started seeing Maxine two months after he was diagnosed. She didn't notice that he couldn't lift his right arm above his elbow or that he always positioned himself to her right so he could hold her hand with his left. He might've slurred his words a touch in the evening when his energy waned, but they'd just shared two bottles of wine. Then one morning she caught him weeping, his hands in his lap at the piano, and he confessed everything.

Instead of running for the hills, she rolled up her sleeves. An acupuncturist, she was convinced she could save him. But no amount of needling, cupping, or burning moxa could prevent his right arm from steadily filling with concrete. She kept at it, but they both knew the effort had become insincere.

Decency laced with guilt prevented her escape. The situation wasn't healthy for either of them. Sex became quick and unimaginative. She became afraid of his body. He became indifferent to hers. He focused on her imperfections. She wore too much eye makeup. She had bad breath. She wasn't beautiful enough, interesting enough, challenging enough. Her list of complaints was just as lengthy.

For four months, they argued and sulked and danced silently around the real reason the relationship had to end. It took him that long to accumulate the courage he needed to break up with her. She didn't protest. They hugged for a long time, then she walked out the door. It was the most unselfish act of his life.

"Anyone looking after you?"

"No. I'm doing okay on my own."

"You're going to need help. Your parents, a relative, friends. You can hire private nurses, home health aides, but that will get expensive. Can you call on someone?"

"Uh-huh."

His mother died of cervical cancer when she was forty-five. Richard is forty-five. Apparently, a rough age in his lineage. He hasn't spoken to his father in years. His two brothers live in New Hampshire. They work fulltime, and their wives are raising young kids. They aren't options. Grace is in school, and that's where she belongs. He still hasn't told her. He doesn't know how. He draws Karina's name next but immediately returns that card to the deck. There's no way.

"How's your living situation? Did you find a new place?"

"No. I'm still good where I am."

"Richard, you're on the fourth floor of a walk-up. Really, you have to get into a new place ASAP, before you need a wheelchair. You're going to need elevators, ramps. Okay?"

He keeps his gaze steady, refusing any sign of agreement. He can still walk. How could he be in a wheelchair ASAP? He knows this is where the disease goes, yet he can't bring himself to fully imagine it. He looks into Kathy's big brown eyes. She can. Easy-peasy.

"So tell me what's going on."

"It's starting in my left arm. I can't raise my hand above my shoulder, and my fingers are a bit weaker. I can't lift anything heavy. I'm dropping things. Walking is still mostly okay."

"Mostly."

"Yeah."

"Okay. What about eating, drinking, talking?"

"Mostly okay."

"Okay, we'll check out these mostly's, see what's happening. Let's start with your left hand. Spread your fingers and don't let me bunch them back together."

He spreads his fingers like a starfish. She scrunches them together with one second's minimal effort.

"Hold your hand straight out in front of you and don't let me push it down. Resist me."

She applies a bit of pressure, and his arm collapses to his side. The last time he was here, he still had the use of both arms and could raise both hands when asked. But his right arm crumbled with the mere suggestion of force on Kathy's part, and he remembers the terror that rushed through him like a cold blue current, chilling his heart, realizing that he possessed almost no strength in that arm and that he was about to lose the use of it entirely and forever. He remembers thinking, *At least I still have my left arm.* He glances now at his left hand, defeated and shamed by his side, and he knows what this profoundly simple exercise will look like in three months' time.

"Make an A-OK sign with your thumb and index finger and lock them into a ring. Don't let me pull them apart."

She pulls them apart.

He wants to punch this nice lady in the face with his feeble hand.

"Show me a big smile, so big it's fake. Like Hillary."

He does.

"Now pucker. Like Trump."

He does.

"Open your mouth and don't let me shut it."

He opens his mouth, and with the heel of her hand under his chin, she steadily closes his bottom jaw.

"Stick your tongue out and don't let me move it."

She pushes down and right and left on his tongue with a Popsicle stick, shifting it in each direction.

"Lick your lips all the way around."

Her eyes track his tongue in a circle.

"Fill your cheeks with air and don't let me pop them."

She does.

"Are you having any trouble blowing your nose?"

"No."

"Any trouble with saliva?"

"Like, am I drooling?"

"Yeah."

"No."

"How about coughing? Any trouble clearing your throat?"

"Not really."

"Let me see. Cough from deep down. Give me a big throat clear."

He tries to take a deep breath but hits a wall sooner than expected, and so his cough comes out shallow and sputtering. He's embarrassed. He was going for the cough of a lion, but instead he's a kitten hacking up a hair ball.

"Take a big breath and expel a note for as long as you can. Ready? Go."

He chooses middle C and runs out of air at about fifteen seconds. Is that normal? Kathy doesn't say.

She goes to the sink and fills a plastic cup with water.

"Here. Take a few sips and then chug the rest."

He does while she appears to study something about his Adam's apple.

"Is taking your meds giving you any trouble?"

"No."

"Good. Taking pills is the highest level of swallowing. So that's great. Water's the fastest liquid and will give you the most trouble. You drink coffee?"

"Yeah."

"How do you take it?"

"Black."

"Okay, you need to switch now to cream. Thicken all of your liquids. Make them slower. Thin liquids can lead to aspiration. How's your weight?" She looks through the pages of his various charts.

"I've lost a few pounds."

Eating has become a joyless, necessary chore. Anything that requires a knife and fork is out. Gone are medium-rare filets mignons at Grill 23. Opening jars and the packaging to his favorite cheese and the twist tie on a new loaf of bread requires a collaboration between his left hand and his knees and his teeth and a patient persistence he often doesn't possess. Unable to lift his hand to even shoulder height at the end of the day, he has to lower his mouth to meet his fork or spoon. It's painstaking and sloppy, and he looks ridiculous, and because he can't get over worrying about what he looks like, he refuses to eat in public. Dining used to be a social and savored experience. Now he mostly orders takeout and eats alone.

And he's started choking. The muscles that coordinate the safe movement of food from the back of his mouth down the esophagus to his stomach must be weakening because sometimes food gets lodged halfway down the tube or, worse, sucked down the wrong pipe. And as they just witnessed, he now has the coughing capacity of a kitty cat, so a small bite of cracker has been a life-threatening endeavor more than once. Almost killed by a cracker. He doesn't share this with Kathy.

"Okay, yup, you've lost seven pounds in three months. We need to stabilize your weight. You need to eat more. High-fat, high-density foods and liquids."

"Okay."

"Cream in your coffee, butter on your bread, pies à la mode."

"Everything my cardiologist recommends."

"We're not going to worry about heart disease."

Right. A heart attack would be a blessing.

"Can you lift your right leg for me and don't let me push it down?"

He resists her for many sustained seconds through increasing pressure before he finally fails. They do the same exercise on the left until he fails.

"Good. You experiencing any foot drop, any falls?"

"No."

He's lying, and his heart beats faster as he waits to see if she catches him. He clipped his right toe on a step going up his front stoop last week, and he fell hard, bashing the right side of his chin and trampling his paralyzed forearm underneath his body. He's wearing a long-sleeve shirt, hiding the massive bruises covering his right arm, and his beard is apparently thick and dark enough to mask the scabbed gash on his chin.

She taps his knees, checking his reflexes. She performs various strength tests on his feet. He gets a passing grade.

"Any cramping?"

"No."

"Your legs are looking good for now. But your arm is going, so you won't be using a cane or a walker once your legs weaken. The power wheelchairs take three to six months to get, so we'll have PT put in an order for you now."

Again, he stares at her with a flat gaze. She can go ahead and order the chair, but he won't endorse this decision with a blink or a nod.

"I'm worried about your dysphagia and the weight loss. Have you thought at all about whether you want to get a feeding tube?"

Only in that he doesn't want to think about it. "No."

"Okay, Dr. Prince will talk you through what's involved and schedule you for the procedure if you decide to go ahead."

He was scheduled to play in Chicago, Baltimore, Oslo, Copenhagen. He's supposed to schedule piano concerts, not feeding-tube surgery. His head swims.

"Your breathing still seems strong. Dr. Kim's going to see you next to check you out more thoroughly there."

Dr. Kim is the pulmonologist.

"Have you banked your voice yet?"

"No."

"Is this something you want to do?"

"I'm not sure."

"It might be a good idea to look into that now. When the time comes, you can always use the synthetic, computer-generated voice, but it's really nice to have the option of still using your own. The guy who does the banking is at Children's Hospital. I'll make sure you have his contact information before you leave today. If you want to do it, I wouldn't put it off much longer."

Kathy flips through his charts, pencils in some additional notes that Richard can't decipher, then looks up at him and smiles, satisfied.

"That's all for me. Do you have any questions? Anything you need that I can help you with?"

Let's see. What does he need? He needs to bank his voice because he'll soon be unable to speak, and the alternatives are to sound like Stephen Hawking or be totally mute. He might need a feeding tube. He's going to need a wheelchair ASAP. He needs a new apartment with an elevator and ramps. He needs someone to look after him.

It's too much to take in. Too many losses and needs at once. He tries to focus on what is most immediate. The loss of his left hand.

He'll have no hands. He'll no longer be able to feed himself, dress himself, wash himself. He'll empty his bank accounts and hire help. He won't be able to type on the computer. He'll use his big toes.

He's going to lose Ravel's Piano Concerto for the Left Hand. He'll never play the piano again.

This is the loss he's imagined in microscopic detail from the first hints of this disease, the one that guts him through his center and keeps him from sleeping and makes him want to swallow a bottle of pills and end his life now. Because without the piano, how can he live?

Yet, this isn't the loss that has him suddenly stunned and panic-stricken, unable to swallow his own pooling saliva. He's thinking about Maxine again, and he's revisiting their good-bye hug. He can still feel her body in this remembered embrace, her breasts pressed against his chest, her wet cheek on his shoulder, her breath on his neck. He can feel the apology, the tragic love story in the memory of that hug. He let go first. Maxine quickly followed his lead, slipped out of his arms, and left his life. He wishes now that he'd hung on a little longer.

He's about to lose his left arm. Three

months ago, he hugged Maxine for the last time. Could that be the last embrace of his entire life?

He swallows hard, but he chokes on his spit, and the coughing quickly turns to crying. Kathy offers him a tissue. Humiliated, he takes it. But then again, he decides he doesn't care. What hasn't she already seen in this room? He sputters, coughs, cries, and drools through three more tissues, then collects himself just enough to find his voice.

"I need a hug."

Kathy sets the tissue box aside without hesitating and stands in front of him. Richard rises to meet her, and she wraps him in a firm embrace. He's dousing her sweater with his tears and runny snot, and Kathy doesn't flinch. He hugs her with his left arm, pressing her into him, and she responds, hugging him back, and their contact creates a human connection that feels as vital to him as the air he can still breathe.

He can't name the element at first. The connection isn't about hope. It doesn't contain sympathy. It's not made of love.

It's care.

Richard exhales and doesn't let go. Kathy stays with him.

This is care.

CHAPTER EIGHT

While her neighborhood still sleeps, Karina is standing on the sidewalk in front of her house, waiting for Elise. The cold air crowds her, penetrating her clothing, and she wishes Elise would materialize so Karina can get her blood moving. She hugs herself as she watches her exhales, white puffs that lift and disperse into the sky as if returning to the clouds. Realizing that she's standing beneath one of the towering oak trees lining her street, she shifts her position a few feet to the middle of the road. She tilts her face toward the sky, searching for warmth from the sun, but it hasn't risen yet. The door finally opens, and Elise emerges.

"Sorry. I couldn't find my gloves."

They fall in step and walk wordlessly through their tidy neighborhood of land-scaped yards and two-car garages, still-darkened windows adorned with school-made ghosts and witches, front porches hosting impressively carved jack-o'-lanterns, pots of green and purple kale, and golden hardy mums. Without stopping, Karina plucks a Tootsie Roll wrapper from the street and pockets it. Karina and Elise won't break into conversation until they reach the reservoir. Anxious to get there, Karina walks a touch faster. Without questioning, Elise keeps up.

They've been walking together one morning a week for three years. Although only recently neighbors, Karina and Elise met at a faculty dinner at the New England Conservatory of Music twenty years ago. Richard had just accepted a highly coveted teaching position in the piano department. They'd moved from New York City because of this prestigious job offer, from the jazz scene at Smalls and 55 Bar, the network of rising musicians Karina jammed with and loved, the steady gigs she played on weekends, and a promising footing in the career she dreamed of.

She didn't realize this at the time, how one-sided the move would be when she agreed to it. She's often wondered how much Richard understood before they packed up and left. Not being from this country, she simply assumed Boston would have a significant jazz culture. Surely, she would find other hip clubs, other talented artists, other opportunities for expression and hire. Boston loves the classical concerts of the Boston Symphony Orchestra and the Pops at Symphony Hall and the Esplanade. Bostonians are fanatically loyal to the rock and pop music of hometown bands such as Aerosmith, the Dropkick Murphys, and New Kids on the Block.

Jazz in New York, New Orleans, Berlin, Paris, and even Chicago is considered a renegade and revered art. There is no jazz scene in Boston. The musicians who play at the handful of jazz clubs in town are one-night guests. They come and they go. They don't live and breathe here. Even before she'd unpacked their dinner plates, she realized this devastating truth and hated herself for being so naïve, so easily duped, as if she'd been promised sushi at a Mexican restaurant and never even asked to see the menu.

Elise was Karina's beacon of hope at that first faculty dinner. A bassist and professor of contemporary improvisation, Elise talked about ragtime and Wynton Marsalis and African jazz. She'd recorded an album with her students the previous year, a campus production, not exactly Blue Note, but still exciting. Karina couldn't wait to connect with her again, to ask her about playing somewhere, anywhere, maybe auditing one of her classes, possibly even teaching, but Elise was missing from the next faculty dinner. She'd been diagnosed with an aggressive form of breast cancer and had taken a leave of absence to undergo treatment.

Then Karina became unexpectedly pregnant with Grace, and Richard left New England Conservatory for what became an endless year of touring, so there were no more faculty dinners. Over time, Karina forgot about Elise. She retreated into the intensity, responsibility, and loneliness of full-time motherhood, resigning herself to living in Richard's immense shadow, darker, lonelier, and far more inescapable than the pre-dawn sky of a grim November morning.

While she never planned on being a mother, she loved Grace fiercely from the moment she was born and couldn't imagine choosing the kind of life Richard was living — gone for weeks at a time, devoting his days and weeks and years so singularly to his career. Even when he was home, he'd practice for eight to ten hours a day. He was there but not there.

She couldn't bear the thought of being separated from Grace, of missing any milestone. She wanted to witness her daughter discovering the world — the magic of seeing her first rainbow, the feel of a dog's fur and tongue, the silky sweet taste of vanilla ice cream. Karina wanted to be the person Grace saw when she awoke from her naps, who hugged her when she cried, who kissed her a hundred times a day. She couldn't abandon this enormous, precious love, this gift. She loved Grace more than piano.

And if she chose Grace over piano because she loved her daughter more, then Richard must not have loved Grace at all. This is the script she wrote and read to herself for years. He must be some kind of selfish monster to not love his own daughter, and she hated him for it. She built this case against him, black-and-white and indefensible. But now, looking back, she admits to herself that her conclusion was too extreme and not necessarily true. Love isn't measured by the number of hours a person logs. For the first time, she wonders if his affairs started before or after she began hating him.

At some point, she can't locate exactly when, she abandoned any possibility of a career in jazz piano. The goal became too implausible, childish, foolish. She thinks about it now as she walks, the vague dream of that intended life she never lived, and it feels like a comet she'd once seen long ago blazing across the night sky, witnessed for the briefest breathtaking moment and then gone for another hundred years.

While Karina was raising Grace and resenting Richard, Elise beat breast cancer, joined the faculty at Berklee College of Music, divorced her husband, and started dating her radiologist. They married and four years ago moved from Boston to the suburbs, directly across the street from Karina. Kindred spirits reunited. Karina still marvels at this serendipity, and her Catholic mind can't help but wonder if God led Elise here for a reason.

As they walk past Oak Hill Cemetery, the date returns to Karina's consciousness. Today is November 1, All Saints' Day, a national holiday in Poland. As a child, she would spend the entire day at the cemetery with her family. Everyone did this. Having lived in the United States her entire adult life, this tradition now seems a bit morbid and creepy, even in comparison to Halloween, but she always liked it. She remembers the white votive candles placed on the raised gravestones, dots of light sprinkled around her as far as she could see like stars spread across the universe.

She remembers her family gathered, her

parents, aunts, uncles, and cousins telling stories of those who'd passed away. She savored the stability she felt listening to those stories, in being connected to that history, a single bead strung on an infinitely long, uniquely beautiful necklace. She loved hearing how her grandparents on both sides met, courted, married, had children. She remembers studying their names etched on the gravestones, imagining the lives she barely and never knew, and that double-edged feeling of importance and insignificance, of fate and random chance this still generates, that every moment of those four lives had to unfold exactly as it did or she wouldn't be here.

They reach the dirt path along the reservoir and begin the three-mile loop. Here they'll begin chatting, as if they're finally out of earshot of their neighbors, their words safe among the trees, the Canada geese in the water, an occasional jogger, dog and dog walker.

"How was school this week?" This is always Karina's first question, inviting the conversation that both inspires and tortures her, like a recovering addict asking for a sip of wine.

"Good. I'm loving that new student I told you about, Claire. She's got such a great ear, and she's so totally open to listening and failing. You've got to come hear her play. There's a class show in two weeks."

"Okay."

"And we're planning the student trip to New Orleans. You should come this year."

"Maybe."

Karina won't go to either. Elise invites her to all kinds of shows and classes and guest lectures and every year to the New Orleans trip, and Karina declines it all. Her excuse used to be Grace. She couldn't go because Richard was out of town, and she was needed at home. Now that she's divorced and her excuse is at the University of Chicago, she has to come up with some other reason. She'll be too tired the evening of the class show. And maybe she'll plan a visit to see Grace the same week Elise and her students are in New Orleans. The thought of being immersed in the jazz scene in New Orleans, that magical hodgepodge of Delta-blues guitar riffs, brassy ragtime horns, and sultry French Gypsy music is too painful for Karina to stomach. Every girl loves a wedding unless the groom is the lost love of her life.

"And maybe one of these days, you'll come play with us, please."

"Someday."

Elise plays bass in a contemporary improvisation band called the Dish Pans with faculty from Berklee, New England Conservatory, and Longy, mostly in bohemian restaurants and hipster bars that have a rotating roster of live music. *Someday* is always Karina's reply, and she'd like to believe that it's true. While she plays and teaches piano almost every day, she's restricted herself to the classical music of Chopin, Beethoven, Schumann, Mozart. The dots are already on the page, and she plays them with the obsequious reverence of a Catholic priest reading from the Bible or an actor quoting Shakespeare.

Jazz improvisation is a speech without a script. It's twelve notes and doing anything she pleases. There are no rules, no boundaries. Verbs don't have to follow nouns. There is no gravity. Up can be down.

And it's collaborative. She hasn't played jazz with anyone since before Grace was born. It shatters her heart every time she realizes how many years it's been. She could remedy this by taking Elise up on her offer. What if someday was today? Her breath goes shallow, and the wind off the reservoir chills the sweat on her forehead. She's too out of practice. It's been too long. A runner laid up for years with an Achilles injury can't simply show up at the Olympic trials. Karina imagines playing with such practiced and accomplished musicians, and the fear of her certain and overwhelming inadequacy locks her life's greatest wish in a box.

"So I need to come clean," says Elise. "I visited Richard."

Karina stops walking, every muscle's action suspended, stuck in stunned betrayal.

Elise pauses several steps ahead and turns around. "Roz from the Conservatory called. It was nice of her to remember me. She organized a bunch of the staff who knew him from his teaching days, and we all went over. I felt like it was the decent thing to do."

Begrudgingly satisfied with this explanation and fueled by curiosity, Karina starts up again. The two women walk side by side.

"So how is he?" Karina asks, a reluctant toe edging into muddy water.

"His arms are completely paralyzed. That was upsetting to actually see."

The previously dormant pit in Karina's stomach, planted months ago, sprouts roots. *This is really happening.* Aside from not being able to open the bottle of wine, he'd looked and acted perfectly normal when she last saw him in July. She'd been holding on to the possibility that his diagnosis was a rumor or a mistake. She still hates him, but palpably less than she did last year, and hasn't wished him dead since before the divorce. She wouldn't wish ALS on anyone, not even Richard. She kept waiting to see a correction in the newspaper, his tour back on, that the reports of his imminent death had been greatly exaggerated.

"I'd planned on giving him the stink eye for you, but his arms were just hanging off his body like dead branches, and there was his piano in the room with all of us trying to pretend it wasn't there. None of us mentioned it. It was too sad."

Richard without the piano. A fish without water. A planet without a sun.

"How did he seem about it?"

"His spirits were good. He was happy to see us all. But you could tell he was trying really hard to be positive, like he was performing."

They continue walking in silence, and soon the silence fills with sound — the muffled steps of their sneakers on the dirt path, softened by a bed of brown pine needles and then the crunching of dry, brown-paper-bag oak leaves; Elise sniffling; the huffing of their exhales.

"Does Grace know?" asks Elise.

"Not unless someone else told her. I

would know if she knew. No, honestly, I wasn't even a hundred percent sure he had it until this very conversation."

Grace. She's in the middle of midterms. It would be cruel to break this news to her right now. She might get distracted and fail her exams. And why hasn't Richard told her? Of course he hasn't told her.

"Maybe I should go see him again," says Karina.

"That's your Catholic guilt talking."

"No."

"Remember what happened last time."

"I know."

"Seeing him is not good for you."

Richard always seemed invincible to Karina, as if he could conquer anything, and he did. He was an unstoppable force that awed and intimidated her and, at times when she was most vulnerable, trampled her. Now he's the vulnerable one, and she can't help but wonder what it would feel like to sit at the other end of the table.

"Yeah, but —"

"What are you hoping for? Tuesdays with Morrie?"

"I don't know."

"He's still Richard, honey."

"Believe me, I know who he is."

"Just don't get hurt."

"I won't," Karina says, her voice utterly void of conviction.

CHAPTER NINE

Karina is carrying a foil-covered plate of pierogi in one hand, a $50 bottle of red wine in the other, and several months of unrelenting guilt down Commonwealth Avenue. It's a gunmetal-gray November morning, raining hard, and she has no hands for an umbrella and four more blocks. She picks up her pace, almost running, and the wind whips the hood off her head. *Damn it.* She has no available hand to pull it back on.

The weather hits her like an assault, and since she's the only pedestrian in sight, the attack feels personal. Raindrops pummel the aluminum foil like machine-gun fire. The bitter-cold wind stings her face raw. Rain soaks through her socks, pants, and hair, chilling her skin like a punishment. She blames Richard. She wouldn't be subjected to this misery if he hadn't provoked her. Of course, she reacted. Just as she always did. It's as if she were programmed to respond to him, an unthinking and immediate ouch to his pinch.

It was already raining when she left the safety of her house, and she knew she wouldn't likely find a parking space within four blocks. She could've waited another day. Tomorrow's weather forecast is cold but clear. But she made the pierogi last night, and she needs to make at least this one thing between Richard and her right, clean up her side of the street, deliver her penance, and be done. Carpe diem. Weather be damned.

Focused on the numbers on the door and the promise of shelter, she barely registers the FOR SALE sign planted in the minuscule square patch of front lawn as she races past it. Out of breath and shoulders hugging her ears at the top of the stairs, she presses the doorbell and waits. Her hands, wet and lacking circulation and painfully cold, are aching to let go of her peace offerings and find comfort inside her coat pockets. Without a greeting or question as to who's there, she's buzzed inside.

When she reaches Richard's unit, the door is ajar. She knocks as she edges the door open a bit more to be heard. "Hello?"

"Come on in!" a man's voice, not Richard's, hollers from somewhere inside. "We'll

6.13

be done in a minute!"

Karina enters, steps out of her shoes at the door, and returns to the kitchen, the scene of the crime. The lights are on. The room smells of coffee. The kitchen island and counters are wiped clean and are bare but for three glasses filled to the top with what looks to be vanilla milk shake, a tall straw standing erect in each. There's no noise, no sign of anyone. She sets the wine and pierogi down on the counter, removes her raincoat, and drapes it over one of the barstools. She waits, not knowing whether to sit or stand, growing increasingly uneasy. Maybe she should find a piece of paper and pen, write a note, and leave.

Her attention wanders to the living room and screeches to a sudden stop, stunned. A wheelchair. A wheelchair unlike any other she's ever seen. The tipped headrest and seat resemble a dentist's chair. The two strapped footrests remind her of the stirrups on a gynecologist's exam table. There are six wheels and shock absorbers and a joystick affixed to one of the arms. This is not a chair for a broken leg. It looks futuristic and barbaric. Cold rainwater drains from her hairline, trickling down her neck. She shivers.

The chair is positioned next to Richard's

piano. She looks again, and the piano is as unfamiliar and formidable as the wheelchair. An inner chill more penetrating than the rain on her skin drips down her spine. The key cover is shut. The music rack is bare. The bench is pushed in. She approaches Richard's Steinway as if she were trespassing on sacred ground, her mind still disbelieving the incongruity of the sight before her. She hesitates, gathering courage, then slides her index finger along its lid, clearing a thick layer of fine dust, revealing a snail trail of the piano's glossy black finish.

"Hi."

She spins around, heart pounding, as if she were a criminal caught in an illicit act. Richard is standing behind a bald man with black-rimmed glasses.

"I'm Bill." He wields an energetic wide smile, extending his hand to hers. "Richard's home health aide."

"Karina." She shakes his hand.

"Okay, well, that's it for me. Gotta run," Bill says. "Melanie will be here for lunch, Rob or Kevin for dinner and bed. You've got three shakes in the kitchen. You all good?"

Richard nods. Bill checks something on Richard's iPhone, worn on his chest and attached to a lanyard hung around his neck like a conference badge.

"Okay, my friend. Call us if you need us. See you in the morning."

Richard stares at Karina as Bill leaves and says nothing. His hair is wet, combed, and parted too severely and neatly to the side. He looks like a young boy on school-picture day. He's clean shaven, his face gaunt. His black sweater and jeans hang on him, long and baggy, as if they belonged to a big brother or were borrowed from Bill. Unsettled by the wheelchair, the abandoned piano, Richard's emaciated appearance and prolonged silence, Karina forgets why she's here and begins to wonder if he can speak at all.

He notices her apology on the counter.

"Pierogi," she says. "I'm sure the wine is below your standards, but it's the thought that counts."

"Thank you."

He walks into the kitchen, and that's when she notices. His arms don't swing. They sag from his shoulders, still, lifeless. And both hands look wrong, inhuman. The fingers of his right hand are stick straight, flattened. The other hand is fixed in a grotesquely curled claw. He positions himself in front of one of the milk shakes, lowers his head to the straw, and sips.

His arms are completely paralyzed. He watches her absorb this information. She smiles, trying to mask her real reaction, a trench coat wrapped around her naked horror.

"Want to have a seat?" He returns to the living room. "I don't recommend that one." He nods at the wheelchair.

The melody in his voice is gone. Every syllable is the same note, softer in volume, and slow, as if each monotone word is being dredged through molasses.

"You can still walk," she says, confused.

"Ah. That's my future. You have to order the chair before you need it or I guess you end up getting it six months after you die. I told Bill they might as well deliver my coffin, too."

He laughs, but the sound of his amusement quickly turns into something else, a runaway choking wheeze, sounding nasty and villainous, gripping him tighter and tighter around the throat as if it aims to kill him. She sits a few feet in front of him, watching, a silent bystander, holding her own breath and strangely paralyzed, not knowing what to do. His final wheeze ejaculates a gob of spittle that lands on the face of his iPhone. She pretends not to notice as

104

it oozes down the screen.

She looks away, over her shoulder, back at the piano and the wheelchair. Richard's past and future. She thinks of all the time he used to fill learning, practicing, memorizing, perfecting — nine to ten hours and more a day. She looks back at Richard, at his useless hands. What on earth does he do all day now?

"Once you need that, how will you ever leave your apartment?" He's on the fourth floor of a 150-year-old brownstone. No elevators. No ramps.

"I won't."

He'll be trapped inside this apartment, locked inside his body, a Russian nesting doll. She suddenly remembers the FOR SALE sign out front.

"So you're moving."

"Trying. I can't afford a new place until this one sells. Even to rent. Keeping me alive is already an expensive project. Might not be worth the investment. Don't expect any more alimony checks."

"No. Of course."

She goes silent. The checking-account balance, her meager piano-lesson income, the monthly bills. She begins doing math, mostly subtraction, equations that scare her and can't be entirely solved right now in her head.

"How's Grace?"

"Richard, she doesn't know. She doesn't know any of this. I didn't realize you would change so much so fast. You have to tell her what's going on."

"I know. I was going to. Many times. I just kept putting it off. Then my voice. I sound like a robot. I don't want to call and scare her."

"Write her an email." Karina's stomach cringes, and her eyes widen, embarrassed. His hands. He can't type.

"I have speech-recognition software and toes. I can still email. But she doesn't return my emails about school and the weather. I couldn't stand it if I wrote her about this and she didn't reply."

Given what Grace knows and doesn't know, it's not surprising she took sides. Loyal to her mother, Grace hasn't spoken to her father in over a year. Karina can't help but enjoy the victory in this allegiance and has done nothing to encourage an end to his daughter's cold war. Karina looks down at the floor, at her damp socks.

"I didn't want to drop this bomb on her while she was at school. I thought it could wait —"

"For the coffin to get here?" Karina asks,

transforming her shame to blame, an alchemy she's long mastered.

"Until she was home for Thanksgiving. To tell her in person. And I know this is dumb, but I think I thought if I didn't tell people I had ALS, maybe I really didn't have it."

Four months ago, she couldn't tell if he had ALS by looking at him. But now, it's unmistakable. How could he be in such crazy denial? Her heart tightens as she imagines Grace absorbing the news, this view of her father for the first time, this threat to everyone's well-being.

"She's not coming home for Thanksgiving. She's got a boyfriend. Matt. His parents live in Chicago. She's staying out there for the long weekend. We won't see her until Christmas."

Just over a month away. Only a few weeks. Richard looks past Karina to the wheelchair behind her. His eyes well up, and he blinks repeatedly, working hard to keep his tears contained.

"Can you tell her for me?"

She considers his request and him, sitting opposite her, so vulnerable, a fragile bird with no wings. He's lost his arms. He's losing his voice. He's going to lose his legs. His life. She should pity him, this flightless, dying bird. But she doesn't. He's not a bird.

He's Richard. She feels her posture harden, a familiar numbness.

"No."

Her reply is cruel, but she can find no other, and the thickening silence between them is pressing on her walled-off heart, begging her to reconsider. She crosses her arms, steeling her resolve. She feels his eyes on her as she stands.

"I have to go."

"Okay. Before you do?"

She looks at him, trying not to see him.

"Would you scratch the top of my head? Please?"

She takes a breath, crosses the impossible distance between them, sits on the couch next to him, and scratches his head.

"Oh my God, thank you. A little harder. All over, please."

She uses both hands. Her nails are unmanicured, but they're hard and strong, and she rakes them all over his head, messing up his neatly combed schoolboy hairstyle. After a good scrubbing, she stops and checks on him. His eyes are closed, and a deeply satisfied closed-lipped smile is stretched across his thin face. It's been a long time since she's touched him, since she gave him any kind of pleasure. Without her permission, a sweet memory massages an unhardened piece of her heart.

"I have to go now. You okay?" She stands.

Richard opens his eyes. They're glossy. He blinks, and a couple of tears escape, spilling down his face. He can't wipe them.

"I'm okay."

She hesitates but then grabs her raincoat, slips into her wet shoes, and leaves without another word. As she's descending the stairs, she thinks of the many times she's left Richard — walking away in the middle of innumerable arguments; storming out in the middle of dinner, deserting him in a restaurant, leaving him to take a cab home alone; the last time she was here, marching out of his apartment after breaking his bottle of wine; leaving the courthouse on the day the judge declared their marriage irretrievably broken, the dissolution no-fault, the divorce absolute. As she walks out the front door, fixing her hood onto her head, shoving her hands into the cozy safety of her coat pockets, she remembers walking down the courthouse steps, scared that it was she who was irretrievably broken, knowing there was plenty of fault to this failure, and daring to admit that she might be as much to blame for it all as he was.

CHAPTER TEN

Richard closes his eyes against the muted morning light, wishing he could fall back to sleep, knowing he can't. He used to sleep through the night without waking, oblivious to the stirrings of his wife or whoever might be next to him, deaf to car alarms and police sirens and phone alerts. He used to sleep for six to seven hours straight every night, lifting gently out of slumber into consciousness each morning with no memory of dreams or thoughts beyond shutting off the bedside light. He turns his head to see the time. He just spent eleven hours in bed, and he's exhausted. He doesn't sleep well anymore.

With two lifeless arms, he's essentially stuck on his back all night. He can rock himself to one side, but it's risky. The last time he did this was a few weeks ago. His right arm became trapped at a painful angle under his torso, cutting off the circulation, and he had a hell of a time freeing it.

And he can't risk beaching himself on his stomach. Because his abdominal muscles have weakened, he's not able to draw in enough air when lying flat either prone or supine. Propped up on three pillows, he sleeps with his torso angled upright so that gravity can assist him with breathing. When three pillows and gravity aren't enough, the solution won't be four pillows.

His pulmonologist says Richard will need a BiPAP machine likely within the next month. It's already been ordered for him. He'll have to wear a mask strapped over his nose and mouth, and pressurized air will be forced in and out of his lungs all night long. His pulmonologist says it's no big deal. The BiPAP is noninvasive. Chronic snorers with sleep apnea use a similar machine all the time. But to Richard, the BiPAP is a very big deal. And everything he needs feels invasive.

The introduction of each new medicine, adaptive device, specialist, and piece of equipment comes with a corresponding loss of function and independence. The new medications for drooling and depression, the new voice-to-text phone app, the ankle foot orthotic he's supposed to wear to keep his right foot from dropping, the feeding tube he'll soon need, the power wheelchair waiting for him in the living room, the Bi-PAP already ordered. Each one is his signature on the dotted line of a contract agreeing to the next phase of ALS. He's standing in a lake of dense quicksand, and every offer of assistance is a block of concrete placed atop his head, sinking him irrevocably deeper.

And although Richard can't bear to talk about it, he's keenly aware of the last concrete block in the queue. When his diaphragm and abdominal muscles quit their jobs entirely and he can't produce any respiratory pressure on his own, the final offering from his multidisciplinary medical team will be mechanical ventilation through a tracheostomy tube. Twenty-four/seven life support. Up to his eyeballs in quicksand, he'll be asked to blink once if he wants to live.

It's ten after seven, and Bill won't be here until nine. Richard has almost two hours to fill. Not long ago, it wouldn't be unusual for him to spend an entire day alone with his Steinway, perfecting the sonatas and preludes of Schubert or Debussy or Liszt. He'd begin in the morning, the sun streaming in through the bay windows, a spotlight for his private stage, and he'd be stunned to look up, seemingly only minutes later, to see his reflection in the darkened windowpanes. An entire day, here and gone in a snap. He was never lonely when he was alone with his piano. Without the piano, two hours is seven thousand two hundred seconds. An anxious eternity.

Torn between competing desires, aching to sleep and aching to move off his back, he spends several minutes doing neither. He turns his head to the side, pressing his nose into the pillowcase, and inhales the smell of freshly laundered sheets. He breathes steadily there, and the experience is heavenly, as sensually enveloping as walking into a bread bakery, but more specific, more personal. He can't remember the brands of detergent and fabric softener his mother used, but Trevor, who instead of managing Richard's career is now managing Richard's bills, services, and the delivery of groceries and household supplies, must be purchasing the exact combination Richard's mother bought. He inhales as deeply as he can, and just as the smell of onions sautéing on a stove puts him in his grandmother's kitchen, he's transported to his childhood bedroom.

He's Ricky, seven years old and waking in his twin bed on a Saturday morning. He'll have bacon and pancakes drenched in maple syrup for breakfast before his piano lesson with Mrs. Postma. He'll play Chopin and Bach. His feet don't yet reach the pedals. Mrs. Postma loves teaching him. She sometimes gives him a pack of Life Savers at the end of his lesson as a reward for being such a good student. He likes the five-flavor rolls best. Cherry is his favorite. A feeling of safety and innocence washes over him as delicious as creamy hot soup, but it passes through him too quickly and without pausing. He's Richard, back in his adult body, in his adult bed, and he wants to cry for that little boy, for what he's destined to face as a man, for all that he'll lose.

Eleven hours of locked-up pain in his hips and spine intensifies, annihilating any hope of sleep, so he shimmies himself out of bed. He walks through his darkened bedroom. He can't draw back the drapes. He can't pull up the shades. He flips the bathroom light switch on with his mouth.

Naked, he straddles the toilet and empties his bladder into the bowl, aiming with his hips. His stream is accurate at first but then, as usual, goes astray. Before he's done, he's sprayed urine onto the back of the lid, splattered it across the seat, and dribbled some onto the floor. He hears his mother's voice in his head. In a household inhabited by a husband and three boys, she was regularly scolding one of them about the god-awful filthy state of their toilet. He assesses the mess he's made, powerless to wipe any of it up. *Sorry, Mom.*

He looks down at his distended stomach. He's not fat. Despite a steady diet of milk shakes, he's alarmingly underweight. His abdominal muscles have started loosening their grip, letting go. He stands sideways in front of his bathroom mirror and examines his profile. He's got the tummy of a toddler, the beer gut of an old man.

He's also five days constipated. His neurologist recently put him on glycopyrrolate, an anticholinergic that decreases the secretion of saliva in his mouth and throat, so there's less drool, less pooling in the back of his mouth. Before going on this medication, he had several unrelenting coughing fits that carried on for so long that Bill and whatever aide or therapist was in the room believed that Richard might drown right then and there in a puddle of his own spit. Thankfully, the drug works, but it comes with a trade-off. Less spit but full of shit.

His overall lack of mobility and the mostly liquid, rather fiberless diet he's on can also cause constipation, but since this is a new issue, he's blaming the glycopyrrolate. He's also on Rilutek. It's said to prolong survival by 10 percent. Richard did the math. The average duration of this disease is twenty-seven to forty-three months, so he stands to gain about three months of life on Rilutek. A single bonus season. According to his most optimistic calculations, he won't see his fiftieth birthday.

Not necessarily, people say. *Look at Stephen Hawking,* they say. Sure, the disease will paralyze every muscle he owns but for those in his intestines and his beating heart, but he could live on artificial ventilation for thirty more years! This is the hope people want him to adopt, the inspirational speech aimed to fuel his will to live and persevere. Although Richard hasn't reached a definitive decision on a tracheostomy yet, if he had to choose today, he would rather die than rely on invasive ventilation. Stephen Hawking is a theoretical physicist and a genius. He can live in the realm of his mind. Richard can't. He looks down at his dangling hands. His world, his fascination, his reason, was the piano. If he were a brilliant theoretical physicist with ALS, he might hope for thirty more years. As a pianist with ALS, he's not buying any new calendars.

Hungry, he walks into the kitchen out of habit. He faces the refrigerator and tries to penetrate it with his eyes as if he had X-ray vision, imagining the food inside that he can't eat unless Bill or Melanie or Kevin opens the door and prepares it for him. His stomach growls. Two more hours until breakfast. For some reason, he pictures the bottle of balsamic salad dressing in the door and thinks about its expiration date, wondering if it will outlast him. He imagines Trevor, tasked with sorting through Richard's belongings after his death, fixing himself a salad, pouring the balsamic dressing over a bowl of mixed greens.

Richard leaves the refrigerator and now stands in front of his bookcase, reading the spines of his books. He can't pull one from the shelf and flip through it. Photo albums from his various tours and concerts are stacked on the shelf below the books containing pictures he can't see of himself playing at some of his favorite venues — the Sydney Opera House, Roy Thomson Hall in Toronto, the Oslo Opera House, Merkin Hall, Carnegie Hall, Tanglewood, and of course Boston Symphony Hall. The cover of the photo album on top is blanketed with dust. He can't wipe it off. Programs from several hundred shows line the bottom shelf. There will never be another program to add to the line, never another picture to slide into the next clear plastic sleeve of his dusty photo album. This realization isn't a new loss, but he never gets used to it. He'll never play again.

His chest tightens, and his heart and lungs feel sluggish as if filling with wet sand. Despite the glycopyrrolate, tears well at the back of his eyes. He coughs several times and steps away from the bookcase.

He continues walking through his apartment, a tourist in his own home, a visitor at a museum where he's allowed to look but not touch. He wanders over to his desk and visits the two framed photographs of Grace. Baby Grace with no hair and one bottom tooth. Grace in her cap and gown, her long chestnut hair worn down, one of the few times he can remember it not in a ponytail. He wonders if she's wearing it up or down these days.

He imagines the space between the two photographs. He missed so much of her childhood. His heart twinges with regret, wishing he could go back. He thinks of the framed moments he'll likely never see — her college graduation, her wedding day, her children. He sits at his desk and leans in to get a closer look, hoping to see something in the tilt of her head, the light reflecting in her eyes, to absorb something new and lasting about her while he still can. The hunger within his distended stomach widens, aching for more than breakfast.

And that single, lonely frame on his desk hurts his heart. There should've been more. When he and Karina were first married, he dreamed of a traditional family with great excitement — three or four children, a house in the suburbs, the regular hours of an instructor at New England Conservatory, and Karina teaching or playing somewhere. He hoped for a son especially, a boy who played piano or violin or any instrument, a young man Richard could inspire, mentor, and celebrate. He promised himself as a young man that he'd be a better father to his children than his father was to him.

He studies Grace's face in the photograph, and his heart is pummeled by regret, anger, blame, and shame. He didn't live the life he intended, and there's no way to do it over. Maybe he's no better than his father after all. He blinks back tears and clenches his teeth, swallowing over and over, stuffing these ancient and new emotions down, absorbing them into his body.

Richard's father was the quarterback captain of his high school football team, division champions class of 1958, married to the prettiest cheerleader on the squad, and Pop Warner coach to two of his three boys. Walt Evans felt no pride or joy in his awkward skinny son who loved classical piano. He still doesn't. Real men love Tom Brady, not Wolfgang Mozart. Although Richard hasn't been back home in years, he'd bet that his brothers' football trophies are still standing gleaming tall on the fireplace mantel in the living room, proudly on public display. His father is probably still bragging about Mikey's one-handed touchdown catch that won the Thanksgiving Day game against Hanover High. Richard's many piano competition awards were kept in his bedroom, hidden, private. If they haven't been thrown away or donated to the YMCA, they're now most likely in an unmarked cardboard box in the attic.

Growing up, Richard felt his father's disinterest in him as disdain, disgust, dishonor. He's not sure Grace's experience of her father is much better. She had two highly trained pianists for parents, and no matter how he and Karina sold it, zero interest in the piano. She loved sports. Soccer and volleyball. Oh, the irony. For the first time in his life, Richard empathized with the disappointment his father felt in him. But he swore he wouldn't pick up the thread in the pattern his father had woven, that he wouldn't in turn reject his daughter. She could love anything she wanted, even if it involved nets and balls instead of strings and keys.

He understood this, yet her nonmusical interests created real distance between them. They literally had no common ground — she was on a field or a court, and he was in a practice room or on a stage. The demands on his time, both rehearsing and performing, kept him from being home much, and when he was, he had trouble relating to her. He's always loved her, but they were never close.

Then he and Karina split. Karina lobbied hard for Grace's allegiance, disclosing all of Richard's many sins. He hated Karina for doing that, accused her of stealing his only daughter's love, and threatened to reveal his side of the story. But in truth Karina didn't need a smear campaign to secure Grace's love and loyalty. Karina already had it. And pointing out the rotting heap of trash on Karina's side of the street wouldn't have served to clean up his.

Hidden behind the photo from Grace's graduation is a picture of Richard and Karina on their wedding day. He almost didn't bother taking it with him when he moved out, and he almost tossed it in the trash when he needed a frame for Grace's graduation picture. He and Karina are holding hands and smiling in the photo, young and in love, assuming everything will work out for them. Oblivious. He thinks of how far they strayed from the life he wanted in that photograph, of what she stole from him, of the second chance at happiness that he'll now never have, and a wild anger snakes through him, coiling in the dark emptiness of his stomach. If he could use his hands, he'd remove that hidden wedding photo from the frame and rip it to shreds.

He needs something to do, something to distract him from the bottomless sorrow and anger inside his gut, from the tortured thoughts circling like vultures in his head. He can't use the computer until Bill affixes Richard's Head Mouse, a reflective-dot sticker stuck to the tip of his nose. Well, he could go "old school" and peck at the keys with a pen held by his teeth or with his big toe as he did before getting the Head Mouse, but he doesn't feel like it.

He considers watching TV. The remote is taped to the hardwood floor where he can press the on-button with his big toe. Once the TV and cable are on, he can press the voice-command button with his toe and say,

"Channel Five." He could watch CNN or PBS or a movie, but it's too passive.

He wants to run, scream, cry, punch something, break something, kill something. Instead, he sits on the couch, powerless, laboring to breathe, staring vaguely at his pathetic reflection in the glassy black TV screen. He tries to imagine the life he might've lived if he hadn't met Karina, if he had forty more years, if he didn't have to sit here alone for two hours with no hands, if he didn't have ALS. His breathing eventually settles as he stares and waits. He thinks of nothing coherent for a long time.

He's playing Debussy's *Préludes* in the TV screen as he falls asleep.

CHAPTER ELEVEN

Richard is awakened by the sound of a key at the door. He looks to his left wrist for the time, an obstinate and futile habit. He hasn't worn a watch in six months, since the fingers of his right hand lost the strength and dexterity to work the latch on the band. His eyes find the time on the cable box as the door opens: 9:00 on the dot. Ever punctual.

"Mornin'!"

Bill bursts into Richard's condo, whistling an upbeat song Richard doesn't recognize, jingling a metal ring of keys like a tambourine. The kitchen and living room lights flick on, and Richard squints against this assault on his senses. Bill puts something in the refrigerator, places an earth-friendly grocery bag on the counter, removes his hat, and hangs his coat on the back of one of the bar chairs. He's all movement and high energy, a diametrical contrast to the silent inertia he entered. He walks past Richard and lifts the window shades.

"Let there be light!" he says in a dramatic stage voice as he does every morning. "Where you at with the BM?"

"Nothing yet."

Bill smiles and heads toward the kitchen. Richard can't imagine how this answer can be a cause for joy, even considering Bill's often-inappropriate sense of humor. Richard assumes he must've misunderstood and is about to correct him when Bill pulls a small white bottle from the bag on the counter.

"This'll fix you."

Knowing that breakfast with a side of laxative is not the first item on his morning menu, Richard stands and waits for his Rilutek. Bill pops the pill into Richard's mouth, tips a glass of water gently at Richard's lips, and studies Richard's eyes as he swallows, watching for signs of distress. Richard gets the pill down without any fuss and then follows Bill into the master bathroom.

He doesn't flinch about being naked in front of Bill. Any modesty Richard had was pulverized to fine dust after their first week together. Bill's seen it all. He cared for his partner who was diagnosed with HIV in

1989 through full-blown AIDS, Kaposi's sarcoma, and the pneumonia that killed him in 1991. The experience catalyzed a change in career from travel agent specializing in excursions to exotic destinations on private islands to home health aide specializing in excursions to exotic diseases in ordinary living rooms.

On the books, he's officially Richard's morning home health aide, but Richard has come to think of him as equal parts brother, doctor, therapist, and friend. Richard wishes every day that he didn't have ALS and therefore no reason to have ever crossed paths with Bill, but since Richard does have ALS, he thanks God every morning for this strange, beautiful man. God bless Bill.

Bill turns on the shower, rolls up a sleeve, and checks the temperature several times with his hand before he's satisfied.

"There you go. Hop in."

Richard steps up and over the wall of the tub, less than two feet high, an elevation he's actually measured and is acutely concerned with. Clearing it already takes concentration and conscious effort. At some point in the coming months, his legs won't possess the strength to raise his feet over the wall. Maybe by then he'll be in a new condo with a walk-in shower, one he can shuffle his feet into while he can still walk, wide enough to accommodate a shower chair that can roll right into the stall when walking becomes a memory. If not, Bill will have to sponge bathe him. So many wonderful changes to look forward to.

Richard stands with his back to the showerhead, grateful for the heat and pressure and touch of the water spraying his skin, one of the few moments of each day when he still enjoys being in a physical body. He pees. No mess to clean up in here. Just outside the open shower curtain, Bill is rubbing a dollop of shampoo between his latex-gloved palms.

"Let's have that gorgeous head of yours."

Bill is bald and openly jealous of Richard's head of thick, wavy black hair. Richard is openly jealous of Bill's healthy motor neurons and strong muscles. Slightly taller than Bill, Richard bends over, offering the crown of his head as if he were being knighted. Bill works the shampoo into Richard's hair, and Richard smiles with his eyes closed, diving deep into this newly discovered carnal indulgence. Head scrubbing for Richard is a hedonistic experience approaching nirvana, almost as sensually pleasing as a blow job. If Bill were an attractive woman, Richard's pretty sure he could climax off an intense head scrub. He channels every unresolved, agonizing itch he's suffered through since yesterday's shower into the sublime satisfaction of Bill's nails combing the base of Richard's skull, raking the top of his head, scratching circles above his temples.

The scrubbing stops, and Richard peeks his eyes open. Water is spraying past the open curtain, and suds are dripping down Bill's forearm. Bill adjusts the curtain and continues. He massages Richard's scalp well past the point of clean hair. Again, God bless Bill.

He finishes, and Richard rinses. Bill squirts bath gel onto a sponge, and Richard moves out of the shower's spray to be washed, front side first, then back. Rubbing the sudsy sponge along every inch of Richard's body, Bill sings "They Say It's Wonderful" from *Annie Get Your Gun*.

The whistling and the singing drive Richard nuts. Bill is a Broadway buff and a karaoke fanatic. Every morning he belts out a medley of songs from every era of Broadway, from *Porgy and Bess* to *Oklahoma!* to *The Lion King* to *Hamilton*. Richard sits proudly on the other end of the musical spectrum. He loves classical piano, the notes alone evoking powerful emotion, each wordless composition translating a privately interpreted journey. Listening to Schumann is like looking at a Picasso, like breathing in God. Listening to Bill serenade him with Broadway tunes is a fork dipped in vinegar, stabbing him in the eye.

But Richard hasn't shared his distaste for Broadway with Bill. He figures it's not wise to risk offending the man who washes his penis. So he quietly endures every maddening medley. He's thought about asking Bill to play music from Richard's iTunes playlists. They could enjoy getting bathed and dressed to Bach's *Goldberg Variations,* Schumann's fantasies, Chopin's preludes. As there are no lyrics, this would shut Bill up.

But Richard can't bear it. He can't bear to listen to the masterpieces of these great composers, the music playing in the practiced circuits of his mind, never again to be executed by his fingers. The exquisite agony in hearing the music he loves but can never play is far more painful than Bill's rendition of "Everything's Coming Up Roses." So Richard tolerates Bill's singing. In a million ways, living with ALS is a practice in the art of Zen.

Bill shuts off the water and dries Richard with a towel. The two men move over to the sink. Bill wipes shaving cream onto Richard's face, finger painting his cheeks, chin, neck, and upper lip. Bill stops singing once he has the razor in hand. Richard watches Bill's brown eyes devote themselves to every contour of Richard's face. Bill is breathing deeply and audibly through his nose, and as if it has its own gravitational pull, Richard finds himself inhaling and exhaling in sync. When Bill is finished, he wipes Richard's face clean with a hot, wet facecloth.

"You look tired," says Richard.

"Queeraoke last night. I was up late."

"With anyone special?"

Bill hesitates. "No."

"Anyone unspecial?"

"I'll let you know when Ryan Gosling realizes I'm the one for him." Bill works some styling gel through Richard's hair and combs it. "You lucky bastard. Look at this head of hair."

"Yeah, I'm the lucky guy in the room."

Richard hears the monotone sound of his own voice, still unfamiliar to him, every last syllable of one word bleeding into the first syllable of the next, every word a single note played over and over. D-D-D-D-D-D. Every sentence is the same song. It's the ALS anthem, lullaby, number one hit.

"You're not getting any pity parties from

me, Handsome. Open."

Bill brushes Richard's teeth with an electric toothbrush and wipes the white froth off his lips with the now cold, wet facecloth when finished. The last step of their morning bathroom ritual is the arm massage. Bill begins with Richard's right arm. He rubs moisture cream onto Richard's shoulder, biceps, elbow, forearm, and hand, Bill's strong fingers sliding along Richard's skin, pressing into abandoned muscles. As with the shampoo, it feels like heaven to be touched.

His right arm and hand are flaccid and passively accept everything Bill does. He wiggles and pulls on each finger. He holds Richard's arm, the elbow in one hand and the wrist in the other, and gingerly rotates the arm at the shoulder, circling forward, then backward, moving this frozen joint. He lifts Richard's arm above his head, dragging his fingers down Richard's skin, squeezing from wrist to armpit, trying to drain some of the edema that plagues Richard in this hand. His limp fingers look like tight sausages due to the fluid that seeps from his leaky veins, pooling in his hands.

Richard watches this exercise somewhat detached, as if his fingers and arm belong to someone else. Yet he feels everything Bill does in vivid detail. Each touch reminds Richard that his arms aren't completely severed from his body. Even though the efferent pathways are forever out of order, his arms are still connected to his nervous system, the afferent signals of pain, pressure, temperature, and touch completely intact. Somehow, this is comforting.

Bill moves over to Richard's left arm. Although both arms are completely paralyzed, they look and act nothing alike. While his right arm is hypotonic, a limp noodle of skin and bones, his left arm is rigid, his fingers locked in a deformed claw. The spasticity in Richard's left arm resists Bill's touch as if in rebellious disobedience. Bill has to work hard to rotate the arm, to uncurl each stiff finger. Richard tries to will his misbehaving fingers to relax. He has no influence over them.

Done in the bathroom, they walk to Richard's bedroom dresser. Bill knows where everything is. He chooses underwear, socks, jeans, and a gray crewneck, each with Richard's approval. Bill then dresses Richard like a parent dresses a small child, like a girl dresses a favorite doll, like a home health aide dresses a grown man with ALS.

Bill pulls a pair of old loafers from the closet, and Richard worms his feet into them. Lastly, Bill loops the lanyard holding Richard's iPhone over Richard's neck as if it were an Olympic medal, clips the Bluetooth connector to his shirt collar, and presses the Head Mouse target sticker to the tip of his nose. There. Richard checks himself in the mirror. As always, Bill did a fine job. Richard is dressed and ready to go out, as if he has somewhere to go, as if he'll ever be expected anywhere other than the hospital ever again. Except for the ghoulish hang of his arms, his protruding belly, the extreme thinness of his face, and the absurd sticker on his nose, he still recognizes himself in the mirror. He wonders if at some point he won't.

They make their way to the kitchen. Bill opens the refrigerator door, that impenetrable vault, with an easy, unremarkable tug and begins pulling ingredients for this morning's smoothies. Richard's favorite recipe is peanut butter, banana, yogurt, and whole milk, with dashes of protein powder, flaxseed, citalopram, and glycopyrrolate. Today's special will include the addition of a laxative. Yum.

Richard looks out the living-room window. He knows from Bill's winter coat, hat, and gloves that it's cold outside, but the day appears sunny, inviting. He looks at his desk, the bookcase, the TV, the piano, exactly as they were earlier this morning, yesterday, the day before that, the month before that.

"I think I'd like to go for a walk when you leave."

Bill removes the lid from the blender and gives Richard a long, serious look. Richard hasn't gone out alone, unattended, since his left hand went dead.

"I'd feel better if you waited for Melanie."

Melanie comes at 1:30, three hours after Bill leaves. Richard hates that he needs Bill's permission to leave his own home, but there's no other way. If Bill shuts the door behind him when he leaves, Richard is trapped inside his condo, his living tomb.

"I'll be fine. Just leave my door open."

"What about the front door?"

"I have my neighbors' phone numbers. Someone will let me back in."

"Who's home?"

"Beverly Haffmans should be around."

Bill approaches Richard and leans his mouth over the phone resting on Richard's chest. "Launch voice control," Bill says slowly and clearly. "Call Beverly Haffmans."

The phone rings on speaker.

"Hello?"

"Hi, Beverly, this is Bill Swain, your

neighbor Richard Evans's home health aide."

"Oh, hi there. Is everything okay?"

"Yup, everything is fine here. He's going to go for a walk this morning. Are you going to be home to let him back in the building?"

"Oh, yes. I'll be here. I can do that."

"Okay, great. Thank you, Beverly. Bye now."

Bill returns to the blender and peels a banana. "I still don't like it. If I didn't have my next client right after you, I'd go with you. You sure you can't wait until Melanie?"

"I'm sick of being in here. I can still walk. I'll be fine."

"You're wearing your brace."

"Okay."

Bill makes four smoothies without singing, a sure sign that he's uncomfortable with this plan. Worried that conversation might lead Bill into verbalizing his concerns, and that might in turn convince him to change his mind, Richard keeps quiet. Bill plops a straw into each drink and then leaves the kitchen.

Richard steps up to the counter, bends his head to the straw of the first glass, and sucks the smoothie steadily down. He was so hungry. And while these drinks are thick

135

and filling, they're far from satisfying. What he wouldn't give to chew on a steak. Or even a piece of toast.

Bill returns with the foot brace and a winter coat, hat, and mittens and squats down in front of Richard. Familiar with this drill, Richard lifts his right foot without direction. While holding Richard's leg to stabilize him, Bill removes the shoe, fits the ankle foot orthotic over Richard's sock, and returns the shoe to his foot. Bill then threads Richard into his coat, pulls the iPhone out so it lies on top of the zipper, clips the Bluetooth connector to the coat collar, fits his hat on his head, and works his lifeless hands into the mittens.

"I'm putting a key to your building in your right coat pocket in case Beverly doesn't answer. You'll ask someone to open the door for you, okay?"

Richard nods, knowing this won't be necessary.

"Okay, my friend." Bill dons his own coat. "You're all set. I'm still not a fan of this idea. You sure I can't set you up with something on Netflix?"

"No. I want to get out of here. I know you have to get going. Let me just drink one more."

He finishes a second smoothie while Bill

slips on his hat and gloves.

"Okay, let's do it."

Bill opens the door, and they leave without shutting it behind them. Richard takes each step down the stairs consciously and carefully, wanting to prove to Bill, who is walking backward in front of him and most certainly assessing the competence of every step, that he's perfectly capable of walking alone. They pass through the grand foyer, Bill opens the front door, and they walk outside.

The air is face-pinking cold, but it's clean and breezy and instantly feels far more vital than the confined air Richard has been stewing in for too long inside. He takes a deep breath and sighs out the exhale. He takes in the passing traffic, the people walking on the sidewalk and in the park, a baby stroller, a bicyclist, a dog, a squirrel. He smiles. He's among the living again.

Bill pats him on the back. "You'll be okay. See you in the morning, Ricardo."

"Thank you, William."

Before he sets off on his own, Richard watches Bill hurry down the street, an angel on his way to the next bathroom, bedroom, and kitchen, to someone with MS or cancer or Alzheimer's, washing hair and teeth and genitals, massaging and dressing and feeding, singing show tunes to all as he does, and, for some, giving them the freedom to do as much as they can while they still can.

God bless Bill.

CHAPTER TWELVE

Three blocks from home, Richard walks through the gate of the Public Garden and is already exhausted. When he's simply standing still or walking from his bedroom to the living room, his legs feel sturdy beneath him, still capable and responsive, normal. At home, he can convince himself that ALS might only ever affect him from the waist up. Maybe he'll return that hideous $27,000 wheelchair that wasn't covered by insurance. But in his fourteen-hundred-square-foot, one-bedroom condo, he's not asking much of his quads and hamstrings and calves.

Three blocks from the front step where Bill left him, he's completely sapped. His legs have become sandbags, his bones filled with rocks, impossibly heavy, and he lacks the energy to move them. Even standing still is shaky. He needs to sit down. Around the bend past the statue of George Washington on his horse, Richard spots the nearest bench and tries to estimate how many steps away he is. He guesses about thirty and seriously wonders if he can make it.

This is not normal. It's not normal for a three-block walk to wear out a forty-five-year-old man, potentially defeating him thirty steps shy of his destination. There's no denying it. ALS has crawled its way into the motor neurons that feed the muscles of his legs, and walking three blocks is the pathetic molehill large enough to unmask its sinister invasion. He imagines his body's resistance to this attack, the molecular war in the fight against ALS at every neuromuscular junction, an invisible army, outnumbered and outgunned, deployed to fight this insidious enemy for as long as it can. The army holds its ground in Richard's legs when he is home, but when it has to divert half its soldiers to the mission of walking to the Public Garden, the resistance becomes compromised, ALS advances, and the enemy is poised to take control. His army calls back the troops. Every soldier is needed in the trenches. No more walking!

But he presses on, every step a grueling punishment. He hears Bill's, Kathy DeVillo's, and his neurologist's voices scolding him in his mind. It's dangerous for him to keep walking when he's tired like this. His coordination gets sloppy. He's especially worried about the possibility of dragging one of his tired feet, stubbing a toe on the uneven pavement, tumbling him to the ground. With no arms or hands to break his fall, every wipeout is a potential head trauma, broken bone, and trip to the emergency room.

Twenty feet from his goal, he's fast running out of gas and faith. Still heavy, his legs now also feel flimsy, a teetering tower of wooden blocks that threaten to collapse beneath him with every step. His blood races through the vessels of his body, rushing through the chambers of his heart, begging him to hurry up and get to the bench before he falls. He looks around. He counts five other people close enough to hear him if he yells, but they might as well be in Timbuktu because he'll never ask any of these strangers for help.

And he'll never ask his father or brothers in New Hampshire or his daughter in Chicago. And he can't ask Trevor in New York or his medical team at Mass General or even Bill, who is somewhere with his next client. He is alone in the Public Garden. He's alone in his home. He's alone in his ALS. And he's suddenly, overwhelmingly terrified.

He can barely breathe, but it's fear that's strangling him, not ALS. Each inhale seems to stoke a building terror, as if his blood now carries panic instead of oxygen. The fear grips his entire body like a vise, a cage around his lungs, more paralyzing than his disease, and he can't move. Sipping sharp tastes of air, he has to keep going if he's going to make it to the bench. He finds a pep talk, a mission statement. *Keep going.* He takes small steps, small breaths. His eyes are married to the bench, and when he's close enough, he leans forward, forcing his legs to *keep going.* It's the bench or bust. *Keep. Going. Keep. Going.*

Two more wobbled steps, and he crash-lands face-first into the bench. His right cheek, shoulder, and hip already throb. He'll have bruises by morning, which Bill will demand explanations for. He rights himself and sits victorious but feels nothing like a winner. The panicked fear flushes out of his system, leaving him rattled, wrung out, warned. He looks back along the path he traveled and beyond the garden gate. A little more than three blocks and a long way home. Too many steps to estimate. Too many steps, period.

Worst-case scenario, he'll spend the next

two hours on this bench. Melanie will call him at 1:30 and retrieve him. But he hopes for better than the worst-case scenario. Always has. He'll rest awhile and hopefully recharge his leg muscles and courage enough to make the journey home on his own.

The garden is tranquil this time of year. He spots a couple of ducks in the pond, but the swans and swan boats are gone for the season. The tourists are gone, too. The people walking by him are Bostonians: a young Asian man, likely a student, bent over at the waist, hauling a backpack thicker than he is; a woman in sneakers and a massive black winter coat carrying a large black umbrella, her eyes focused on the ground — Richard looks up at the clear blue sky, perplexed — a corporate woman carrying her dry cleaning with two fingers, the winter wind blowing the clear plastic sheath covering her hanging clothes behind her like a sail, her purse bouncing off her hip on the downbeat of every left step, her heels beating the ground in a half-time tempo, late for something; a short Italian guy, his stomach leading way out in front of him, gabbing on his phone in a thick Boston accent, his walk a swagger in expensive-looking leather shoes.

Most of the people who pass Richard are traveling alone, stone-faced, white cords dangling from their ears as if they're robots powered by the devices they hold. No one looks at him. It's not that they see him and look away. They never notice him in the first place. He's part of the background, as uninteresting as the bench he's sitting on.

A sparrow leaps onto the wooden seat a brazen few inches from him and tilts its head from side to side. They make eye contact, and then the sparrow hops to the ground. It pecks at something there and flies away.

Everything living is in motion, going somewhere, talking, walking, pecking, flying, doing. Life is not a static organism. Every day, he's a little more shut down, shut in, turned off. A little less in motion. A little less alive. He's becoming a two-dimensional still-life painting, slipping inexorably into the alternate dimension of the sick and dying.

A woman passes him. Something about her reminds him of Karina twenty years ago. Her long hair and that purple scarf. He met Karina in Sherman Leiper's Technique class. Although he noticed her on the very first day, it took him most of the semester to talk to her. Fresh out of public high school in New Hampshire, he had no experience with girls yet. When he was a teenager, his father regularly discredited Richard's masculinity in obvious digs and under-his-breath derogatory comments. In a home and town where jocks ruled, a boy who loved tickling the ivories was seen as unmanly and decidedly uncool. Already cast aside by his father and brothers and boys in his grade, he couldn't risk adding more rejection from Jenny or Stacey or any of the other cute girls he had crushes on. Instead, he channeled his private feelings of longing and unrequited love into his playing. He devoted his attention to piano instead of girls, and he insulated his young heart from the pain of being judged weird or wrong or not good enough by pretending not to care what anyone thought of him.

At Curtis, music ruled, not athletics. Every girl there was attracted to music, and even better, to musicians. Like a seed waiting for healthy soil and sunshine, Richard's confidence around girls blossomed at Curtis.

That first day of Technique class, Karina was wearing a lavender scarf wrapped around her long brown hair. He remembers her big green eyes and pale skin, her plump bottom lip distracting him from the lecture as he imagined how soft it would feel to kiss it. Then she spoke, called upon by Sherman Leiper. He can't remember the question, but he can still remember the sound of her answer in that Polish accent, her perfectly charming broken English. He sat there captivated, fascinated, turned on, jealous that she wasn't speaking to him. Her voice was a melody of exotic sounds and intonation, a song he wanted to learn.

He loved the melody of her voice, but it was her fearlessness that he eventually fell in love with. At eighteen, she'd left her country, her family, her first language, everything she knew. Although his story was less dramatic, he felt a kinship in this. They had a common independence, a sense of no return, that music would be their savior, that everything was riding on this education. Curtis was Richard's path to freedom and fulfillment, and he found Karina on that same path with him, matching him stride for stride, holding his hand, smiling next to him. Their mutual passion for playing the music of Chopin and Schumann bled into a passion for each other. Their relationship at Curtis was heady and intense, their days and nights consumed in classes, lessons, practice, and sex.

Richard sighs as the bitter memories rise

up from the shadowed corners of his mind, dialing into vivid focus. He's surprised they held back from intruding for as long as they did. It's hard for him to visit those old, happy memories of Karina without every horrible memory demanding equal viewing. *In good times and in bad.* The good and the bad — insoluble elements, prime numbers, oil and water. His good and bad memories of Karina don't blend, balance, neutralize, or cancel each other out, and he's stuck holding both, perfectly intact.

Videos from his memory bank play — their first coffee date in the student lounge, the first time they had sex, the last time they had sex, watching her play piano, which was always feeling her play piano, her green eyes loving him when he got his first big break, playing with the Cleveland Orchestra, her green eyes hating him at the dinner table after they moved to Boston, the morning Grace was born, Karina's surgery, the day everything he believed unraveled — and too many emotions run through him. He's happy, in love, betrayed, heartbroken, overcome with lust, disgust, rage, regret. The release he needs is laughter or crying or screaming or possibly all three, which would be fine if he were home and not on a bench in the Public Garden. The people walking by will think he's nuts. He feels a little nuts.

He needs to get Karina off his mind. He'll walk back home now. Walking will consume all of his mental energy and focus.

He's standing next to the statue of George Washington when the laxative kicks in. A massive cramp seizes his large intestine, followed by urgent pressure, a five-day-late freight train barreling into the station, right now. The pain and fear of losing control keep him pinned in place, unable to move. But he must. He's three blocks from home.

A few steps onward and the cold air against the sweat on his forehead makes him feel clammy, sick, as if he might pass out. He's not going to make it. He has to. He reinstates his pep talk. *Keep going.* Five days of stagnant waste are now in motion, insisting on evacuation, and the struggle to walk combined with the struggle to hold it all in brings tears to his eyes. *Keep going. Keep. Going.*

Through sheer will and some kind of a miracle, he reaches his front step. The urge to shit is now screaming full tilt, a peristalsis of feces and water churning inside him, pressing downward. He won't be able to hold it in much longer.

Dipping his chin to his chest, he summons

all of his strength and pours it into his voice.

"Launch voice control. Call Beverly Haff-mans."

The phone rings and rings and rings and rings.

"Hi, you've reached Beverly Haffmans. Please leave a message after the beep."

"Beverly, it's Richard Evans, your neighbor. I'm at the front door. Are you there? Open the door if you get this message. Please. I need to get in. . . . End call."

Shit. Where did she go? He presses her doorbell with his chin. No one answers. Unable to think of what else to do, he tries calling her again. The phone rings once and goes straight to voice mail.

"End call."

He literally held his shit together with the promise to his body that he would relieve himself when he got home. He can't pull down his pants, but he imagined soiling himself in the privacy of his own bathroom. Now that he's on the stoop, he has no reserve left. His bowels have run out of patience and composure, and he swears he can feel the pressure in his eyeballs.

He has nowhere to go. Public restrooms aren't an option. He has no hands. He could call 911, the lesser of two humiliating options. Wait. He remembers his other neighbor.

"Launch voice control. Call Peter Dickson."

The phone rings twice.

"This is Peter."

"Hi, Peter, this is Richard Evans, your neighbor. Are you home?"

"No, I'm in New York. What can I do you for?"

"Nothing, never mind, thanks."

"Everything okay?"

"Yup. I gotta go. End call."

He remembers the key in his pocket. In his fucking pocket, and he can't reach it. He turns to the street to look for help. A young woman is jogging on the sidewalk, approaching his stoop.

"Excuse me!" he yells from the top step, unable to walk down fast enough to meet her, unable to wave his arms.

She notices him. Thank God. She removes an earbud and slows down.

"Can you help me get my key out of my pocket and open my front door for me?"

Her face closes off, scared. "Sorry," she says quickly, and jogs away without looking back.

"Wait! Please!"

She practically sprints down the street.

150

He can only imagine what he looks and sounds like — a sweaty, bashed forehead; his arms hanging; his torso bent over; his voice monotone and creepy. He'd run, too.

No one else is on his side of the street, and his voice is too weak to reach the dog walker he sees in the park. He looks down at his phone. It's 12:20, over an hour until Melanie arrives. He won't make it. Maybe they can send someone else, someone now. Yes!

He activates the voice control on his phone. A wave of pain and pressure rolls through him, doubling him over at the waist. He knows this is his last chance. He can barely speak.

"Call Caring Health."

It rings three times.

"Hello?"

"This is Richard Evans. Can you send someone out right now? I can't wait for Melanie. It's an emergency."

"Richard? This is Karina."

What? How? His voice, his slurring, sloppy, barely audible monotone voice. Caring Health. Karina.

"Sorry, I . . . I —"

"I'm in the city. I'll be there in five minutes."

CHAPTER THIRTEEN

"Please just leave me. Melanie will be here at one thirty."

"Shut up."

In the pause that follows, the last kicks and screams of their mutual dread settle into surrender. They're in Richard's bathroom. She could leave him here. But for some reason that she doesn't yet understand, she's not going to, and so it's not worth discussing.

She unclips a device labeled BlueAnt from his coat collar, lifts his phone up and over his head, and places both on the vanity counter. She then unzips his winter coat, unsealing the stench that had been trapped beneath the insulating layers of down and weather-resistant outer shell. She covers her nose and mouth with her hand, an utterly ineffective shield against the noxious odor that is quickly saturating the air in the room.

She flashes to a summer afternoon when

Grace was two. Armed with nothing but the innocent intention of retrieving a beach chair from the car, she popped the trunk and was assaulted by the putrid, violent stink of a forgotten diaper filled with poop, baked in eighty-degree weather for several days. The smell emanating from Richard right now is similar but far worse. She removes her useless hand from her face and gags.

About to take a deep breath as she would before attempting anything potentially painful or scary — striking the first key of Bach's *Goldberg Variations* in a recital a million years ago; pushing in concert with the labor contractions that delivered Grace; picking up the phone today, knowing it was Richard calling — she thinks better of it. Taking a deep breath now would mean consuming more of this aerosolized cesspool. Instead, she lifts the top of her sweater and hangs it over her nose, creating a mask, and breathes short, timid breaths through the woven fibers.

She looks up and finds herself accidently eye to eye with Richard. His thin, clean-shaven cheeks are wet with untouched tears, and his eyes, ever formidable in her experience, submit to her gaze, humiliated, apologizing, holding an expression so stunningly uncharacteristic of him that she can't look away. He closes his eyes and keeps them shut, likely unable to bear being seen like this, and she's grateful for the curtain between them, that he's not able to see the tears welling in her eyes.

While music, especially live music, can easily overcome her — the swell of the notes, an overwhelming awe of the artistry before her, the sorrow in the story of the song — she never cries for the crying. Raised under Russian oppression, she'd seen more than a lifetime's worth of weeping before she could tie her own shoes. At a young age, she learned to pretend that nothing bothered her, to dam up any tears of pity or compassion with great, impenetrable walls. She watched dry-eyed as scrawny toddlers wailed in the bread line where she stood dutifully for over two hours every day after school; as Mr. Nowak, who lived across the street, was hauled off to prison in front of his hysterical wife and six crying children for stealing a pig's head from a neighboring farm; as her mother wept while Karina packed her suitcase, leaving for a six-month job as a nanny in Switzerland, knowing that six months was a lie and that the nanny job was simply the plausible excuse necessary to obtain a passport, a way station on the way to school in America, and that she might never see her daughter again.

So it unnerves her that Richard's tears have somehow found a wormhole. She clears her throat, attempting to shake it off, reorienting her focus toward the task at hand. She unbuttons and unzips his jeans, grabs the waistband of his pants and boxers at both hips, and, in one hard yank, pulls them down to his knees.

It took her longer than five minutes to get to Richard's front stoop. She was only about a mile away when he called, but parking took several additional minutes. Some of the wet, runny shit that had dripped down his legs has already dried, his coarse black hairs poking through like weeds in droughty earth. A substantial heap is in his under-wear, and the rest is stuck like cake frosting to his ass and balls. More than she bar-gained for.

"Okay, can you balance on one foot?"

"I'm too tired. I don't want to fall."

"Hold on to my shoulders."

"I can't."

"Oh, right. Here, lean against the wall behind you."

She holds him firmly by his bare waist, and he shuffles back a few steps until he's flush to the wall. She squats down in front of him.

"Lift." She taps his left shin with the palm of her hand.

His shoes already off, she tugs the pants and boxers down and off one leg. In doing so, she slides his leg through the soiled clothing, and now his entire leg is smeared with shit. A substantial hunk of it falls out of his boxers and onto the bathroom floor. The white wall behind him has been painted brown by his rear end. Good God.

"Switch."

He lifts his right foot, and she drags the pants and boxers down, threads them over his socked foot and off. She looks at her hands and wishes she hadn't — Richard's shit on her right thumb, across her knuckles, beneath her freshly painted nails, pressed into her neatly trimmed cuticles. Her sweater mask has fallen off her nose, but she doesn't want to touch her sweater with her contaminated hands, so she leaves it. The stench, the mess, her hands. She wretches twice.

"I'm sorry," he says.

She can't pause now to clean herself up or she won't be able to finish. She has to keep going.

"Lift."

156

She peels the left sock off, then the right. She stands and grabs the bottom of his crewneck and tries to pull it up and over his head, but his arms won't cooperate, and he's stuck, a puzzle she can't solve.

"You have to go one arm at a time," says Richard.

She wrestles his left arm through the hole, then the right, then his head. He's now totally naked, smeared with shit and tears and shame.

She runs the shower. Richard steps in. She grabs the sponge on the tub's edge and saturates it with liquid soap.

"I'm good like this. Melanie can do the rest."

"Shut up."

As she begins to wash him, to touch his shoulders and chest and stomach, she has the split-second recognition that, although much bonier than she remembers, this is Richard's naked body before her, a body she has loved, kissed, hugged, held, spooned, sucked, fucked, avoided, despised, resented, cursed, hated. A comprehensive menu of memories and feelings related to this body, inappropriate to this bizarre situation, scrolls across her consciousness. She refuses it, ignoring his body's history, and focuses instead on the impersonal job in front of her. The sponge, the bum, the soap, the leg, the water, the penis, more soap, the balls, the sponge, the other leg.

Finally, the water circling the drain is clear. She leaves him there, goes to the kitchen, finds a trash bag, and returns to the bathroom. She locates a clean segment of his pants and, fashioning her hand like a pair of tweezers, transfers his trousers into the trash bag. She does the same to the socks, boxers, and shirt, then knots the top of the bag to seal off the smell. Even though she's sure she didn't touch any poop, her hands feel contaminated again. She washes them thoroughly in the sink under the hottest water she can stand and then washes them again.

She returns to the shower and shuts off the water. Richard steps out of the tub, and she dries him with a clean towel. They then walk wordlessly to his bedroom. Without input or direction, Karina finds his clothes and dresses him.

There. It's done. They look at each other now.

"Holy shit," says Karina.

Richard laughs. She didn't mean to be funny, but she's too adrenaline buzzed to remain straight-faced and joins him. They laugh deep, hard, sighing cackles, and the release feels good. It's been a long time since she's been on the same side of joy with Richard.

"I'll wait until Melanie gets here," she says, realizing that it's now almost 1:30.

"Okay."

She follows Richard into the living room and sits next to him on the couch. He turns the TV on by stepping on a remote control taped to the floor. He surfs a few channels, finds nothing of interest, and shuts the TV off. They sit side by side in silence, waiting for Melanie, and the lack of anything to say or do stretches on well past uncomfortable, feeling somehow more awkward than the shit show they just endured in the bathroom.

"So what were you doing in Boston?"

"I had a doctor's appointment."

"Oh." He doesn't ask what for or if she's okay. She doesn't blame him. Pandora's box is better left locked shut.

"I was just leaving the parking garage when you called."

She was at her annual gyn physical, not due to be in that office again for another year. What are the odds that she'd be barely over a mile away and available when he called? She looks around the room — the piano, the wheelchair, the desk and chair, the TV and coffee table. She looks at him.

"How long does Melanie stay with you?"

"About an hour."

"Does anyone else come here to help you?"

"Someone comes in the morning, usually Bill, for an hour and a half. Then another person comes at night to help me with dinner and get ready for bed."

"So about four hours a day?"

"Yeah, about that."

She thinks about the twelve or so waking hours in each day when he's alone with no help and all the trouble he could get into. What if he falls? What if he's hungry? What if he chokes? What if he shits his pants on the front step and is locked out of the building?

"You need a lot more help that that."

"I know. I don't work anymore. I can't afford it."

She thinks about the stairs and that wheelchair. This situation is untenable.

"You're selling this place."

"My realtor says I have it priced too high, but I don't want to come down or I'll lose money on it. Suppose it doesn't matter. I have a huge mortgage. It won't free up enough cash."

She doesn't point out that leaving here

160

might be more about living somewhere without stairs than the potential for liquidity. She knows his father and his brothers. His father won't help, and his brothers can't. It's too bad his mother isn't still alive. She would be here for him. His agent is in New York City.

"Is there a girlfriend?"

"No."

"You can't go on like this."

Isn't that exactly what she said to him when she finally asked for a divorce, but with an *I* instead of a *you*? She pinches her mouth shut, trying to withhold what she's about to say next, thinking that maybe if she makes it past this moment, if Melanie walks through the door and takes over the conversation, then she won't say what she's about to say.

She looks at Richard, and he nods, and she can't tell if he's agreeing with what she said or what she's thinking, believing suddenly that he can read her mind. This is nuts. She can't do this. She can't say what she's about to say. She'd have to be a masochist, an idiot, insane. Elise will call her crazy for sure. She can't undo all that has happened by saying what she feels compelled to say.

Just as she's sliding down a slick hill to

panic, a sense of calm settles over her instead, leveling her tilted inner landscape, and she realizes that it doesn't matter whether she says it now or not. She sighs. She looks at Richard and his lifeless arms and the wheelchair and his piano, and it's already true and done, as if this moment, this whole day, her entire life, were fated, and she agreed to say what's next before she was even born.

"You need to come back home."

"I know."

CHAPTER FOURTEEN

There aren't any Hallmark cards illustrated with doe-eyed characters or inspirational quotes that celebrate the life moment when a man moves back in with his ex-wife. For eight days now, Richard has been living at 450 Walnut Street, the house he lived in with Karina and Grace for thirteen years, the house he left when he and Karina separated a little over three years ago, the house conveyed to Karina free and clear in the divorce settlement. More specifically, he's been living in the old den, now his new bedroom, on the first floor.

Practically speaking, the move was a summer breeze. Aside from his clothes and toiletries, he needed only to move his computer, his TV, his Vitamix, and his wheelchair. He left everything else behind for his real estate agent to use in staging his condo. She says the piano in particular shows well, helps potential buyers to imagine a cultured life there, especially once they learn whom it belonged to and that it comes with the unit if they want it. She was ecstatic to see the wheelchair go. In her thirty-two years in the real estate business, she says that nothing ruined the feng shui of a home more than a power wheelchair.

He even left his king bed, as his occupational therapist convinced him that now was the perfect opportunity to order the hospital bed he needs. Weakening abdominal muscles plus no arms equals one hell of a time getting up from a flat mattress. He hated agreeing to it, but he has to admit that he sleeps much better in the twin hospital bed with the back raised to about sixty degrees than he did propped up on two or three pillows on his horizontal Posturepedic, and getting up without assistance is infinitely easier.

Emotionally speaking, the move was a Category 5 hurricane. Getting out of this house, away from Karina and the unsettled turmoil between them, and starting over in his own place in Boston had felt like a glorious victory, as if he'd won some grand prize or been released from prison or been allowed to graduate despite failing a required class for years. He remembers those first few mornings alone, the delicious moment upon wakening when he realized that she wasn't next to him or anywhere under the same roof, and he felt relieved, revitalized, ten years younger. And now, here he is, back under the same roof, demoralized, pathetic, emasculated, dying.

His new bed sits where his piano used to be. Where his passion, his love, his life, used to be. Now, in all likelihood, unless Karina panics and calls 911, this is where his death will be. He tries to ignore his deathbed, but there's no avoiding it. Even when he's not sleeping or sitting on it, when he's at his desk or watching TV from the easy chair, he feels it near him, waiting for him.

He is grateful to be living on ground level, to no longer have to negotiate three flights of stairs or a locked front door if he wants to go for a walk. He can open and close the garage door though voice activation of an app on his phone, and Karina keeps the door from the garage to the foyer propped open. So he can come and go without the need for keys or contingency plans.

But there's a rub. In Boston, he could go anywhere anonymous, unseen. Here, he knows all the neighbors. Despite their well-meaning smiles and hugs and conversation, he wishes he could step outside and be alone, unnoticed. He doesn't want to be seen like this.

His wheelchair is currently stored in the back corner of the garage, blessedly out of everyday sight. When he needs it, a construction project will be necessary. Karina assumes that it'll fit through the doorway, but she hasn't checked. He's spent countless hours alone in his living room sitting opposite that chair, as if they were staring each other down, and he's memorized the size and shape of his enemy. A quick eyeball of the entryway and he's already surmised that the geometry doesn't work. Twelve steps lead up to the front door. They'll either need to widen the doorway from the garage to the foyer or build a ramp over the front steps. The ramp will likely be cheaper. That or a bottle of pills.

He's at his computer, writing the seventh letter to his father that he won't send. He hasn't sent the other six. All are saved, but none are sent. Saved for what? When? Later. Later, which used to mean some nebulous, indeterminate time in his infinite future, has taken on a sense of immediacy since his diagnosis. Diagnosed a year ago with a disease that comes with an average life expectancy of three years, later is right fucking now. Yet, time for him is strangely both compressed and spun out. A day can seem to drag on for a week by midday, then pass by in a skinny minute during that same evening.

Is he saving these letters for his deathbed? His funeral? Will his father even come? The father he wants would be heartbroken to read that his youngest son has ALS. He'd drop everything to be by his son's side, supporting him with whatever he needs, his biggest champion to the end. The father he has might not even reply, which is probably why Richard can't bring himself to hit SEND. Maybe he'll print the letters, roll them, stuff them in glass bottles, and toss them into Boston Harbor for some other father to find. Maybe he'll delete them.

He's using a Head Mouse to type. A camera clipped to the top of his laptop screen detects the shiny target stuck to the tip of his nose, and the cursor moves wherever he points his face. When this technology was first introduced, the directions suggested sticking the mouse target to the user's forehead, hence the name. But most people wear the sticker on the bridge of their glasses or, like Richard, on their noses.

The door to his old den/new bedroom is intentionally left open, a lack of privacy traded for the ability to come and go without needing to call for Karina to come and open the door. Like letting the dog out. He's an animal in a cage. A pig in a pen. An ex-husband in the old den.

Despite being able to come and go, he restricts the majority of his time to this room, mostly for fear of stepping on any number of unresolved eggshells and land mines hiding beneath the floorboards of this home. And in the private company of his desk, TV, and hospital bed, he can sometimes forget that he's living under the same roof, under the care of his ex-wife. While he feels some relief in knowing that Karina is around should he need help, he's also loath to ask her for it.

He's hungry. He'll wait two hours for the next home health aide to come and make him a smoothie. He's cold and could use another layer. Think warm thoughts. He has to move his bowels and will need to be wiped. It doesn't matter that Karina already dealt with far worse on that fateful, humiliating day at his condo. He'll hold it in.

He lost Melanie and Kevin and the other home health aide regulars in the move due to geography. They serve only clients who live in the city of Boston. But Bill worked his magic and stayed on even though Richard now lives nine miles outside Bill's official territory. God bless Bill.

Through the open door, he can hear Karina's piano student playing in the next room. The student is dreadful. Richard leaves his unfinished letter to his father and peeks through the open door. A girl, a teenager. She has terrible posture, neck and shoulders slumped forward and down. Karina should correct that. It takes him a minute to figure out that it's Chopin's Nocturne no. 2 in E-flat Major that she's slaughtering. Her playing is uninspired and sloppy with many fits and starts, and Richard agonizes through every hesitation, the unfinished phrases hanging in the air, and he keeps impatiently begging her under his breath to strike the proper next note. To top it all off, she keeps forgetting the flats. This girl clearly didn't practice last week on her own. If he were her teacher, he'd send her home without finishing the lesson.

He returns to his desk but grows tired of using the Head Mouse. He switches to pecking the keys with a pen held in his mouth, but that's even more painstaking, and he soon gives up altogether. Instead, he sucks a sip of the milk shake left over from lunch. He doesn't care for this one. It's bland and too chalky, probably Ensure. His new early-afternoon aide, Kensia, left it on the desk for him. He takes another sip. It's definitely from a can and definitely not one of the freshly made elixirs from heaven that Bill concocts for him. But he's hungry and needs the calories, and Karina is busy, and Bill won't be here until the morning, so Richard sucks it up.

This is his new mantra, for Kensia's tasteless milk shakes and most everything else about this disease. He can't play piano ever again but has to listen to some shit student butchering a masterpiece in the next room. Suck it up. He can't live safely alone so he has to move back into his old house with his estranged ex-wife. Suck it up. An itch at the tip of his nose is intensifying every second that he doesn't address it, but if he scratches it by rubbing his nose against the edge of his desk or the wall or his bed comforter, he risks wiping off his Head Mouse sticker and not being able to use the computer again without pen pecking until the next aide comes. Suck it up.

He returns to his chair and stares out the window, listening vaguely to the piano lesson through the open door. As his thoughts often do if given too much unstructured time, they wander into the unsolvable realm of whys. Why did he get ALS? Why him? He runs up and down the familiar streets of these frequently traveled neural circuits in

170

his mind, knocking on doors and ringing bells, not in a self-pitying way, but more in a scientific-discovery kind of questioning. It's always an answerless quest.

Ten percent of ALS cases are purely genetic. One of his parents would've had to have had ALS for his ALS to be this hereditary kind. His father is alive and well, as far as Richard knows, and will probably live to be a hundred. His mother died of cervical cancer when she was forty-five, so he supposes that she could've had the mutation and would've developed ALS had she lived longer. But he dismissed this possibility seconds after he first considered it shortly after his diagnosis. First, it's just too freakishly unlikely and cruel that she would've been dealt cervical cancer *and* ALS. Second, and more convincing, his mother's parents, Gramma and Papa, died in their eighties. Both from strokes, if he remembers correctly. No ALS. So his ALS didn't come from his mother.

Five to 10 percent of ALS cases are familial, caused by a collaboration of genetic mutations. Conspiring DNA. Without genetic screening, the quick and dirty test to identify ALS as familial is the diagnosis of ALS in two other blood relatives. There is no ALS on either side of Richard's family tree. He's the only bad apple, rotting on a withering branch. So he doesn't have familial ALS. This is the single satisfying part of his why line of ALS questioning because it means that Grace is safe from this hideous monster. Or at least as safe as anyone else.

His form of ALS is called sporadic, caused by something other than or in addition to the DNA he inherited. He must've exposed himself to something or done something to cause this. But what? Why did this happen to him? He's not a vet and has never been a smoker. Both, for reasons no one understands, increase a person's odds of developing ALS. Did he have some degree of lead poisoning, mercury toxicity, or exposure to radiation that led to this? Did he have undiagnosed Lyme disease? Could Lyme trigger ALS? There is no scientifically based evidence to support any of these speculations.

Was he too sedentary? Maybe too many hours sitting at a piano bench causes ALS. He pictures the warning labels printed on all future Steinways: NEUROLOGIST'S WARNING: PLAYING MAY CAUSE ALS. Obviously not.

He grew up in the seventies and eighties, when processed foods were all the rage. Maybe his ALS was caused by consuming too many chemical preservatives or additives or saccharin. Maybe it was a dietary deficiency, a lack of some necessary vitamin at a critical age. He ate and drank almost nothing but bologna, Doritos, and Tang in 1977. Is that why he has ALS? Did he drink too many cups of Kool-Aid? Did he eat too many Steak-Umms, Twinkies, and bowls of Lucky Charms?

Maybe ALS is triggered by a sexually transmitted disease, a virus yet to be identified. Are virgins safe from ALS?

Who gets ALS? From what he's witnessed at the clinic, the answer is anyone. He's seen a twenty-five-year-old medical student, a sixty-five-year-old retired Navy SEAL, a social worker, an artist, an architect, a triathlete, an entrepreneur, men and women, black, Jewish, Japanese, Latino. This disease is as politically correct as they get. It has no bigotries, allergies, or fetishes. ALS is an equal opportunity killer.

Why did a forty-five-year-old concert pianist get ALS? Why not? He hears his mother's voice: *Don't answer a question with another question.* But this is the only answer he can find.

Only when the playing from the next room stops does he realize that his jaw has been clenched. God, how can Karina stand it?

The music begins again, but this time, it's Karina playing, showing her student what the piece is supposed to sound like, what's possible given those same notes. Her playing is beautiful, a soft blanket calming his agitated nerves. He gets up and walks to the slightly open door to hear her better.

Why did Karina stop playing piano? Teaching kids half-hour lessons after school doesn't count. Why did she give up on her career as a pianist? He pretends as he often does when he first flirts with this particular why that he doesn't already know. Unlike the ALS whys, this why has at least one verifiable answer, one that he's never admitted aloud.

As students, she was inarguably more talented and technically proficient than he was and might've stayed the better player and had his career and more, but she abandoned classical piano for improvisational jazz. It was heartbreaking for him, disgusting even, to watch such God-given talent go misdirected, unappreciated, wasted. Granted, he's more than a little biased, but to him, Mozart and Bach and Chopin are gods, and their sonatas, fantasies, études, and concertos are timeless masterpieces, every note divine brilliance. Playing them on a world stage requires education, talent, passion, technical precision, and endless hours of disciplined practice. Few people on the planet can do this. Karina was one of them. He finds jazz sloppy, incomprehensible, unlistenable, played by mostly untrained amateurs in dive bars, and he never understood how it moved Karina's soul.

His admittedly snobbish preference for classical music aside, her singular pursuit of jazz was a doomed decision, and he told her so, many times, which probably only glued her faster to it. If a stable, well-paying, and respectable career in classical piano is a fringe endeavor, then a sustainable life playing jazz is akin to landing a job on the moon. The only shot in hell a jazz pianist has of making it is to play with the very best, to develop and nurture and elevate her playing with the other elite musicians called to do this rarest of things. Karina needed to be where these musicians were — in New Orleans, New York City, Paris, or Berlin.

After Curtis, he and Karina lived in New York. She found a regular gig playing with a phenomenal saxophonist and drummer at the Village Vanguard, which paid squat but made her so happy. She was at the beginning of something real and possible, and they both felt it. Who knows what might've happened for her had they stayed?

Instead, he relocated them to Boston, accepting a coveted teaching offer at New England Conservatory, a faculty position he sold to her as necessary for his career, a job that, as it turned out, wasn't so necessary, as he readily left it barely two years later for a life of touring. He knew that moving to Boston put the brakes on Karina's momentum and was potentially cheating her out of her life's dream, but he never admitted this to her. And he knew this not just in retrospect, but while they were on the train from Penn Station to Boston's Back Bay. And he said nothing. Looking back, this was possibly the most selfish thing he'd ever done.

Until eight days ago.

But that wasn't her only chance. When he began touring, playing with a different symphony orchestra in a different city every week, every month, for years on end, he was willing to move and told her so. His home could've been based out of any city, out of New York or New Orleans just as easily as Boston if she wanted. Karina chose 450 Walnut Street in a suburb nine miles outside Boston. He'll never understand why she did this to herself. Maybe fearless Karina had become afraid. Maybe that's when he began falling out of love with her.

Karina switches to Mozart's "Rondo alla Turca." He listens to her play, remembering how remarkable she is and the choices they made and didn't make and where it all got them — Richard in the den with ALS and Karina in the living room teaching a moron — and Mozart's light-hearted notes suddenly turn dark and sinister. An anger rises inside him, not a logical notion or a fleeting feeling, but a deeply stored thick black poison.

Why is she teaching pitiful high school students when she should be a world-class, revered musician? What does she earn — maybe $50, $100 an hour? Does she do four half-hour lessons a day? How is she going to live on this?

Grace's college tuition is already in the bank, thank God, but what little savings he has beyond this is dwindling fast. He hates himself for not having long-term disability or life insurance. But he didn't work for a company that offered benefits. He was the company, and he was relatively young and healthy and had forever in front of him to earn more than enough money to suit his lifestyle. The worst he could imagine was a career-ending injury to his hands. But in that highly unlikely case, he'd then teach, go on a lecturing tour, take a faculty position at some school. There would always be options. He never considered the possibility of needing insurance. He assumed nothing bad would ever befall him. Certainly nothing catastrophic. Now look at them. Living catastrophes.

After all the lies and betrayals, he's still devastated that she gave up such a rare, God-given talent for classical piano to chase jazz and then never even catch it. His mind sends fruitless signals to clench his hands into fists. His anger mixes with impotence.

It's not all his fault.

She blames him for everything.

She lied about everything.

She would say that he betrayed her first.

Cold and wishing for a fleece for the past couple of hours, he's now running hot. Sweat is soaking his undershirt beneath his paralyzed armpits. He feels shaken, disturbed, as if he needs to sit down or leave the house, but instead he stays pinned to the open door.

Karina's playing stops, and now it's the student's turn with "Rondo alla Turca." Nothing about it is sweet or lighthearted. He's reminded of Grace reading aloud when she was five or six, stammering through each syllable of *Frog and Toad,* despairing several times a page, losing any hope of comprehension as every ounce of focus was drilled into the effort of microscopically sounding out the letters. A joyless experience. Except he loves Grace. He hates this student.

He shouldn't do that. He shouldn't hate this poor student. But a poisonous black hate lives inside him, and his hatred needs a subject. The easy choice would be ALS, but ALS doesn't have a face or a voice or a heartbeat. It's hard to hate something that isn't human.

He hates Karina. Her excuses. Her lies.

He hates himself. His selfishness. His infidelities.

Why does a forty-five-year-old concert pianist have ALS? Maybe it has something to do with karma. Maybe his ALS is retribution for something he did equally horrendous in magnitude. Or maybe it's because of what she did. Maybe his ALS is punishment for their mutual sins.

Or, strangely, maybe ALS is their chance to make amends. If they admit where they'd been wrong and apologize for all the hurt they caused each other and are forgiven, if they settle their bad karmic debt in this other way, maybe he'd be cured. Or, if not cured, maybe healed in some way. For both of them. He realizes that this kind of mystical wondering is akin to wishing on a star, praying to God, or believing in the prophecies of a Magic 8 Ball.

But why not try?

He pulls the door shut with his foot. He can't tolerate one more second of listening to this wretched piano lesson. And he'd rather go on hating Karina and himself than answer that why.

CHAPTER FIFTEEN

From his reclining chair in the den, Richard can hear Karina singing "Baby, It's Cold Outside." She's been in the kitchen all day preparing for Wigilia, a traditional twelve-dish Polish supper served on Christmas Eve, her favorite day of the year. She's been singing and cooking since early morning, determined to enjoy this day even if no one else at 450 Walnut Street will join her. Or maybe she's hoping that her dogged cheerfulness might hitch a ride with the velvety smells of cooked onions, garlic, ginger, and yeasty dough permeating the house and infect her daughter and ex-husband.

As far as Richard knows, Grace has always helped her mother cook for Wigilia. They wear matching red aprons. Grace specializes in baking the *makowiec,* a sumptuous poppy-seed rolled cake. They're an adorable team, singing and chatting while preparing this special feast from scratch.

181

Not this year.

Grace has been holed up in her room since walking through the front door two days ago. Her muttered excuses for reclusion have so far included exhaustion, headache, and reading. Every now and then, Richard hears the water running in the pipes overhead, so he knows she's in the bathroom above the den. She came downstairs a couple of hours ago for a wordless visit to the kitchen, probably to grab some food to go, and scurried back to her cave. It's now 6:00 p.m., and she's still up there.

He and Karina agonized over how much to tell Grace before she came home for Christmas break. Karina didn't want to risk distracting her from her studies and cause her to bomb her finals, but Richard didn't want her to come home to his ALS with absolutely no warning. There was no good choice here. They compromised. Since Karina's voice doesn't sound like Siri on a bender, she called Grace and gave her a hint of what she'd be coming home to.

Just wanted to let you know, your dad is living here back at the house. . . . No, we're not getting back together. He needed some help, so he's staying here for a while. . . . I'm not crazy. . . . It's fine. We'll talk about it when you get home.

He keeps replaying the shock on Grace's face at the first sight of him. It was more than the simple discomfort of seeing her divorced, estranged father living back at the house. That would've been mind spinning enough. It was his ALS — his slumped, hanging, lifeless arms; his slurry, monotone voice; his emaciated frame. He's had a year to get used to this creeping metamorphosis. He adjusts to each incremental loss, each distortion along the way, and so when he looks in the mirror or hears the sound of his voice, he usually notices only the most recent change. He registers the difference from ninety-nine to one hundred and adapts to it. He doesn't have to start from zero with every new symptom, every pound or consonant lost. He mostly still sees and hears himself. Every week, a new normal.

But Grace hadn't seen him since before he was diagnosed. He watched her absorb the entire transformation, from zero to one hundred, in less than a second, and the stunned impact on her face made him breathless, horrified to be the source of it. She averted her eyes and forced a soft hello. Stiff and mute, she endured their carefully planned introduction to ALS 101. Then, without a word, she withdrew to her room.

Karina announces that supper is ready.

Richard emerges from his room, and Grace materializes, hovering at the edge of the dining room like a nervous rabbit about to dart. Karina calls her into the kitchen. Alone in the dining room, Richard sits at the head of the table, where he sat for holidays and dinner parties for thirteen years, but instead of feeling familiar, it feels strange, unsettling, wrong. The dining room is exactly as he remembers — same oak table and ivory slip-covered chairs, same crystal chandelier, same silver and china, same mint-and-copper-colored abstract oil painting on the wall. Everything is the same.

But he couldn't be more different. He's an ex-husband, an ALS patient, a former concert pianist. In this chair, he's an interloper, an uninvited guest, a walk-on assuming a starring role. As is Polish tradition, Karina has included an additional place setting for an unexpected visitor, someone who might be lost in the night and needing a meal. Richard stands and changes seats. There. Far more suitable.

Karina and Grace shuttle in and out of the dining room, making several trips, transporting plates and platters and bowls and serving spoons while Richard sits and watches like a powerless king. The table fills up with colors and smells and memories.

Barszcz — a tangy bright red beetroot soup. *Uszka* — little ear-shaped pastas filled with sautéed wild mushrooms. Pierogi, braised sauerkraut, herring in sour cream. Twelve dishes in all. A splendid feast before him.

Returning from her last trip to the kitchen, Karina pauses, noting without objection that Richard has changed seats, then places a vanilla ice-cream milk shake smack in the middle of his plate. She sits, recites a quick prayer, blessing them for the upcoming year, then breaks off a piece of bread from a loaf instead of using a traditional wafer and passes the loaf to Grace. Grace does not pass the loaf to Richard. Karina and Grace begin eating this decadent meal, and Richard sips his shake.

Although he's still capable of eating certain soft foods such as mashed potatoes and macaroni and cheese, and he could certainly handle the soup and pasta on the table tonight, he can't stand being fed. He's tried it, gone along with the song and dance a few times with various home health aides. He wore the bib and opened wide. It made him feel helpless, emasculated, infantile. He quickly put a stop to it, trading beloved flavors and textures and favorite foods that require forks and spoons for the rather limited menu of drinkable soups, smoothies, and shakes. He's losing control of his muscles, his independence, his life. While he still can, he's going to feed himself.

So he sips his vanilla shake while watching Grace and Karina eat Wigilia supper in front of him, annoyed that Karina didn't think to offer him the beetroot soup in a glass with a straw. He's too stubborn, too stupidly offended, to ask. Instead, he keys into the sights and sounds of them eating — the clinking of the silverware against the china, Karina slurping the soup off her spoon, steaming bowls being passed, Grace chewing with her mouth open. The entire sensory experience — every festive, forbidden molecule of it — disgusts him. Even Bing Crosby singing "White Christmas" is a personal affront.

No one is talking. Naturally chatty, Grace hasn't offered a single word. Silence has always been the cloak she wears to conceal her anger or fear. She's shoveling one forkful after another into her mouth, clearing her plate as if she were in a race, gunning for first prize. She's done before Bing Crosby finishes his song. She pushes back her chair, stacks her soup bowl onto her plate, and stands, on her way to the kitchen.

"Hold on there," says Karina. "You're not excused from the table."

"Why not? I'm done."

"You didn't have any *piernik or makowiec.*"

"I don't want any *piernik* or *makowiec.*"

Grace loves *piernik* and *makowiec.* So does Richard.

"Fine, then sit and keep us company. Wigilia isn't over."

Grace relents and sits but doesn't add any dessert to her plate. Richard catches her stealing fast, microscopic glances at him, as if looking directly at him for more than a moment might be dangerous. It's one thing to read about ALS on the Internet, as he assumes she's been doing up in her room over the past two days, it's quite another to sit across the table from it, a plate of *piernik* and a couple of flickering candles away, to witness it live and in the flesh, residing in her father.

"How were your finals?" Karina asks.

"Terrible."

"Oh no, why?"

"I didn't study because I was too busy reading about ALS."

Richard and Karina turn to each other, stunned.

"But how —"

"You tell me Dad is back living with you, and you won't tell me why? I texted Hannah Chu and told her how freaky this was, and she told me."

"I'm sorry, honey —"

"So Hannah Chu and God knows who else already knew that my father had ALS, and I didn't. Glad I'm part of this family or whatever you want to call this."

"We didn't want to tell you before finals for that very reason."

"This didn't happen overnight. Why didn't you tell me sooner?"

"I didn't know myself until recently," says Karina.

She's known since July if not before. Always deflecting blame, always right, always innocent. Richard wants to pounce on this lie, argue the facts and for once expose Karina in front of Grace, but his voice is too slow to produce to jump in, and he lets it be.

"What about you?" asks Grace, addressing her father for the first time. "Why didn't you tell me about this?"

He was diagnosed just before Christmas last year. He didn't want to ruin Grace's holiday with his grim news. Then full denial set in. He couldn't have even whispered, alone in his condo with no one to hear him, that he had ALS, never mind speak the three letters aloud to his only child. He continued to tour, pretending everything was fine, and didn't reveal his diagnosis to Trevor for three more months. Shortly after, his right hand weakened further — threatening his playing, his reputation, his life — and the jig was up. Still, he didn't announce his disease to the world. Trevor hid it behind the guise of tendinitis for a while. So at first, keeping the news from Grace wasn't personal.

Then it was. He was afraid of giving her yet one more reason to push him away, that she might reject him so completely that they'd never have a chance to recover. Before ALS, he had no idea how to make things right between them, if it was even possible. Admittedly, he was lazy and figured they had time. And now he has ALS, and they don't have twenty years of therapy or living to sort it all out, and he still has no idea how to make things right. He's not off to a good start.

"I tried to, many times. It's hard. You had finals and then the second semester of your first year of college. I didn't want to ruin this exciting time in your life."

"Don't worry, you won't."

Born loyal to her mother, Grace has always blamed Richard for Karina's unhappiness and the divorce. As she sits across from him, arms crossed, eyes glaring, Richard sees an additional edge to Grace's anger, one that has probably been there for years, but that he'd never noticed until just now. Betrayal.

Every time Richard cheated on Karina, he was also cheating on Grace. He repeats this theory in his mind, chewing on it like a fresh stick of gum. It's one thing to have missed Grace's Saturday soccer game or Sunday dinner or an awards night at school because he had a concert in Miami. It's another to have missed those things because he chose to linger in Miami with a woman whose name he can no longer remember. Grace spent much of her childhood without a father at home, and some of those days and nights were because of his various infidelities. So in that sense, he cheated on Grace, too.

He looks at his daughter, who has always so closely resembled her mother with her wide-set green eyes and espresso-brown hair, and sees resentment in those green eyes, defiance in her strong jaw, her mouth a weapon. He sees himself in his daughter's face, and his heart aches. Neither of them got the father they wanted.

"So what happens next?" Grace asks.

Barring any special weekend trips or time

off, Grace won't be home again until the end of March, if she doesn't go to Daytona Beach or Key West or wherever college kids go these days for spring break. Three more months. Any number of depressing changes could transpire in that time, changes that could necessitate a feeding tube, a BiPAP, a wheelchair, eye-gaze communication, a trach tube and invasive ventilation. Hopefully, he won't be dead.

"I don't know."

Both the ultimate certainty and immediate uncertainty of Richard's future, imaginable and unimaginable, hang in the air over Wigilia supper. No one says a word, and no one eats. The last track of the Bing Crosby Christmas album ends. The room is silent. Richard examines the uneaten meal on the table, the comfort food Grace has refused, refusing to be comforted, the twelve dishes Karina cooked from scratch by herself, recipes handed down from her parents and grandparents. He focuses on the untouched *makowiec* — a sweet poppy-seed cake, his favorite — and decides to take a risk.

"Karina, would you please feed me a bite or two of the *makowiec*?"

She doesn't react at all at first, her blank face not seeming to comprehend his request. He's never asked her to feed him.

Apprehension fills her eyes as she registers his question.

"I don't know. Is that allowed?"

"Just a couple small bites. I'll wash them down with milk shake. It's not Wigilia without *makowiec.*"

That won her. Karina's a sucker for tradition. Still unsure, she cuts a thin slice of the cake and sets it onto Richard's plate. She then sits in the empty chair next to Richard and faces him. She pinches off a small piece of cake between her thumb and finger, barely the size of a corn kernel, and holds it up.

"I'm not a bird. A real bite, please."

Still uncertain, she takes an unused fork from the unexpected guest's place setting and cuts a modest helping of cake. She makes eye contact with Richard and gingerly sends the piece of *makowiec* into his open mouth.

Richard closes his lips and lets the cake sit on his tongue. If his taste buds could weep with joy, they would. His mouth is watering, so maybe they are. The moist cake, the sour cream and butter, the sweet honey, a hint of lemon, the bumpy poppy seeds. He chews. He chews! He can't remember the last time he chewed. It might've been a bagel. Whatever food it was, it wasn't memorable. This cake is divine, every taste and texture swirling through his mouth a scrumptious celebration.

Once he's mashed this small bite of heaven into a liquid paste that could be sucked through a straw like a smoothie, he begins consciously swallowing. No problem. He sticks his tongue out like a child to prove that it's gone.

He raises his eyebrows and tips his head toward the plate. Karina loads up another forkful. Richard opens his mouth, and she feeds him. They stay connected through eye contact as he chews, Karina vigilantly searching for any issues, Richard wordlessly letting her know that he's all right.

He clears that bite and asks for another. As he chews, he looks into Karina's unwavering green eyes, and the cruel awkwardness and pity he dreaded in being fed by her in particular isn't there. Instead, a gentle intimacy, a quiet tenderness passes between them that he never expected. After the next bite, she wipes his bottom lip with a napkin, and he feels appreciative instead of ashamed. She smiles. He wishes he hadn't sworn off being fed so many months ago and is imagining all the delicious chewable meals and lovely moments he's unnecessarily forgone when he begins to choke.

Maybe he got a little cocky. Maybe he was distracted by the unexpected connection with Karina. He inadvertently moved the bolus of cake to the back of his mouth before it was entirely pureed, triggering the swallowing reflex before he was ready. He doesn't know if he panicked first and caused the problem, or if a piece of cake went down the wrong pipe and caused him to panic, but he's got a hunk of gooey *makowiec* paste stuck in his windpipe, and he can't breathe.

Worse, because his abdominal muscles and diaphragm are weak, he can't produce the simple cough a normal person could to blast the gob of food out of there. His eyes bulge wide-open, unblinking, and Karina stares back, terrified but unmoving, paralyzed. He's straining every muscle and vein in his neck, trying desperately to cough, to breathe, to yell for help, silently choking.

"Mom!" Grace screams, waking her mother into action.

Karina starts pounding on his back with the heel of her hand as if he were bongo drum. It's not working. He envisions the half-chewed lump of cake as a wet concrete stopper in his trachea. He looks across the table at Grace, who appears fuzzy and scared through his watery eyes.

Karina switches tack. She stands behind his chair, wraps her arms around his middle, and starts rapidly pumping her fisted hands into the soft space below his sternum, between the bones of his rib cage. Over and over she thrusts her fists into his abdomen. The *makowiec* won't budge. He tries and tries to help her, but he can't cough with any real force. His head begins to tingle. Grace and the entire room blur. Karina's saying his name, and he knows she's right here, pounding on him harder and harder from behind his chair, but she sounds far away.

Maybe this is how it ends. Maybe this is what happens next.

CHAPTER SIXTEEN

Karina uncaps the plastic MIC-KEY button that lies flush against Richard's skin two or so inches above his belly button, attaches a small length of tubing, and begins pressing on a fifty-milliliter syringe plunger, delivering a total of 500 cc of Liquid Gold over the next half hour directly into his stomach, his fifth and final "meal" of the day. They watch a rerun of *Friends* on TV while they wait for the syringe to empty.

The past three weeks have been all about tubes. After his nearly fatal choking episode on Christmas Eve, Karina took him to the ALS clinic. His neurologist, pulmonologist, radiologist, speech-language pathologist, and gastroenterologist listened to what had been going on and assessed his breathing and swallowing. Two major things were discovered. Two monumental decisions, both involving tubes, were made. The mother of all decisions, involving the mother of all tubes, still awaits a verdict.

First, he had a swallowing study. He drank barium dissolved in a thin liquid and sputtered as he swallowed. He next consumed barium mixed in applesauce and had to swallow several times to clear the feeling of mush stuck to the side of his throat. He then suffered a violent coughing fit trying to eat the tiniest bite of a barium-sprinkled cookie. A radiologist and the speech-language pathologist studied the X-ray video and determined that his ability to reliably and safely swallow had become significantly compromised in the past three months. No kidding.

The muscles of his tongue and palate have further atrophied, making them weak and lazy. Most dangerous, his epiglottis is slow to close off his larynx while swallowing, which means that food can be aspirated into his trachea and lungs. This is what likely happened with the *makowiec* on Christmas Eve. While liquid milk shakes won't lodge in his windpipe like poppy-seed cake, they can drain down the wrong pipe and drip into his lungs, causing aspiration pneumonia. Anything that goes into his mouth now could easily kill him.

Not yet ready to surrender to dying, he surrendered to a feeding tube. He had the surgery the day after Grace returned to school. The twenty-minute procedure was straightforward and routine for his surgeon. Dr. Fletcher fed an endoscope through Richard's mouth, down his esophagus, and into his stomach. He then threaded a thin plastic tube through the scope and out a small hole incised in Richard's abdominal wall.

Karina waits a good ten minutes after the first 250 cc for his stomach to settle before delivering the rest. When given too rapidly, he gets too full too fast, nauseous, and vomits. Liquid Gold has a foul, acidic, nutty flavor on the way up that makes him cringe just thinking about it. That stuff was never meant to be tasted. Thankfully, Karina takes her time.

When *Friends* is over and the final food syringe is emptied, Karina dissolves his evening meds in water and delivers that through the syringe as well. The water feels cool and refreshing and weirdly quenches his thirst without ever touching his lips. She then flushes the tubing two more times with water, recaps the MIC-KEY button, and lowers Richard's lifted shirt. There. Done with dinner or his nightcap or his feeding or whatever this is called. His stomach is now filled with five hundred calories in a half liter of liquid. He can't say that he's hungry, but he's hardly sated. Although the service was impeccable, he'd give the meal itself a one-star Yelp rating.

He remembers when he first started touring, he ordered steak from room service every night. By maybe the eighth or ninth night, he couldn't stomach even the thought of one more steak. He'd had his fill. He ordered pizza and didn't touch another steak for months. The only item on the room-service menu now is Liquid Gold, every meal for twenty-three days straight and counting. What he wouldn't give now for a medium-rare dry-aged New York strip.

He tries not to think about food. For one, it's torture to imagine what he can never again have. Second, like Pavlov's dog anticipating the steak his master is about to plop in its dish after the bell is rung, remembering food makes Richard's mouth water. While the PEG tube eliminates the potential threats of eating and drinking, he still has to contend with his own saliva, which, like any liquid, can go down the wrong pipe when swallowed.

Even with the help of the glycopyrrolate, his drool, which has for some reason become the consistency of Elmer's glue, is constantly accumulating, either spilling over his bottom lip and hanging from his chin in shimmering, stringy ribbons or gurgling at the back of his mouth. Thinking about steak turned the faucet on. He's gurgling.

Karina flips on his new suctioning machine, pokes the wand into his mouth, and slides it around in there, vacuuming between his teeth and gums and under his tongue, slurping up his excessive spit, drying out his flooding mouth. He feels like he's at the dentist every time she does this.

The second big discovery at his clinic appointment was the treacherous state of his breathing. His forced vital capacity, the amount of air he's able to forcibly exhale, was down to 42 percent. Over the past three months, he'd started to notice that he was regularly out of breath when walking from room to room, that he had to pause every four or five words when talking because he was out of air, and that he was speaking only on the exhales.

"Are you waking up throughout the night?" asked his doctor.

"Yes."

"Are you starting the day already fatigued?"

"Yes."

"And do you have a headache when you wake up?"

He did, almost every morning for weeks.

"You're hypoventilated during the night. You're not getting in enough oxygen, and you're retaining too much carbon dioxide. I want you on a BiPAP."

He had no idea that his insomnia and morning headaches were due to a continual lack of air throughout the night. So now he sleeps with a mask attached to a machine by a long tube. It's ten o'clock, and the only thing left on his exciting daily itinerary is getting hooked up to the BiPAP.

Karina fills the humidifier and plugs it in. Richard watches her weary but focused eyes as she works. She applies Vaseline with her pinkie to the many raw sores on his face. The moist air and prolonged contact of the mask against his skin every night have caused it to break down, creating a painful rash. He tried switching to nasal pillows instead of a full-face mask, but he couldn't keep his mouth closed while sleeping and found wearing the chinstrap to keep it shut too aggravating. So he wears the full mask and endures the sores. Karina wipes her hands on a towel, turns the BiPAP on, then secures the mask over his nose and mouth.

The relief is instantaneous. Initiated by his own inhale, air is forced in. His lungs fully inflate, and his rib cage expands. When he exhales, the machine inverts the pressure, and air is forced out as if his lungs were a pair of bellows and the machine were pressing the handles together. Every night, in this moment when Karina seals the mask onto his face, he realizes exactly how labored and shallow his breathing has been all day, as if he's been wearing a tight corset around his lungs since morning and Karina finally released it. With the mask on his face, he breathes an abundant flow of sweet oxygen in and carbon dioxide out, and a deep tension lifts out of his body like steam rising off a hot cake. He won't suffocate in the night.

His pulmonologist says that his forced vital capacity appears to be declining at about 3 percent per month. The BiPAP is only capable of producing pressure that supports breathing. It doesn't breathe for him. It breathes with him. At some point, the Bi-PAP will no longer sustain him. The only options then will be death or a tracheostomy tube coupled with mechanical ventilation and 24-7 care. Like the medium-rare dry-aged New York strip, he tries not to think about it.

While the introduction of the BiPAP has meant a better night's sleep for Richard, it has meant the opposite for Karina. She adjusts the mask, making sure it's entirely sealed, knowing without question that, like all things, the seal is temporary. When he yawns, when he scrunches up his nose because it itches, when he turns his head to the right, the mask can come loose. If it does, the machine will then sound an alarm, and Karina will have to get up to readjust the mask. Several times a night. She sleeps on the couch in the living room now to shorten her commute.

He's like a newborn, and Karina is the sleep-deprived new mother, a walking zombie. But with newborns, there is light at the end of the tunnel. The baby starts eating solid food or gains weight or turns one—some developmental milestone is achieved and miraculously the baby sleeps through the blessed night. There is no light at the end of this tunnel, no developmental milestone that will graduate Richard from needing assistance all hours of the night. Unless they consider his death a milestone. Maybe Karina does.

He watches her face, her pretty green eyes. She's inspecting the perimeter of his mask, but because the mask is over the midline of his face, it looks as if she were studying him. Her eyes appear dull, disconnected from the source of any internal spark. Her long hair is gathered into a low ponytail, but a section from the front has fallen loose, draping over her right eyebrow. He wants to reach out and tuck it behind her ear.

She looks him in the eye and sighs. He wants to tell her that he's sorry that she's so tired. He's sorry that he has this and had nowhere else to go. He's sorry he's become such a burden to her. And then suddenly, strangely, for the first time, he wants to tell her that he's sorry for all of it.

And he's sorry without the usual accessories, the excuses that absolve him or an equivalent list of her crimes weighing down the other side of the scale, blaming her, making them even. There is only his apology. He's sorry he was so careless with her, their family, their life. He's sorry that he cheated on her, that he didn't know what to do with his loneliness, that he felt unappreciated, unseen, unloved by her and didn't know how to talk to her about it. He was lonelier in bed with Karina than anywhere else on the planet. He never told her. He remembers those green eyes looking straight at him, simmering with resentment, punishing him, looking straight through him, indifferent, shunning him. He was too afraid to ask her what was wrong, too afraid to hear her answer. They never talked about any of it. They were complicit in their mutual silence.

Her exhausted eyes, likely praying that the mask stays put for at least a couple of hours, connect with his. He wants to tell her now that he's sorry, before she leaves the room, before this revelation and urge to confess evaporate, before he goes to sleep and, as if it were a dream in the nighttime, he awakens in the morning with only the vaguest sense of having known something. He holds his apology like a helium balloon, the slipknotted string fast loosening from his wrist, soon to be a dot in the stratosphere. He has to say it now or possibly never.

"I'm sorry."

But his voice, already thin and weak like the rest of him, can't be heard through the mask, over the vacuum-cleaner-like whir of the BiPAP.

"Good night," she says.

Karina turns off the TV and the light, leaving the door open a crack as she disappears from his room without ever hearing him, not knowing.

CHAPTER SEVENTEEN

Finished with his morning shift, Bill walks into the sunlit but chilly living room, leaving the door to the den wide-open. Cuddled under a blanket on the couch and draining the last still-hot sip of her second cup of coffee, Karina is distracted by this, bothered even, as if she'd witnessed someone leave a bed unmade or the cap off a tube of toothpaste, nagging her like an aggressive itch she can't yet scratch. She doesn't keep the den door wide-open. She can't shut it entirely as she would prefer, as Richard would be trapped inside, but there needs to be some physical, visible barrier between them. She keeps the den door positioned open only a crack, creating at least a semblance of separation and privacy. She feels safer that way. Not wanting to reveal this probably diagnosable compulsion to Bill, she'll close the den door to an inch shy of shut after he goes. Then she'll finally take a shower.

Karina anticipates their daily good-bye as Bill checks a text on his phone. Done, he looks up at her, but instead of offering his usual cheery hug and a kiss on the cheek, he stands there with his arms crossed, studying Karina as if she were a math problem he can't quite figure out or a piece of art that sort of offends him but he's not sure why.

"Okay, girlfriend, my one-thirty just canceled. Kensia will be here with Richard then. You're meeting me for coffee."

"I can put on a pot here if you want some coffee."

"No. You're getting out of this house, and we need to chat."

"About what?"

"About you," he says, assertive and concerned.

"Me?" She's suddenly self-conscious about her bedhead and sweatpants, that she's not wearing a bra under her T-shirt or any makeup, and that she doesn't smell so good. "I'm fine."

"You are so not fine. Ryan Gosling in *The Notebook* is fine. You're Mickey Rourke in *The Wrestler*."

Mortified, she wants to pull the blanket

she's wrapped in up and over her head.

"I'm just tellin' it like I see it."

"I haven't showered yet," she confesses, as if this weren't obvious. "And I've already had two cups of coffee and can't have any more caffeine or I won't sleep at all tonight."

"You can order decaf."

"Honestly, I'm okay, Bill."

"Decaf coffee at one thirty, or we're going for martinis after I get off work tonight at six thirty. And don't throw any more excuses at me 'cause I have a really big bat, and I'll just keep hitting 'em back at ya."

"I'm good."

"You're bad."

"I can't leave at six thirty. Kevin's only here until six."

Bill squints at her through his black-rimmed glasses as if he were contemplating his next move in a game of chess. "You're driving me nuts." He checks his phone again. "Okay, my next visit lives nearby, so let's do this now. Come."

He marches into the kitchen, a man on a mission, and not knowing what else to do, Karina follows him. They sit opposite each other at the square breakfast table. He looks into her eyes and says nothing, taking her in, and she feels so utterly exposed and yet safely held in his gaze that she finds herself working hard not to cry.

"Okay, honey, tell me what is going on. I need to know more about this situation."

"What do you mean?"

"I mean about the two of you. Not for nothing, but the tension in this house is killing me."

Karina sits back in her chair, blinking, stunned. She thought she'd been nothing but perfectly civil, polite, and dutiful around Richard, especially in front of Bill, whom she adores and admires and wants to impress. She can feel the razor-sharp point of every edge between Richard and her, but she assumed their animosity was traveling on a private, restricted highway. She didn't think Bill or anyone else visiting or tending to Richard could possibly pick up on it.

"Really?"

"You both do anything to avoid making eye contact with each other. Seriously, if you're in the same room, your eyes dart around so much I practically have to sit down I'm so dizzy."

"Well, you know we're divorced," she says in a hushed voice, not wanting Richard to hear her through the wide-open den door, wondering what details he's already shared with Bill.

"Are you ever going to talk about your

whole history?"

"To you?"

"To Richard."

She pauses. She didn't see that coming. She picks at a flake of skin on her chapped bottom lip with her thumb, smelling her coffee breath on her hand as she does. The skin peels too far without letting go, and a quick pinch stops her from continuing. She licks her lip, tasting blood.

Bill waits, watching her.

"Part of the reason we're divorced is because we don't know how to talk to each other."

"Look, I don't walk in your shoes, but I see what I see, and I've been through a lot. I've lost people close to me, and in the end, it's all about peace of mind and closure. You've gotta get to forgiveness."

She has taken Richard in. She pulls down his underpants so he can pee, she wipes his urine off the toilet seat and the floor when he's done, she suctions mucus out of his mouth all day, she reseals that damn mask onto his face all night, she pushes liquid food and water through a syringe into his stomach, she makes sure the den door is cracked open instead of shut so he can come and go. And a thousand other things. Now she's supposed to forgive him, too?

She wants to do the right thing, and she wants to please Bill, but she's maxed out. Totally tapped.

"I can't do any more than what I'm already doing for Richard." She crosses her arms over her chest.

"Sweetheart, forgiving Richard is for you. Not for him."

She softens her stance, surprised to be considering this perspective. *Forgiving Richard would be for me. Could that really be true?* She tries it on, but instead of feeling true like *the sky is blue,* it feels more like *the sky is infinite space extending through more than one hundred billion galaxies.* It could be true, but she can't comprehend it.

"I don't know if you've fully grasped this, but he's probably not going to live to be ninety."

"I know."

"I wouldn't wait too long then. You might just miss your chance."

Bill looks her straight in the eye, making sure his words landed, and her heart beats faster as if it's been warned or dared or threatened. She nods but has no idea yet what she's agreeing to.

"I gotta run. But also, honey, please. You gotta take care of yourself. I've seen too many caregivers burn out. You gotta get out of this house and have time that's just for you."

"I walk with Elise every week."

"That's not enough. What about meeting someone?"

"Like a man?"

"Yes, a man. Or a woman if you're into it. Whichever. A date."

"No." She shakes her head for emphasis, dismissing the suggestion.

"Look at you. You're beautiful. Or, you would be after a long shower and some makeup and maybe a trip to the mall."

"The last thing I need is another man to take care of, thank you."

"I'm not telling you to marry him, for God's sake. I'm talking someone to wine and dine you. And getting laid wouldn't hurt either, girl. I'm just sayin'. You know I love you."

"Thanks. I just . . . I'm good."

"Okay." Bill stands, not believing her, but satisfied enough for now, needing to go. "But find something outside of this that's just for you. ALS is going to take Richard down. Don't let it take you, too."

He kisses the top of her head and leaves the kitchen. She stays in her seat, listening to the squeaky sound of his rubber-soled footsteps on the hardwood floor of the liv-

212

ing room and then the front foyer, the rising chord progression of his coat zipper, the questioning intonation of the front door as it creaks open, and the satisfying thump of it closing all the way shut.

CHAPTER EIGHTEEN

Karina and Elise walk together every week, regardless of the weather. Neither snow nor rain nor heat nor gloom of early dawn keeps them from completing their three-mile loop. It's an admirable policy in theory, but questionable on mornings such as this when the temperature, with the windchill, is below zero. They leave the paved roads of their neighborhood for the dirt path that encircles the reservoir, walking much faster than they normally do. The sharp, frigid air stings Karina's cheeks and seems to penetrate her brain through her exposed eyeballs, every blink a temporary shield, a noticeable moment of relief. She wishes she'd remembered her sunglasses. The normally soft pine-needle-strewn dirt path has no give, feeling petrified beneath her feet, the earth frozen solid. Frequent bursts of wind slice her body and steal her breath. It's too cold to be out here. It's almost too cold to talk.

"She definitely needs more help," says Grace, walking fast behind Elise's heels as if pursuing her.

Grace arrived home yesterday for a long weekend. Before bed, Karina invited Grace to join her and Elise in the morning but didn't pin any hopes and dreams on Grace's actually coming. A night owl who hates the cold and hasn't seen 6:00 a.m. since elementary school, Grace didn't verbalize any interest, and Karina took her nonanswer to mean *Thanks, but no thanks.* So Karina was more than a little surprised, and happy, to see her daughter dressed and waiting at the front door when Karina was ready to leave.

It's been a month since Grace was last home. It feels like a year. In December, Karina came and went without too much thought regarding Richard's safety. He could always reach her on her cell. But his voice has significantly weakened since Christmas, and the voice-activation app on his phone can't reliably comprehend his muted, slurred speech. His whole life has changed in one month. He needs Karina's help regularly, throughout the day and night, and so her whole life has changed, too. She worries about leaving him alone, but she's not giving up her weekly walk. He'll be fine.

"What about his father and brothers?" asks Elise.

"They're not going to take him in," says Karina.

"How do you know if you don't ask?"

"Believe me, I know."

"They can at least give you some money for more help."

"I can do it."

Richard has thirty hours a week of home health aides, not covered by insurance. The rest is on Karina.

"But why do you want to?"

"Yeah, Mom, what are you trying to prove?"

Karina's not sure. Maybe having Richard in the house gives her something useful to do, something that fills the many hours every day when she's not teaching children to play piano. When Grace moved to Chicago, an enormous, lonely void moved into Karina's home and heart. No amount of therapy, chocolate, wine, sleep, or Netflix could evict it. Richard in the den with ALS has elbowed out some of the void, which is admittedly strange, as his presence had never before been the cure for her loneliness. Are these really her only two options — live with Richard or live with the void?

She must be a saint. Or a martyr. Or

screwed up.

"It's not forever."

"That's what Jane Wilde thought."

"Who?" asks Grace.

"Stephen Hawking's first wife," says Elise. "They were in their twenties when he was diagnosed, and she married him anyway, thinking he had only a couple of years left. He's in his seventies now."

"So Dad could live that long?"

"If for some reason the disease stops progressing," says Karina, not believing this is possible in Richard's case, given the decline he's experienced in the past month. "Or if he gets a trach and goes on a ventilator."

"You can't do this indefinitely, Karina."

"I know. If he goes on a ventilator, he needs to move to a facility."

She's not a nurse. And she's not his wife.

"He'd probably qualify for some kind of assisted living now," says Elise.

"I'm okay for now."

"I don't get it," says Grace. "You couldn't stand living with him. You said the day he moved out was the happiest day of your life."

Karina bristles. She shouldn't have said such a thing within ear's distance of Grace. Karina's hoping she didn't lack all judgment and say this directly to Grace. She might've. She doesn't ask.

"Let me look after him for a few hours here and there. How about Tuesday and Wednesday evenings?" asks Elise.

"No. I couldn't ask you to do that."

"You're not asking. I am."

"No, really, I'm okay."

"I could at least come over and keep you company."

Reluctantly, Karina acquiesces. "Okay."

Elise puts an arm around Karina and hugs her as they walk.

"I'm worried about leaving you alone with Dad."

"I'm not alone. Elise is coming over Tuesday and Wednesday evenings. Don't worry, honey. I have plenty of help."

"You don't. And this is only going to get harder. You realize this, right?"

Karina does, but she doesn't answer Grace or acknowledge her with a nod. Karina keeps walking, her frozen eyeballs focused on the ground. One step at a time.

"Maybe I should stay home and take this semester off."

"No, you're not doing that," says Karina.

"What if I figured out a way to do the next semester at BU or Northeastern?"

"No. We're not discussing this. Your father

218

would never want you to do that for him."

"I'd be doing it for you, not him."

As much as Karina would love for Grace to stay, to help with Richard and fill the void, she won't risk Grace's future. Karina knows all too well that a life derailed, even for a short time, can't always find its way back to its original track. She never even made it back to the station. No, she won't let Grace pause her studies, her relationship with Matt, her pursuit of happiness for a semester. For one second. Especially not for Richard. She won't let Grace make the same mistake she made. That pattern ends with her.

Restless ghosts of unresolved resentment rise to the surface, as full and fresh and haunting as they were twenty years ago, ten years ago, last week. Karina lets the aching pain run through her, the tragic story of how Richard ruined her life, welcoming it for its familiarity, for the way it makes her feel justified.

"You're not disrupting your life out there."

"You're disrupting yours," says Grace.

"That's different."

"She has a point," says Elise. "You're not exactly moving on if Richard is living in the den. Can you see your mom bringing a date home? This is the living room, and that's my ex-husband in the den."

"Richard isn't keeping me from dating. I'm not interested in dating."

"What are you interested in then?" asks Elise.

Getting warm. Ending this conversation.

"How about coming with me and my students on the New Orleans trip?"

"I can't this year."

"Why?"

Her ex-husband in the den.

"I think you like having Richard around to blame for things. It's like a comfortable habit."

Karina hates to admit it, but there is truth to this. If she blames him, she never has to blame herself.

"You can hire help for a few days, someone to stay the nights," says Elise.

"I can't."

"You won't."

"Fine. I won't."

"Why?"

Karina doesn't answer because she doesn't know. Or maybe she's beginning to but can't yet articulate it. She senses something like a program running in the background, an awareness creeping up the basement stairs of her subconscious.

Maybe this horrible, bizarre living situation is giving her and Richard a chance at resolution, at forgiveness. She considers this possibility, first suggested by Bill last week, as the three walk in silence, Elise and Grace waiting patiently for an answer. Karina would like to forgive Richard for uprooting them to Boston; for missing most of Grace's childhood; for cheating on her, betraying and humiliating her, robbing her of happiness. She's tried many times over the years. After giving it much thought, she believes Bill, that forgiving Richard would be good for her. What's the saying? Not forgiving someone is like drinking poison and expecting the other person to die. But she hasn't been big enough or spiritually evolved enough or brave enough to do it. Richard is sick and dying, and she still can't let him off the hook. Making him wrong allows her to feel right, and feeling right is her drug of choice.

And she'd like to be forgiven. But she can't bring herself to apologize to Richard, to say the words. She's handcuffed by shame and a stubborn, self-righteous logic that supports her side of the story. She had her reasons. Maybe her actions now can be the words she's still too afraid to offer.

"I don't know," says Karina.

"I could come back for that," says Grace.

"Go to New Orleans."

"No, you don't need to."

"How many days is it?" asks Grace.

"Four," says Elise. "Thursday to Sunday. First week of March."

"I can do that."

"It's too much," says Karina.

"It's four days, Mom."

"I mean it's too much, taking care of him. I'm up all night."

"I'm young. I stay up all night all the time. I got this. You're going to New Orleans."

Elise smiles, patting Grace on the back. "I love this girl."

They reach the beginning of the trail, where they began. Before stepping off the path and onto the paved road of their neighborhood, Karina looks back for a moment at the frozen reservoir, at the loop they just completed. Like her morning walk, her thoughts and emotions run in circles. Richard is living with her again, and caring for him is more than she can handle, but she can't ask him to leave, and her entire life is a circle. She's trapped, never getting anywhere.

"Okay, I'll go to New Orleans."

Grace and Elise high-five, celebrating their victory, but Karina doesn't join in. The trip is a month a way. As she's recently learned, anything can happen in a month.

They stop in the street in front of their houses to say a brief good-bye. Grace and Elise hug, and Elise wishes her good luck at school. Karina checks the time on her phone. They've been gone for forty-five minutes. She hurries to the front door, anxious to get inside, to sit at the table in her warm kitchen with a cozy hot cup of coffee.

She swings open the door, and her stomach drops. Without thinking, she runs toward the den, toward the piercing sound of the BiPAP alarm.

CHAPTER NINETEEN

Karina barrels into the den, breathless. Richard is propped up in his hospital bed, the mask askew on his face, much like it was at 4:00 a.m. He smiles sheepishly beneath it. She quickly sizes up the situation: he's fine. But instead of feeling relieved, she's pissed, as if he's played the same cruel trick on her for the millionth time, and she stupidly fell for it.

"Is he okay?" asks Grace, running in right behind her mother, her voice high and terrified.

"He's fine."

Grace looks him over, assessing the state of her father herself. His face is alert and calm. He's clearly breathing.

"Jeez. Okay, I'm gonna take a shower," says Grace, only temporarily inconvenienced by the false alarm, her spiked emotional temperature already back to normal.

But Karina's heart is still feverish, adrenaline whipping through her body, searching for danger. The shrill sound of that damn alarm sends shock waves through her nervous system, activating some automatic primal instinct for crisis. She can't seem to override her response to it. But nothing about the BiPAP machine is yet life-and-death. He can still breathe without it. He breathes entirely on his own without it all day long. It only *assists* him at night.

So the sound of the BiPAP alarm shouldn't send her running. The sound of his choking on rivers of goopy spit *is* life-threatening. He could aspirate and develop pneumonia. But oddly, she often ignores the first minute or more of these routine, seismic coughing fits, listening patiently and somewhat annoyed from another room, hoping he'll work it out on his own. He almost never does.

She turns the BiPAP and the humidifier off, silencing the alarm, then pulls the mask up and over his head.

"I-ha-fa-pee."

Of all the undignified ALS-related chores, she hates the morning pee the most. She swears he yawns or turns his head on purpose, breaking the seal on the mask, sounding the alarm so she'll magically materialize before him. He then wants her to unhook him from the machine so he can get up and use the bathroom.

She shouldn't resent him for having to pee in the morning, but she does. It's always about 7:00 a.m. when he makes this request, shocking her out of a dead sleep. She begins almost every day exhausted, hollowed out and nauseated from lack of sleep. Granted she's already up today, but normally, she's out cold at seven. Bill comes at nine. Why can't he just lie there and wait for Bill? She should be grateful that he doesn't piss the bed.

He swings his legs over the side of the bed and worms his butt to the edge. Using his weakening core, he works to pull himself to standing. She watches him struggle and doesn't offer a hand. She follows him out of the den, through the living room, and into the first-floor bathroom.

He stands in front of the toilet, waiting for her. She pulls his boxers down to his ankles, and he steps out. She picks his shorts up off the floor and rests them on the vanity, keeping them safely dry.

He stands over the bowl, thrusts his bony hips forward, and pees. She crosses her arms and grits her teeth, irritated with him for not sitting. Granted, sitting doesn't guarantee that everything will land neatly in the toilet, but she feels the odds are better. What does he care if he misses? He's not the one who has to clean up the mess.

She closes her eyes, an absurd and unnecessary offer of privacy, listening for him to finish. She can tell by the intermittent sound of trickling, of urine splashing into water and then nothing, that he's peeing all over the floor. Just as she predicted. She's sweating, stifling hot beneath her winter coat and hat, which she still hasn't had time to remove. She wonders when she's going to get her cup of coffee.

When he's done, he presents himself to her. She squats in front of him, holding open each hole of his boxers for him to step into. She pulls them up.

"Can-a-pu-on-my Hea-Mus?"

"Give me a minute. I have to clean up this mess."

He leaves her — his ex-wife; his dutiful, unpaid, unthanked nursemaid — to the job of wiping up his piss. She unzips and removes her coat and hat, sprays disinfecting cleaner all over the toilet seat and floor, and wipes everything dry with a wad of paper towels. There. Clean until the next time he pees.

While washing her hands in the sink longer than necessary, she studies her face in the mirror. Her mouth is turned down at the corners, a resting frown. Her skin and eyes are dull. Her hair is flat and oily. She hasn't bothered washing it in days. She needs a long, hot shower. She needs a good, long nap. She needs breakfast and a cup of coffee. But instead, she has to return to Richard's room to stick a silver Head Mouse dot to the tip of his nose. It will take two seconds. But he gets to go first, and she hates him for it.

Back in the den, he's sitting at the desk in front of his laptop, waiting for her. She peels a dot from the sticker strip and presses it onto the tip of his big nose. He begins typing, selecting letters one at a time by aiming his nose at the keyboard displayed on the screen. As usual, Bill will get him showered and dressed when he arrives at nine. While she's in there, she opens the shades and strips the bed. With an armful of bedding, she's on her way to the laundry room when her eyes unintentionally catch the words *Dear Dad* at the top of his computer screen.

"You're writing to your father?"

"Ya-na-su-po-sta see-tha. Don-rea-dova-my-shoul."

"I'm not. Are you asking him for help?"

"No."

"Why not?"

"Why-do-we nee-hel?"

She stares at the back of his head, incredulous. She's pretty sure her frowning mouth is hanging open. Maybe she misheard him. Did he really just ask, *Why do we need help?*

"Bill-an-tha-otha-aides do-mo-satha heavy-lif-ting. You-do-wun meal-a-day but-o-tha-than-that I-mo-sly-stay ou-ta-ya-hair."

She squeezes the sheets in her fists. She wants to pull every strand of hair out of his ungrateful head. Who does he think just wiped up his piss? Who will interrupt every piano lesson this afternoon to suck his mouth dry so the students don't have to listen to him sputter and gag between notes and worry that he's dying in the next room? Who is up all hours of the night adjusting his mask so he can breathe? Who does he think washes his bedding and clothes and takes him to his doctor's appointments? But, otherwise, yeah, he mostly stays out of her hair.

"I'm exhausted."

"Yuh-firs-les-son is-no-un-til afa-noon. Why-don-you go-ba-to bed?"

"Why don't you go to hell?"

She drops the pile of bedding on the floor, marches out of the room, and shuts the door behind her. She doesn't want to see him. He can stay in there until Bill arrives.

229

Standing in the living room, shaking with fury, she's unable to decide what to do. She's too angry to enjoy breakfast and a cup of coffee, too incensed to take a nap, and Grace is still in the shower. Karina stands there, paralyzed in her rage, and wonders what would happen if she stopped helping him. What would happen if the next time he chokes, she doesn't stop her piano lesson midnote to suction him? At some point, the BiPAP won't simply be used for the quality of Richard's sleep. He'll need it all day and night for adequate ventilation. What happens when they reach that point in one month, in two months, this summer, and his mask comes loose in the night, and she ignores the sound of the BiPAP alarm? What if she awakens the next morning, refreshed from a full night's sleep, to find Richard with his mask askew, asphyxiated in the den?

She stands in the living room, exhausted, unappreciated, unshowered, and hungry, wondering if she'd be charged with murder if he dies on her watch.

CHAPTER TWENTY

The first half of every piano lesson is devoted to technique — scales in four octaves, Schmitt exercises, chords, and arpeggios — training fingers and ears. The second half is focused on playing the piece of music assigned to the student the previous week. Ideally, the student has practiced twenty minutes a day at home.

This student has not.

Now that he's finished the technique part of his lesson, Karina waits for Dylan to begin playing, and every minute of waiting increases the temperature of her exasperation. Dylan is thirteen and has probably grown six inches since last year. He's got long arms and fingers, knobby shoulders and knees, and appears uncomfortable in his own body, as if he hasn't quite moved into all that new space. Pink, inflamed acne covers his otherwise pale face. A whisper of fuzzy brown hair has sprouted above his lip.

He's wearing bright golden yellow shorts and a matching sweatshirt. His mother will shuttle him to basketball practice immediately after his piano lesson. Every few seconds, he snorts phlegm from somewhere in his throat up into his brain.

"Would you like a tissue?" asks Karina.

"Huh? No, I'm good."

No, you are not good, she wants to say.

He studies the sheet music in front of him as if reading Greek for the first time. Maybe he has a learning disability or some kind of musical dyslexia or amnesia and she shouldn't judge him. Or maybe, he simply doesn't want to be here. That makes both of them. She was up half the night, and sitting on this bench in silence is draining the last drops of her depleted energy. Her eyelids rest shut for a second or two with each blink. She's desperate for a nap.

Dylan lifts his left hand, but then retreats, placing it back onto his lap. He can't decide where to put his fingers. He won't even sample a note unless he's sure he's got it right. Millennials. They're all afraid to make a mistake. Dylan would rather sit on this bench, paralyzed in fear and indecision, than play the wrong note.

If she just tells him, she can end this infuriating stalemate. But she's not going to. Not today. She provides the answers for this kid every week, and he never learns. She blames his mother. She probably sits next to him while he does his homework and checks his answers, irons his clothes, wakes him up in the morning. The boy is helpless. Well, Karina is done coddling him. She sits and waits and says nothing, letting him sweat it out.

He snorts again as he squints at the music, leaning closer to the sheet of paper, searching for where to put his left hand. She's given him many bass-clef mnemonics. All Cows Eat Grass, for the spaces. Good Boys Deserve Fudge Always, for the lines. Or, Grizzly Bears Don't Fly Airplanes. No matter how it's packaged, he can't retain it and is forever perplexed by the arrangement of black dots on the five lines and four spaces of the bass clef.

She wishes he'd quit. She's tired of teaching students who don't want to play piano. She wishes all of them would quit. Aghast by this reckless thought, by the misfortune she just invited into her life, she crosses her fingers in her lap. How would she keep this roof over her head if that happened? She needs to be more careful about what she thinks.

Dylan snorts again. He shouldn't be here

with a chest cold. If Richard catches it, it could easily lead to pneumonia, and with ALS, that could be the end of him. She thinks about telling Dylan that they need to end the lesson early, but he doesn't have his license. They'd have to wait for his mother to pick him up, and his half-hour lesson would be done by the time she returns anyway.

The indecipherable music in front of him is Prelude in C by Johann Sebastian Bach. No sharps. No flats. It's as simple a piece of music as she can imagine that is still lovely to play and hear. The first note is middle C. Granted, the note is written for the left hand, and so it's on the ledger line above the bass staff and not on the ledger line below the treble staff, as he's used to seeing it. But still. It's middle fucking C.

His awkward presence and the even more awkward silence continue to provoke her, itching her hot, weary nerves, making her crazy. She grinds her teeth and breathes impatiently through her nose, suffering in her resistance. She will not tell him what to do. Not one little hint. These kids are handed everything with a pretty little gold bow tied around it. Everyone's a winner. Everyone gets a trophy. Not on this bench. Welcome to real life, Dylan.

He snorts again, and she wants to scream. *Play a note! Blow your nose! Do SOME-THING!* On another day, she might blame herself. If only she were a better teacher, more inspiring and encouraging, he'd know how to play this piece. Today, she's letting him own the blame. They'll both sit here for the remaining ten minutes in silence if they have to.

She gazes vaguely out the living-room window and notices three birds in the distance, possibly doves, sitting on electrical wires, two on the top line, the third on the wire below them. These round, black birds blur into treble-clef notes that she plays in her desperately bored mind. G-G-E. G-G-E. She begins to compose a piece of music prompted by these avian notes, and her foul mood is somewhat lifted by the sweet melody when Richard's coughing intrudes. Not the sound she was hoping for.

She listens for the shape and meaning of it and hopes that, like young Dylan here, Richard will work it out on his own. The cough is wet and gurgling, unrelenting. Richard's abdominal muscles have weakened considerably in the past month, and he often can't produce a cough effective enough to simply clear his throat. To Dylan, it probably sounds as if someone were drowning in his own spit in the next room, but Karina has grown hardened to these now-familiar noises.

Richard suddenly goes quiet, and it's the silence between the bursts of choking that she never gets used to, that fill her with dread. She can picture him straining, his body shaking and taut with effort as if he were trying to pull the cough up from his toes, the stringy vessels swelling in his neck, frothy spittle dripping over his mouth. She waits, listening, and she's reminded of years ago, lying awake in bed, waiting to hear the sound of the front door creaking open after midnight, the sound of Richard's heavy footsteps in the foyer, the wheels of his carry-on rolling across the hardwood floors. She resented him for being away, and then she immediately hated him for being home. Here he is, back home. And she still hates him.

If the situation were reversed, if she was sick, and Richard was stuck tending to her, everyone would canonize him. No one makes her feel like a saint for doing this. She feels pathetic, foolish, resentful, and stupid, probably how Dylan feels sitting at her piano for thirty minutes once a week.

Richard coughs again, breaking the silence. He hacks and sputters, obviously fighting for air, and the sound of his failing to clear his throat crawls up Karina's spine and screeches in her ear. That's it. She's had enough.

She stands abruptly, leaving Dylan in his endless confusion over Bach's impossible notes, and rages into the den. For the briefest moment, she considers the cough-assist machine. But her heart and mind are saturated in a burning-hot soup of hatred, and she can't take one more minute of any of this. She pulls out one of the two pillows from behind Richard's head and registers the split-second, wide-eyed recognition in his eyes before she covers them and his entire face. His head moves side to side beneath the pillow but not violently so. Paralyzed, his hands lie still by his side, unable to resist. She presses down harder.

It takes only about a minute for his head to go still. She waits a bit longer before lifting the pillow. His eyes are open, his pupils fixed in place, uninhabited.

She hears the sound of middle C.

"Is that right?" Dylan asks.

Karina blinks. The doves have taken flight from the electrical wires outside. She turns her head to see Bach's Prelude in C on the rack and pulls herself fully back into the living room, releasing that sinful, warm chocolate torte of a daydream. She listens as the pleasing tone of middle C fades, and Richard begins coughing in the den.

"Yes, Dylan. That's right. Congratulations."

She checks the time on her watch: 4:00. Lesson's over.

CHAPTER TWENTY-ONE

Grace is sitting at Richard's desk, slumped and sullen, her body swiveled in the seat so she's angled toward the door, the way out, instead of facing him squarely. Aside from Karina and Bill and the other aides and doctors who are used to seeing people with ALS, most people choose not to face him directly. He's gaunt and often drooling, and his arms are lifeless and his voice is messed up. Strangers can tell by the quickest glance, because that's typically all they'll stay for, that something is really wrong with that guy. But he understands that, even if he were healthy, facing him is hard for Grace.

He'd been watching *Game of Thrones* from his easy chair when she knocked on the slightly open door a few minutes ago and asked if she could come in, but she hasn't said a word since. She's clearly been sent in against her will, dutifully obeying her mother's directive. She keeps glancing down at her phone, possibly checking the time, wondering how long will be long enough for her to endure this nonconversation. She's been in here for three minutes going on eternity. Or maybe she's reading texts. He can't tell. She's leaving for the airport in an hour, going back to school. This is good-bye.

"I-wan-you-to-know, how-eh-va-ex-pen-sih thi-gets, yah-tu-i-sha mo-ney-wo-be tussed. Yah-ed-u-ca-sha is-safe."

"Okay. Thank you."

Whatever he didn't give Grace growing up, at least he will have given her this.

"Are there any new drugs coming out soon that might cure it or at least slow it down?" she asks, as if finally remembering something she planned to say.

"I'm-ina-clin-i-ca-tri. May-be-thata-be-a mag-ic-bul-le."

"Oh, good."

She seems satisfied and doesn't inquire any more on the topic. Like most twenty-year-olds, she probably can't imagine death in any real way. So of course something will save him. And there it is, the solution, the clinical trial drug. Problem solved. She can move on to a safer, more palatable topic. Or return to their mutually uncomfortable silence. Either way, no one's dying in this room.

Every morning, Bill dissolves the mystery clinical trial pill in water and pushes it through the syringe into Richard's stomach. He wants to feel some kind of difference when this happens — he can take a deeper breath, his articulation improves, the fasciculations in his tongue subside, he can miraculously wiggle his left thumb. But aside from the quenching cool rush of water filling his belly, he feels nothing.

Maybe he's in the control group. Or maybe, likely, this isn't the cure. But he stays in the trial, not because he's betting on this little white pill. He's not deluded into thinking modern medicine can save him. He's already gone too far down the rabbit hole, and he knows it. It's too late for him to be saved. He's in the trial because he's doing his part, contributing this small step in the long march toward the cure.

He figures every single thing that didn't work before scientists discovered the polio vaccine, for example, was necessary to get them to that cure. How many mistakes did he make in learning to play Chopin's Étude op. 10, no. 3, in learning any masterpiece, before being able to play it flawlessly? On the road leading to any great achievement are a thousand missteps, a thousand more dead ends. Success cannot be born without the life and death of failure.

Someday, scientists will discover a vaccine, a prophylactic, a cure, and people will talk about ALS the way they talk about polio. Parents will tell their children that people used to get something called ALS, and they died from it. It was a horrible disease that paralyzed its victims. Children will vaguely imagine the horror of it for a moment before skipping along to a sunnier topic, fleetingly grateful for a reality that will never include those three letters.

But not yet. Today, there is only one lame excuse for a treatment and no cure, and children like Grace sit in front-row seats, opposite their fathers, witnessing ALS in all its grotesque, unspeakable detail.

Even if, by some miracle, his little white clinical trial pill was the magic bullet, at most it would stop the advancing ALS army from taking over any more territory, arresting the disease where it is. From what he understands, this drug can't rebuild what has already been destroyed. So he wouldn't get any worse, but nothing could be reversed. He'd still have two paralyzed arms and hands, a barely intelligible voice, difficulty breathing, a feeding tube, and a right foot that drops and trips him regularly. As much as the prospect of dying in one year freaks him out, a dozen more years of living like this is even more unappealing. It's downright terrifying if he dwells on it.

He needs a magic pill and a time machine. He'd stop the disease and then go back in time, before ALS stole his hands. And then he'd go back even further, to when Grace was two, when he started touring to play with faraway symphony orchestras; to when Grace was four, when he was traveling to hide from Karina and her discontent; to when Grace was six, and he'd teach her how to tie her shoes and ride a bike, he'd celebrate her 100 percents on spelling tests, he'd read bedtime stories to her and kiss her good-night; to when she was eight, nine, ten. To know his daughter.

But here they are instead, in the den, strangers saying good-bye. They have no time machine and no cure for ALS and no cure for this broken relationship. No supplements can fill all that was lost, no pills can be pushed through his PEG tube to make everything right between them.

She swivels her chair back and forth, back and forth, then stops, her feet planted, as if she's decided something. It must be time for her to go. She folds her arms around her middle as if she were cold or feeling ill or protecting herself and looks directly at him.

"My whole childhood, I felt like you picked piano over me."

It's one thing to house shortcomings and failures within the privacy of his own thoughts; it's another to hear the words aloud, publicly spoken by another, called out by his daughter. He feels a crashing wave of shame, and then, to his surprise, he's washed in relief. He holds his daughter's fierce gaze and feels so proud of her.

"I did."

Her face reads surprised, and her eyes don't know where to look. She wasn't expecting agreement. It's time to take responsibility, to accept blame, to be the grown-up, to be her father, right now or never. She's going back to school. He might not have another chance.

He wants to say more, to let her know that while he chose piano over her, he didn't love piano more. It was just easier for him to love piano than to show his love for her. He was good at piano. What if he wasn't a good father? What if he was like his father? Piano was consuming, demanding his full attention, his passion, his time. He'd have time for Grace later. And later was always later. This is the biggest regret of his life.

He was a terrible father. He didn't play a starring or even supporting role in her upbringing. At best, he was an ancillary, recurring character, and now he's a non-union extra with no lines. When he's thought about his legacy, it's always been about his body of work, the music he's played and recorded, his piano career. He now sees his real legacy sitting opposite him, his daughter, a beautiful young woman he doesn't know, and he's out of time. He likely won't meet her boyfriend, her husband, her children. He won't see her graduate college or where she'll live or what she'll do. He looks at her pale green eyes, soulful like her mother's, her long hair pulled back into a ponytail, and realizes that he's never known her, and now he never will.

Maybe if he'd had more children as he wanted, he would've been a different father. Maybe he would've made better choices, been more involved. Karina was so capable, so totally committed to mothering Grace, he genuinely felt he wasn't needed at home. Over time, he felt he wasn't wanted there either. So he buried his head and dreams in his career and assumed he'd have more chances, that he and Karina would have more children. There would never be any more children. He clenches his jaw, swallows, and holds his breath, but the tears come anyway.

Grace pulls a tissue from the box on the desk, walks over to her father, and wipes the tears from his face and eyes. She returns to her seat and dabs the corners of her own eyes with the same tissue. He gives her a gentle, grateful smile. He wants to give her so much more.

"I have to go."

"Wi-you-be ba-home-fah spa-ring-brea?"

"I was planning on going to Lake Tahoe with Matt and some friends. But, I dunno, maybe."

"Tha-souns-fuh. You-sha-do-tha."

"I'll probably be here for a weekend in March. I'll definitely be home for the summer."

"O-kay."

"See you then."

"See-you-then."

She stands, walks over to him, and with her hand on his shoulder, kisses him on the forehead.

"Bye, Dad."

As she leaves the room, he wants to reach out and touch her, to wrap his arms around her and hug her tight, to show her with touch what he can't seem to execute in words, but his hands are even more useless than his voice. He's plagued with regret and the inability to articulate the apology he wants to give her because of the sweeping scope of it, because his voice production is so damn slow and there are too many and not enough words, because he's entirely unpracticed with this kind of conversation. As she leaves the room, he thinks about the story of his own father — the one he's carried his entire adult life, heavy and cumbersome and painful — and wonders what story Grace carries about him. When her boyfriend asks, "What's your dad like?," what is her answer? How heavy and cumbersome and painful is her story?

CHAPTER TWENTY-TWO

Richard and Karina are sitting side by side in the small office of Dr. George, an augmentative communications specialist. Dr. George has just spent the past few minutes giving them an overview of who he is and what he does, and he's jazzed about all of it. He's probably in his midthirties, pale and thin, wearing metal-rimmed glasses, and is excessively cheerful bordering on goofy, effervescing with energy as if he's had three too many shots of espresso, but Richard suspects that this is simply how this guy rolls. His sunny demeanor is as unexpected as it is disarming, so unlike that of the many other specialists Richard sees. Not that he can blame the others. Treating ALS isn't exactly a barrel of laughs.

"So tell me what's been going on," says Dr. George.

"Well," says Karina, "it's hard to understand him when —"

"I'm sorry, forgive me for interrupting. I'm going to stop you right there. I want to hear straight from the horse's mouth. Make sense? Richard?" Dr. George nods at Richard, eyebrows lifted, smiling. "Giddyup."

"I'm-los-ih my-voice an-we-wa-na-know wha-ta-do so-I-ca-still co-mu-ni-cay."

"Okay, great. I'm a little heartbroken I'm just meeting you now. I wish you'd come in after you were first diagnosed or even a few months ago."

Richard's neurologist, who referred him to Dr. George, said Richard was told about voice banking when he was first diagnosed and many times thereafter, but Richard has zero recollection of it. He was in shock when he was diagnosed and then in denial for at least a season. Dr. George's information was buried somewhere in a packet of other terrifying information he wanted no part of, such as PEG-tube surgery and invasive ventilation and power wheelchairs. Even after he accepted his diagnosis, he didn't accept that he would someday lose his voice. Some people with ALS don't. Maybe he wouldn't. Banking his voice feels like the equivalent of setting up a baby's nursery or creating a baseball diamond in a cornfield. If he builds a voice bank, he will come to need it.

"I-know-I-ma lil-lay-to the-par-ty."

"That's okay. The party's still going. Even though your voice has lost a lot of its melody and isn't as robust as I'm sure it used to be, it's still you. The way you accent syllables, idiosyncratic phrases you might use or even noises you make — your laugh, for example — are all specific to you. By recording these, we can help keep your communications personal and human."

Richard wonders about the sound of his laugh. Is it the same as it was before ALS? He tries to remember the last time he laughed out loud but comes up blank. His life hasn't been funny in quite a while. As every other sound coming out of his mouth has changed, he suspects that his laugh is different, too. He tries to hear it in his mind's ear but finds only silence. He'll have to try laughing when he gets home.

"Even with the sound of your voice being mostly monotone, you'd be surprised. Even the smallest inflection can convey emotional nuance and personality you just can't get from the computer-synthesized voice options."

Dr. George doesn't have to convince Richard of the value of using his own voice versus a computer-generated one. He understands the breadth of what can be communicated in the smallest subtlety of sound. A single key played on the piano can convey the entire range of human experience. Middle C can be played staccato and fortissimo, a loud and sudden *yell*! It could mean anger, danger, surprise. The same note played pianissimo is a whisper, a tiptoe, a gentle kiss. Middle C held down, along with the foot pedal, can convey a longing, a wondering, a fading life.

The same note played by a novice versus a master is a completely different experience. What does Mozart's Concerto no. 23 in A Major have to say? How does it make a listener feel? It depends entirely on who is playing. So, yes, Richard understands.

"I like to think of voice banking as an acoustical fingerprint. Our voices are part of our unique personalities and identities. As you know, with ALS, everything gets taken away. Voice banking is a way we can preserve a piece of who you are before it's gone."

Before *he's* gone.

"Synthetic speech is flat. That's the voice Stephen Hawking uses that you've probably heard. There's no musicality in it. Musicality is so important for conveying meaning, you know?"

More than Dr. George knows. Richard's

voice now is a one-note instrument, a child's annoying party horn. His articulation is indistinct, his once-sharpened consonants filed down to a soft, rounded nub. Even Karina and Bill, familiar and trained in Richard-speak every day, are having a hard time comprehending what he's saying. His production is painstakingly slow, every syllable hard labor, and he runs out of air every three to four words. He often runs out of patience for what he wants to say before he even begins and then doesn't bother.

"You can pick and choose what to record. It can feel like a tiresome process, and it does take time. But I promise it's worth it. Don't record in the afternoon or evening, your voice and energy will be at their lowest quality. That's why your appointment today is at four. I want to hear you when your voice is tired. Record in the morning. Make sense?"

Richard nods.

"And we want to conserve your energy. Things like 'I'm thirsty' can be the synthetic voice generated by the computer. 'Thank you so much' would be better in your voice. You get what I'm saying?"

Richard does, but he can't think of anything to record beyond *Thank you so much.*

"Do-you-ha-va liss?"

"We do! You're so on top of this. Yes, we have a list of ideas to get you started. But there are no rules to this. You can record anything you want. You might also want to record what I call legacy messages. These are longer than a phrase or a sentence and not about the activities of daily living. They can be reflections of who you are or messages you want to leave for the people you love, like your wife."

Dr. George settles his gaze on Karina and smiles big.

"I'm his ex-wife," says Karina, correcting him swiftly, the clear tone and volume of her voice leaving no room for miscommunication.

"Oh. Good for you guys," says Dr. George, still smiling, completely unfazed. "Some people like to record movie quotes, a fun way to inject a little humor into the day. So, like, 'Frankly, my dear, I don't give a damn.' Make it fun."

Yeah, Richard can record movie quotes while he's having his Liquid Gold dinner. ALS is a blast. Although the technology is cool, it sounds time-consuming, and Richard's not sure any of this will be worth it. He has only so much time left.

He often checks the time on his laptop

and on the TV cable box many times an hour, a vague and persistent dread harassing him, as if he needs to buy something at a store before it closes soon, or he's increasingly late for an appointment, or he's waiting for someone to arrive, the doorbell to ring any minute. Yet, he knows that he has nothing to purchase, no appointments to keep, and isn't expecting the arrival of anyone at the front door other than Karina, home health aides, and therapists. It doesn't matter. He still checks the time. Over and over and over.

Every minute that goes by is one less minute. But what exactly is he doing with those minutes? If he weren't in Dr. George's office right now, he'd be in the den sipping on a coffee milk shake and bingeing on the next season of *House of Cards*. He's squandering his minutes, but what else is there for him? He can't play piano. He can't teach piano. He can't even bear to listen to the classical music he loves unless it's played by Karina.

He looks forward to the moments in her lessons when she takes over. He'll notice the antecedent extended pause and imagines her student scooting over, Karina positioning herself at the center of the bench. He stops whatever he's doing when this happens and waits. She begins playing, showing her student how the piece is supposed to sound and feel, developing the student's ear.

He'll close his eyes, and he's transported into the music. He's traveling with the notes, feeling whatever Karina feels as she plays, as if he were no longer trapped in his prison cage of a body, flying. Listening to Karina play is transcendent, as free as he's felt since he was diagnosed. He wishes she'd play more, when her students are gone for the day, just for him.

"Aside from voice banking, there are some other communication aids I can offer you. You'll want this." Dr. George produces a round red plastic button from one of his desk drawers, something that a clown might pull out of his prop bag. "It's a simple call button. So, for example, say you're choking and you can't call for help, you can step on this call button, and the receiver end will buzz loudly like a doorbell, and so even if Karina is somewhere else in the house, she'll be alerted. It's kind of like a baby monitor. This is a great option for you because you're still walking. So you can get to the button and step on it. You're lucky you still have your legs."

While Richard knows he's lucky to still

have use of his legs, and he's lucky that he can still talk, and he's lucky he can still breathe, these kinds of comments strike him as both ridiculous and insulting. But he tries not to take offense.

His legs will soon be leaving him. For the past week, he's felt a long-distance pause between the decision to take a step and stepping, a loosening of body from mind, of muscle from bone, of intent from action. ALS is extending its evil tendrils south.

Maybe he's just being paranoid. Maybe he's imagining the weakening in his right leg, creating a somatization. Maybe it's psychosomatic. His mother used to tell him, *If you're looking for trouble, you'll find it.* That may be true, but he certainly never went looking for ALS. He knew that Lou Gehrig had it, that Stephen Hawking has it, and was peripherally aware of the Ice Bucket Challenge. That was the extent of his knowledge on the subject, and he wasn't seeking to know more.

Trouble came looking for him. He was diagnosed fourteen months ago, and paralysis from the waist down, one leg at a time, is what comes next, whether he's a paranoid hypochondriac looking for trouble or not. But for now, he agrees with Dr. George. He's lucky to still have his legs.

"An-yah-lu-cky you-still-ha-vyah ki-neys."

Dr. George laughs, a high-pitched, tickled, unguarded giggle. Richard should record it and use that as his banked laugh. He likes Dr. George. He wonders if George might actually be his first name and not his last, if he's choosing to be addressed with a title that's less stuffy and more intimate, like Dr. Phil or like an unrelated friend who goes by Uncle instead of Mr. He's Uncle George.

"You're also going to want a bunch of these low-tech alphabet boards and flip charts. I know they're not as sexy as the eye-gaze and Tobii technology, and you'll get your sexy on eventually, but you'll use these first, and they're actually quicker and easier to use. As his voice goes, or maybe later in the day when his energy is low, you'll want to use these, Karina."

Dr. George hands her a stack of charts. Richard reads the tabs: *In Bed; Comfort; Transfer and Position; Wheelchair; Computer; Bathroom.* Karina opens to the *In Bed* chart. Richard scans the page.

Raise/Lower Head
Hot/Cold
Turn on BiPAP
Chap Stick
Nose/Wipe

Take Arm Out of Cover
Take off BiPAP
Mouth Dry/Water
Pee
Scratch My Head
Raise/Lower Foot of Bed
Adjust Mask
TV and Lights Out
Nose/Saline
Wipe My Eyes

In bed used to mean something entirely different. Karina turns the page before Richard has the chance to absorb every option. She spends only a second or so on each additional chart before flipping, looking overwhelmed and scared.

"I know it can feel a bit like being on a game show, and this kind of intense listening can feel awkward and frustrating at first, but you'll get good at it. Ask yes-and-no questions or point to what you're asking. Richard, when you can no longer speak, as long as you can nod and shake your head, great. If you can't move your head, you'll blink for yes and do nothing for no."

The same message is printed at the top of every chart: *You have to keep looking at my face and DON'T guess please!* Richard wonders what happens if he can no longer raise his eyebrows or blink. What happens if his face can't offer any clues? He doesn't ask.

"Okay, I know this was a lot. Only a couple more things, then you're good to go. You're going to love this." Dr. George retrieves something from a box under his desk. "It's a head mic and voice amplifier. We're going to turn Richard's volume way up. Super-lightweight and easy-breezy. Here, try it."

Dr. George hooks one end of the microphone over Richard's ear and bends the wire so the tiny mouthpiece sits in front of his left cheek.

"Try saying something."

He feels like a rock star in concert. Madonna comes to mind.

"Sss-tri-ka-pose."

Dr. George stands up and vogues. "Isn't that great? It can amplify a whisper and make what you said audible. It'll save your energy by a lot. Our goal is for you to be fatigued from talking after four hours instead of two."

Richard's fatigued after talking for five minutes.

"Okay, so you have the call button and the voice amplifier, the alphabet and flip charts, and here's the voice recorder for you to use." Dr. George hands the recorder to Karina. "Each file you create is automatically saved in the format we use to build your bank. You don't have to do anything but hit RECORD. It's not voice activated though. You have to turn it on and off by pressing here, so Karina will have to help you."

Karina holds the recorder out in front of her with both hands as if she's been given something fragile or dangerous or sacred. Maybe it's all of those.

"Okay, that's all I have for today. Please contact me with any questions at all, and come back to see me as things change. And I'd say if you're going to bank your voice, do it now."

The change in Dr. George's voice in that last sentence was subtle but unquestionable. The key was slightly lower, the intonation narrowed, and his articulation crisper. The sound of a spoken sentence can add layers of meaning beyond the mere definition of the words strung together. Dr. George's last sentence was a rich concerto, and Richard clearly heard the subtext.

You don't have much time left.

CHAPTER TWENTY-THREE

Dear Dad,

I'm writing to let you know that I've been diagnosed with ALS (Lou Gehrig's disease). Both of my arms are paralyzed, I'm having difficulty breathing and talking and swallowing. I can no longer safely eat food, so I have a feeding tube in my stomach. I can still walk, but this, too, will go. Despite all of these losses, I'm mainly in good spirits. Because I could no longer manage living alone, I've moved back in with Karina, where she and a wonderful team of caregivers help me get through the days and nights. Just wanted you to know.

Your son,
Richard

This is the simplest of the nine letters he's composed, saved, and not sent to his father.

He reads it again. Nothing but straight-forward information. Just the facts, ma'am. He wrote the first draft of this letter back when he still had use of his left arm, when he still lived alone on Comm Ave. and spent his days and nights obsessively playing Ravel's Piano Concerto for the Left Hand. That was this past summer. He can't decide if August was a lifetime ago or yesterday.

After Bill leaves him showered and dressed and fed, he spends his mornings at the computer. He'll scan the news, but he's conscious not to spend too much time surfing these treacherous global waters. War, terrorism, nasty politics, racial tensions, murders, ignorance, blame — the news either frustrates, angers, or depresses him. He has enough to be frustrated, angry, and depressed about.

He invariably finds himself using this time every day to write and reread the letters he's written to his father. Periodically, he edits his "coming out" letter, updating the list of losses to keep it current, just in case he should decide to send it someday. He added the part about the feeding tube just after Christmas.

He reads the letter again. Pointing the tip of his nose to FILE, he pulls down the menu, then points his nose to PRINT and hovers there just shy of long enough for the computer to register a click before turning his head to the right, his nose aimed at the window, disconnecting the cursor from his mouse target. A game of printing chicken.

He has no idea if his eighty-two-year-old father has an email account, so sending him anything would require actual paper, an envelope, and a stamp. If Richard's ever going to print and mail any of the letters he's written, this would be the one. Unlike the other eight letters he's composed, this disclosure contains no blame or indignant rants. He's almost printed it many times, flirted with the fantasy of his father holding the envelope in his hands before opening it, but Richard's heart gets all twisted as he hovers the cursor over PRINT, and he bails.

Part of him doesn't want his father to know. Keeping his diagnosis from his father fills Richard with an exhilarating sense of winning. He was born into a father-son game he never wanted to play, the rules still cruel and incomprehensible to him, but damn it, he's going to win. He's living with a disease that shaves off another layer of control every single day. Possessing control of whether his father knows or not puts a sword in Richard's hand, a power that's too seductive to resist. He's going to prove, in an ultimate and final test, that he doesn't want or need his father for anything and wouldn't turn to him for help or love even in the most dire circumstances. He won't give his father the satisfaction of knowing he'll soon be rid of the son he never wanted.

But when Richard's bombastic offense tires of wielding its sword and takes a seat, his defense is clearly visible, cowering in the corner. More than anything, he's afraid of his father's indifference. He wonders if his father already knows, if word of mouth has spread north to cow country, and Walt Evans is the one doing the snubbing.

Or his father doesn't know and wouldn't respond if he did. Richard imagines his father opening the envelope, reading the letter through once, crumpling the paper in his fist, and tossing it into the trash. Or he reads it, refolds it, and slides the letter into his coat pocket, where it will be forgotten along with some lint and a gas receipt. In all the fantasies Richard entertains about his father's potential reaction to this letter, Richard's mind won't allow for the possibility of his father picking up the phone or showing up at the door. The father Richard knows would offer no words of shock, horror, empathy, sympathy, or love for his youngest son.

This is why Richard doesn't print the letter.

He knows he'll never send the others. He'll never get what he wants from his father. What does he want? He wants his father to admit that he was wrong for making Richard feel as if he weren't good enough to be in the family. He wants his father to tell him that he's okay exactly as he is. He wants his father to say that he's proud of him. He wants his father to say he's sorry for showing no interest in his piano career, his wife, his daughter. In him. He wants a big fat heartfelt apology.

But Walt Evans is an old dog, and he's not going to change, and he's certainly never going to apologize. And it doesn't matter now. Sorry won't do Richard any good. What's done cannot be undone.

Yet, Richard continues to write to his father. It feels good to get the words out — words Richard felt when he was six but didn't have the vocabulary to articulate, words he wanted to yell when he was sixteen but didn't have the courage, words he wanted to argue when he was twenty-six but didn't have the composure, words he wanted to speak when he was forty-six but literally no longer had the voice. The letters he writes communicate what he could never say, every typed word carrying an ancient scar on its back, every typed sentence fracking a bevy of silenced wounds stored in his deepest, darkest core, releasing a lifetime of outrage and resentment. But it seems no matter how many sentences he writes, the injustices buried within him are never fully mined.

He considers writing another letter, but he lacks the energy. His neck muscles tire faster when sitting up at the desk versus reclined in his chair or propped against the back of his bed. It's becoming conscious work to hold up his ten-pound head. His accuracy declines after typing only a few minutes, the cursor drifting down the screen as his head drops forward. He's probably ready for one of those neck braces, the standard soft white collars people wear when they've been injured in an accident.

He opens the second letter instead. It begins as a résumé, a list of Richard's achievements, appearances, and critical reviews (only the good ones). If he never sends it to his father, maybe Trevor can use it for Richard's obituary.

He graduated with honors from Curtis. He was an associate professor at New England Conservatory. He's played with the Chicago and Boston Symphony Orchestras;

the New York, Cleveland, Berlin, and Vienna Philharmonic Orchestras. He's played at Boston Symphony Hall, Carnegie Hall, Lincoln Center, London's Royal Albert Hall, Tanglewood, Aspen, and many more. His playing has been hailed as "inspirational," "spellbinding," and "possessing great virtuosity."

I was a great pianist. Audiences all over the world applauded me. They gave me standing ovations. They loved me. Why couldn't you applaud me, Dad? Why couldn't you love me? Richard has never found a satisfying answer to either of these questions, but staring at his bio on the computer screen, he's proven, at least to himself, that he's worthy of a father's love. *There is something wrong with him, not me.* It took Richard forty-six years and ALS to get that far, which feels like progress but is probably just shifting blame, the pea transferred to another shell under deft sleight of hand, the truth still hidden from everyone.

Maybe if he'd loved to play something more accessible to his father, if he'd been into playing Billy Joel or the Beatles, if he'd wanted to play in a rock 'n' roll band in a pub instead of classical piano in a recital hall, if he'd also played football and baseball like Mikey and Tommy, his father would've approved. Walt hated classical music. They lived in a one-hundred-year-old three-bedroom farmhouse with thin rugs and thinner walls. Whenever Richard practiced, which was all the time, there was nowhere in the house that didn't fill with sound. If Richard was playing Bach, the entire house was listening to Bach.

Walt Evans hated Bach. Ten minutes was about all he could tolerate before he either stormed out of the house to do yard work or got in his pickup and drove to Moe's, the local bar. If for some reason he wasn't allowed to leave the house, if Richard's mother told them supper would be ready in a few minutes, and Walt was forced to endure a few more minutes of Richard's practicing, he'd explode. "Would you *stop* with all the goddamn noise?!"

Richard opens another letter, and every familiar sentence, every ancient accusation, is a bugle call to his oldest, darkest suffering, summoning an army of resentment and hatred to rise up within him. *You called me a pansy for playing piano instead of football. . . . You called me a fag for loving Mozart. . . . You threatened to hack my piano to pieces with an ax and use the wood for kindling. . . . You never came to my recitals. . . . You never accepted me. . . . You never even knew me. . . . You never loved me, Karina, or Grace.*

Grace. An electric ripple runs through him, decimating the tortured battlefield within, leaving him hollowed out, staring in helpless horror at his computer screen, seeing history repeated. The letters on the screen blur as he imagines a similar letter addressed to him, written by Grace.

You picked piano over me. You never came to my games. And now you have ALS, and you'll never know me. You never loved Mom or me.

Tears roll down his face. *Please don't think that.* He can't stand the thought of this kind of letter, penned by her hand, of this legacy of pain he's leaving her. Maybe what's done can be undone. Maybe that's what apology is for.

After a quick knock on his door Karina enters the room without pausing. It irritates him that she doesn't even allow him to respond, for the possibility that he might not want her to enter. He's still upset, his face wet with tears. He can't wipe them away.

"It's Tommy." She's holding Richard's cell phone, faceup.

"Who?"

"Your brother," a voice says from the

269

phone on speaker. "Hey, Ricky, I'm sorry I'm not calling with better news. But, well . . ." Tommy's voice thins out and disappears. He sighs and clears his throat. "Dad died last night."

Richard stares at Karina. The puddle of agony he was just knee-deep in over Grace's imagined letter evaporates. He waits for what replaces it. He feels nothing.

"Mikey found him early this morning. He was in his chair with the TV on. We think he died in his sleep. Probably a heart attack. . . . You there?"

"Yah."

"I'm so sorry," says Karina.

"Thank you. The wake is Thursday at Knight's Funeral Home and the funeral is Friday at St. Jude's."

"O-kay," says Richard.

"I know. I'm having trouble talking, too. He lived a good life. Almost eighty-three. And dying in your own home in your sleep, no hospitals or long, drawn-out disease, you can't ask for better than that, right?"

Richard and Karina trade a silent conversation about ALS and death with their eyes before Richard realizes that Tommy is waiting for an answer.

"No."

"Hey, I know we haven't seen you in a

long time, but you're welcome to stay with Mikey or at Dad's house. I'd have you here, but we literally got kids sleeping in closets and don't have any room."

Richard looks up at Karina. She nods. She'll go with him to New Hampshire.

"Thaks-Tom-my. We'll-be-there."

"You okay, man?"

"Yeah."

"All right. We'll see you Thursday then."

Tommy doesn't know that Richard has ALS. Neither does Mikey. None of them knows. They're about to find out.

Karina hangs up the phone and eyes Richard's impassive-yet-already-tear-strewn face. "I'm sorry. Are you really okay?"

"Fine." He swivels his chair toward the computer and away from her, showing her the back of his head.

He hears her leave the room without a word. He swivels the chair to be sure that she's gone, then returns to his computer. He takes a deep breath, or at least a deep shallow breath. He points his nose at the screen, holding the position of his heavy head steady, focused on the folder labeled *Letters to My Father.* The folder opens. One by one, he selects each of the nine files and drags them to the trash. He studies the screen. The folder remains. The cursor darts and shimmies and his heart pounds hard in his throat as he works to select and then direct the folder to the trash bin.

There.

In an instant, his father and any possibility of apology are dead and gone.

CHAPTER TWENTY-FOUR

They're the last to arrive at Walt's house after the funeral. Karina and Grace hover awkwardly behind Richard in the living room, waiting for him to continue walking or sit down or do something. He just stands there, paralyzed, observing empty space. His upright piano, a fixture in his childhood home as seemingly permanent as its foundation, is gone. There is nothing in its place. Richard stands still, trying to comprehend its incomprehensible absence, feeling as if the only record of his childhood has been expunged. As he imagines his dead father erasing his past and ALS erasing his future, there is too little of him left. Time feels as if it's collapsing in on him, and his bones are suddenly too fragile, his skin too transparent, his presence sliced too thin, and he wonders if he might cease to exist right then and there.

"Whe-did-he geh-ri-do-vit?" he asks of no

one in particular, his voice barely audible even with the voice amplifier.

Karina moves to his right side, wraps her arm around his waist, and holds him by the hip, offering him stability.

His brother Tommy wanders in from the kitchen. "What's going on?"

"Where's the piano?" asks Karina.

"I have it. Lucy and Jessie take lessons. I hope that's okay."

Relief washes through Richard. He breathes, and he's back in his body. Lucy and Jessie are his nieces, ages nine and twelve. He nods.

"Yes. Thas-per-feck."

"They're really good. I tell them they get it from their uncle."

Richard smiles with his eyes and looks down at his feet, uncertain how to handle this unexpected compliment.

"You guys hungry? We've got food in the kitchen. Grace?"

"Sure." Grace follows her uncle into the other room.

Richard takes a seat in the rocking chair and looks around the living room as if he were visiting for the first time. It may well be the last time. Much like its former occupant, the house is old and outdated. The floorboards are worn and creaky, the paint on the cracked walls is chipped, the ceiling is mottled with water stains. With the exception of the missing piano and the additions of a giant-screen TV and an oversized recliner, the living room is furnished exactly as Richard remembers it.

There are still no curtains on the windows. His mother believed in sunshine and having nothing to hide. She often said she wouldn't do anything she wouldn't mind the neighbors seeing. On this four-acre, heavily wooded property, the nearest neighbor would've needed the Hubble telescope to see Sandy Evans smoking cigarettes in her pink curlers and nightgown.

Even though his mother has been gone for twenty-eight years, it's her absence and not his father's that Richard feels most acutely in this room. She was his only ally in the family, the only one who truly saw and accepted him. Without his mother, he couldn't have played piano. She arranged for his lessons, insisted on the money from Walt to pay for them, drove him to every lesson, every recital and competition, and defended his right to practice.

He remembers the time she put herself between Richard's piano and Walt's chain saw. Richard can't remember what set him off. Maybe he'd had a half dozen beers, and the Patriots lost. Richard does remember the thumping of his heart in his ears playing percussion with the distant buzz of his father's chain saw slicing through the branches of a maple tree in the backyard after Walt stood down, determined to destroy something. Richard remembers sitting at the kitchen table while he listened, his mother's hands shaking as she measured out flour and salt for apple-pie dough. He remembers stupidly asking, "Can I play now?" — his mother answering, "Not now, honey." He remembers he was ten.

She was so proud of him for getting into Curtis on scholarship. She died just before he turned nineteen. She never met Karina, never got to see him graduate or play professionally, never got to hold her granddaughter. She never knew that her son would someday have ALS.

He thinks his mother would've approved of Karina. What little his father experienced of her, he was never a fan. Walt didn't trust anyone from out of town, never mind from out of state, never mind from Poland. His world played out within his zip code, his life revolving around his job at the local quarry, the town church, the bank, the school, and Moe's tavern. He didn't like that he didn't know Karina's parents, that he couldn't judge what kind of family she came from. When asked about her religion, she told him she was a lapsed Catholic. The only kind of person Walt, a Protestant and faithful Sunday churchgoer, trusted less than a Catholic was a godless woman. He found no charm in her accent and didn't appreciate her sophisticated vocabulary, which, even spoken in broken English, was far superior to Walt's. He blamed Karina for his son's name preference of Richard over Ricky when she had nothing to do with it. Walt took her to be uppity, a snob, a heathen, probably a communist, a lazy immigrant only interested in Richard as a ticket to a green card.

The grown-ups filter into the room carrying food and drinks and take seats. No one chooses the recliner. That must've been "the chair." Richard's not sure if everyone is staying off it in reverence to Walt or if they all find it too creepy, knowing he died there a few days ago. On Monday, his father was sitting in that chair watching TV. Today he's in a box in the ground.

Grace says she isn't hungry after all and joins seven of her eight cousins outside, sledding on the hill. They range in age from three to twenty-two, nieces and nephews Richard doesn't know. They were all stone-faced and tearless during the funeral, seemingly more weirded out by their drooling, unfamiliar uncle than their dead grandfather. It's probably easier to bear witness to the graceful exit of an old man than the sloppy, slow-motion, paralytic crawl to death that is ALS in someone who should be in the prime of life. The older kids snuck periodic glances at him as if on a dare, and when caught staring, their eyes fled to somewhere safer, often the coffin.

Brendan, age eight, wiry with a buzz cut, a sharp nose, and curious eyes, doesn't feel like getting wet or cold and is sitting sandwiched between his parents, Mikey and Emily, on the small couch. Tommy and Karina are on the love seat. Tommy's wife, Rachael, is outside, helping her two youngest kids up and down the steep hill. Everyone is eating deli-meat sandwiches and Buffalo chicken wings on paper plates. The men are drinking Budweiser out of cans, and the women are drinking white wine.

Richard watches his brothers eat, massive bites of bread, ham, and cheese churning around in their open mouths like clothes in a circular dryer window while they talk, and he's a kid again at the supper table. Skinny, he ate modest meals, always a single helping, and finished quickly. Never allowed to be excused early, he felt as if he spent hours at the table every night, waiting in lonely silence as his brothers gorged on several platefuls of meat and potatoes. Unlike Richard, they were big boys with big muscles to feed. Athletes who were every day running on a field or bench-pressing at the gym, they were in good physical shape when they were young, but now, they're both overweight. They've got beer guts and full-moon faces and beefy arms and legs that look stiff when they walk, like growing kids stuffed into last winter's snowsuits.

"Want me to get you a plate?" asks Mikey, noticing that Richard isn't eating.

"I-can't-eee-tha."

"You need one of us to hold the sandwich for you?"

"It's not that. He can't swallow the bites without choking," says Karina.

"I-ha-va fee-ding tu."

"There's a tube in his stomach," says Karina to wide-eyed Brendan.

"Can I see it?" asks Brendan.

"Sure," says Richard.

They all sit, watching him, as if waiting in the audience for the curtain to rise and the show to start.

"One-a-you has-to-lif-my shir. I-ca-na do-it."

Richard looks to Brendan and raises his eyebrows twice. Brendan tentatively leaves his seat, walks over to his uncle, and pauses. He looks back at his parents.

"Go-fo-rit."

He gently lifts his uncle's shirt, exposing a quarter-size white plastic disk flush with the upper part of Richard's hairy stomach.

"Ew," says Brendan, releasing the shirt.

"Brendan!" says Emily. "That's not nice."

Brendan quickly retreats to his seat between his parents. Mikey swats him on the head with a rolled funeral missalette. Richard's shirt has fallen back down over his stomach, but everyone in the room is still studying the spot where the tube lives, imagining what they just saw.

"So what goes in that?" asks Mikey.

"It's called Liquid Gold," says Karina. "It's like baby formula."

"Tase-lie chi-cken."

"Really?" asks Tommy.

"No." Richard smiles. "I-am ki-ding."

"What are you doing to fight it?" asks Mikey.

"Wha-do-you-mean?"

"Look at that guy who started the Ice Bucket Challenge, right? And the movie *Gleason*. Did you see it? That defensive back from the New Orleans Saints. He got

ALS and started a nonprofit. Their slogan is 'No White Flags.' Guy's an inspiration. A real hero. You can't just take this lying down, Ricky. You gotta fight it."

Former captain of their high school football and baseball teams, cornerback at the University of New Hampshire, Mikey sees every obstacle as an opponent that can be beaten, a game that can be won.

"How-do-you thin-I-shu fight?"

"I dunno. Look at what those guys did."

"You-wa-me-to dum-pa bu-cket a-ice o-vah-my-head?"

Or block a punt? Get a trach and go on life support when he can no longer breathe? Is living at any cost winning? ALS isn't a game of football. This disease doesn't wear a numbered jersey, lose a star player to injury, or suffer a bad season. It is a faceless enemy, an opponent with no Achilles' heel and an undefeated record.

"I dunno. I'd do something though. Start another challenge or make a documentary or something. Something that helps find the cure. The key is fighting and not giving up."

"O-kay."

"It's good you're still walking. Those other guys are in wheelchairs."

"I-will-be in-one-soo."

"Maybe not. You never know. You gotta

stay positive. You should go to the gym, lift some weights and strengthen your leg muscles. If this disease starts stealing your muscle mass, you get ahead of it and build more. You beat it."

Richard smiles. He appreciates the thought, but that isn't how muscle atrophy in ALS works. The disease doesn't discriminate between strong and weak muscles, old or new. It takes them all. Exercise won't buy him more time. High tide is coming. The height and grandeur of the sand castle doesn't matter. The sea is eventually going to rush in, sweeping every single grain of sand away.

"Goo-i-de-a."

"I don't know how you do it," says Tommy. "I don't think I could ever go without food."

"Then-you-be gi-vin-up. This-tu-bis how-you fi-ALS."

It ain't sexy. Richard's PEG tube and Bi-PAP aren't interesting enough fodder for a movie or a global Internet phenomenon. His fight is a quiet, personal, daily struggle to simply breathe and consume enough calories to keep being here.

"It's good to see that you two are back together," says Emily.

"We're not back together," says Karina.

"Yah." Richard smiles. "We-jus li-vin-in sin."

"No," says Karina. "There's no sinning going on whatsoever."

"That's too bad," says Mikey.

Emily laughs. "Well, that's really amazing then, what you're doing for him."

Karina says nothing. Richard says nothing and doesn't look in Karina's direction, embarrassed that Emily has so easily articulated what Richard has never said. And although he'd like to, he can't blame ALS for his silence.

"So, Ricky," says Mikey. "We want to talk to you about Dad's will. We already knew about this before he died, but he left the house to me and Tommy."

Of course he did.

"But we talked it over and agreed that we're going to sell the house and split it three ways."

Everyone waits.

Richard repeats what he just heard in his head and asks, "Really?"

"Yeah. He had three sons, not two. That ain't right, and we want to do the right thing."

"Yeah, man," says Tommy. "I hate that I never stood up for you when we were kids. Dad was really hard on you."

"He could be a bullheaded bastard," says Mikey.

Tommy nods. "We're standing up for you now."

It never occurred to Richard that his big, brave, tough jock brothers were scared of their father, too. To show any allegiance with their youngest brother would've risked being forsaken, ostracized, disowned. Like Richard. His brothers weren't as macho as he thought they were. And he doesn't blame them.

"He was also a great father," says Mikey, his voice out of air, jaw clamped, wiping the outside corner of his eyes with his fingers. "Sorry you never got that side of him, Ricky."

"You know, you were better at piano than either of us clowns have ever been at anything," says Tommy. "He should've been proud of you. Jessie Googled you, and we all watched your performance at Lincoln Center."

"Holy shit, man," says Mikey.

"Yeah, you're amazing," says Emily.

"I wish Mom could've seen you play there," says Tommy.

"Tha-means-so much to-me." Tears spill down Richard's face.

He never saw that coming. With the death

of the autocratic dictator, their Berlin Wall crumbled, and his brothers were right there, waiting for him on the other side. Karina pulls a tissue from her purse, walks over to Richard, and mops up his wet face.

"Three ways," says Mikey. "That's the fair thing. It wasn't right how Dad treated you. Our son, Alex, is a junior now, hasn't willingly picked up a ball since he was six. He's into musicals. Loves to sing and dance."

"He's really good," says Emily.

"Yeah. And he's a great kid. Can't imagine doing to him what Dad did to you." Mikey sighs. "And I wouldn't be the man I am without him."

Tommy nods. Mikey knocks back his Budweiser. Richard absorbs the acceptance and apology given to him by his brothers, and a space begins clearing inside him, a field stretched to the horizon, a morning sky, a universe of stars. Still overwhelmed and unable to speak, he silently thanks his brothers, one generation healing the wounds inflicted by another.

"I'm sorry to break this up, but we really have to get going," says Karina.

"Can't you stay another night?" asks Emily.

"No, we have to get Grace to the airport. She needs to get back to school."

"Let's do a toast to Dad before you go," says Mikey, cracking open another can. "Can you pour beer into that thing?" He points his finger to the center of Richard.

Karina looks to Richard, and he nods. Every now and then, when he asks her to, she delivers a syringe full of wine through the PEG tube and wets his lips with the smallest taste, one of the few pleasures he still indulges in. It's not the same as drinking wine from a glass. It'll never be the same. But he can still taste a Château Haut-Brion on his tongue. He can still feel its warm infusion in his belly.

Karina attaches the tubing and flushes it with water. She fills a fifty-milliliter syringe with Budweiser and slowly presses on the plunger while everyone watches. Richard belches. Brendan laughs. It tastes like a teenage memory, horrible and wonderful.

"Okay, save some for the toast," says Mikey. "Karina, you have your wine?"

She picks up her wineglass in her right hand, holding the syringe of Bud attached to Richard's stomach in her left. "Ready."

Tommy and Mikey raise their beer cans. Emily and Karina lift their wineglasses. Brendan raises his Coke.

"To Walt Evans," says Mikey. "May he rest

in peace."

Rest in peace, Dad.

CHAPTER TWENTY-FIVE

It's 8:28, four minutes later than last he looked. For the past three days, time has been a fat slug napping on a shady stone. Karina is in New Orleans, joining Elise and her students on their annual pilgrimage to the holy motherland of jazz. Sitting in front of his computer, Richard aims his nose like a conductor's baton, directing the cursor arrow across the letters of the keyboard, typing the names of various jazz artists in iTunes. He plays a few seconds of Herbie Hancock. Then Oscar Peterson. A few seconds of John Coltrane. He can tolerate Miles Davis for just over a minute. The notes wander without any apparent destination, a lost dog in a field, sniffing and tail wagging, scampering here and there, no one calling it home. The compositions are scribbles, run-on sentences without proper grammar and no punctuation, indulgent explorations in incongruous sound.

He clicks on Thelonious Monk, and his mouth cringes as if tasting something noxious, something too sour or bitter or rotten, and he wishes he could spit the sound out. The saxophone and the trumpet sound like an escalating argument, both sides shrill and unreasonable. He hurries the aim of his nose to the PAUSE button. He can't take one more second of this assault, this madness, this noise.

For Richard, music is like language. While he doesn't speak Italian or Chinese, he finds the experience of listening to Italians chatting over cups of espresso to be a melodious pleasure. Chinese, on the other hand, feels like cacophonous machine-gun fire, every word a needle inserted into his spine next to the sound of someone rubbing the surface of a rubber balloon. For Richard, jazz is Chinese.

Or, it's like abstract expressionism. Richard can look at *Number 5* by Jackson Pollock, a supposed masterpiece revered for its artistry and worth millions, and see only unappealing, splattered bullshit, utterly lacking in structure or talent. Jazz is Pollock. Mozart, on the other hand, is Michelangelo, Rembrandt, Picasso, painters who've mastered the art of seeing. To look up at the ceiling of the Sistine Chapel is to be with God.

Bach, Chopin, Schumann, these composers have mastered the art of listening. Richard hears Debussy's "Clair de lune," and every cell in his body has a broken heart and bare feet dancing in the moonlight. Playing Brahms is communing with God.

Richard doesn't feel jazz in his body. It doesn't move through his heart and soul. He doesn't get it. It's always been impossible for him to understand what he can't feel.

While Karina is away, Grace is home, babysitting her father. They've been under the same roof for three days, two lines rarely intersecting, alone together. She mostly stays in her room. She says she has a ton of homework, but to call or come get her or step on the call button if he needs anything. So far, he hasn't needed her for anything other than his last meal of the day and getting hooked up to the BiPAP mask at bedtime. So he hasn't called for her.

While Grace is here, he's been waiting for Bill to arrive at nine in the mornings to pee, saving both Richard and Grace the indignity of a daughter pulling down her father's pants so he can urinate. Two days ago, he asked her if she wanted to watch a movie with him. Any movie. She had statistics, economics, and physics homework and no time for a movie. Yesterday, he asked her if she wanted to go for quick walk. His right leg is too weak and his right foot is too droopy for him to risk going for a walk alone. She said it was too cold outside. Today, he didn't ask her anything.

It's now 8:40 p.m. He keeps looking over to the door, expecting to see her. She pokes her head in the den every couple of hours to check on him. He hasn't seen her since five. *Do you need anything? . . . No.*

But he does need something from her. He needs things to be right between them before . . . He needs things to be right between them before his circumstances force him into finishing that sentence. For now, not finishing that sentence, not squinting his eyes to bring into focus what's blurry and waiting for him on the horizon, or even ignoring what is hovering two feet in front of his face, is his only line of defense against this disease. Denial, blunt and dull and shaped more like a spoon than a knife, is the only weapon he's got.

He's not sure how to go about making things right with Grace but realizes it probably involves being in the same room. Admitting that he chose piano over her has maybe loosened a few bricks in the wall dividing them, but it's still standing strong and tall, an imposing, ancient fortress. Karina comes home tomorrow, and then Grace goes back to school until the summer. She might not be back home again before . . .

It's 8:43, and he's running out of time.

He thinks about asking Grace to help him with the recording device that Dr. George gave him for banking his voice. He's done little so far. He and Karina recorded a few simple phrases: *I have an itch. I have to use the bathroom. Will you wipe my nose? Will you wipe my eyes? I'm cold. I'm hot.* Karina played these back to make sure the device was actually recording, and after hearing what his voice sounded like, he lost all motivation for the project. He wishes he'd gone to Dr. George sooner, while his voice was still robust and full of melody and inflection and personality, while his voice was still his and not this stripped-down, aerated, soulless, robotic monotone. He'd rather listen to free jazz than the sound of his voice. He might as well use the computer-generated speech when the time comes.

It's 8:51. That time is coming.

But the banking project would give him

an easy excuse to need Grace for something. He looks to the door, to the red call button on the floor. He doesn't call for her. He's too tired. He hasn't done a damn thing all day, and he's exhausted.

It feels later than it is. His room is dark but for the glow of his laptop screen and a sliver of light from the hall intruding through the slant of the cracked door. He gets up, stands at the edge of his room, and listens for signs of Grace. He hears nothing. Restless, he leaves the den and wanders the living room, studying the furniture and decor like a curious museum patron after hours. Or a creepy prowler. The living room is dim, gently illuminated by lights Grace must've left on in the kitchen. The cold black night is framed in every window. If Karina were home, she would've drawn the shades.

The living room is neat and tidy, everything in its place. It's too tidy. Sterile. Before he moved out, before Grace left for college, the entire house felt like Grace's home. Her backpack and clothes and books and papers were strewn about. Her music and phone conversations could be heard throughout the house no matter what room she was in. Her personality and presence loomed large here. But Grace doesn't live here anymore. Karina does. Other than revealing that the person who lives here plays piano, observing Karina's home gives little sense of who she is.

But this is her home, her life. Not his. He's not supposed to be living here anymore.

He visits her piano, the same Baldwin upright they bought used when they first moved to Boston. His eyes travel from one end of the keyboard to the other. From watching and listening to Karina and her students play these past few months, he knows the action of the keys is slow compared to that of his grand, and he imagines the frustrating stickiness within the pads of his paralyzed fingers. For years, he tried to convince Karina to upgrade to a grand piano, but she always refused.

The top sheet on the shelf is Beethoven's "Für Elise." One of Karina's students was mutilating this composition in a lesson last week. When Richard was eleven, "Für Elise" was his favorite piece to play. He hesitates, then sits down at the bench. As his eyes travel the notes, he hears the music in his mind's ear, and he is eleven again. He's playing for his mother, and when he finishes, she kisses him on the head and tells him it's the most beautiful song she's ever heard.

He reads the notes to this simple, overplayed, yet lovely piece, and without trying, he feels it in his body — in his beating heart, in his unmoving fingers that still fondly remember, in his tapping foot. This is music.

He aches to touch the keys. While he can feel the imagined music playing in his body, the experience of participating in its creation and hearing it live resonates in his soul. He tries to remember the last time he played, the feelings coursing through his body and soul as he lived the notes of Ravel's Piano Concerto for the Left Hand, and he gets only a faded sense of it. He can't grab on to it. The memory is but a passing ghost. Tears flood his eyes, and he leaves Karina's piano before he's reduced to sobbing.

He follows the light into the kitchen. A bowl of lemons is centered on the square table. One of the lemons has gone moldy. He wants to pluck it out and throw it in the trash. He thinks about calling Grace down from her bedroom and asking her to remove the bad lemon but, assuming his diminished voice couldn't reach her anyway, decides not to bother.

He walks over to the pizza box on the counter, the lid tilted slightly open. He peeks inside. Three pieces left. He inhales the smells of peppers and onions and dough and with a tortured sadness remembers the sensory pleasure of eating, like a lover he'll never kiss again, a piano he'll never play again. He imagines the chewiness of the toppings and cheese, the crunchy bite of the crust, the hot temperature of the tangy sauce and salty cheese in his mouth, the rapid responsive action of his grand piano, his hands in Maxine's thick black hair, his mouth on hers.

Almost dizzy with desire, he notices that he doesn't imagine Karina's hair or lips. He tries to remember the last time they kissed, the last time he held her, the last time he got hard thinking about her. He can't find it. His memories of touching her, wanting her, loving her, feel like yellowed, unlabeled snapshots in someone else's scrapbook. Too much time has passed.

It's 9:03.

Stepping away from the pizza box, he approaches Grace's coffee mug from this morning, next to the sink. He bends over, leans his face into the mug, and inhales whatever he can draw out of the sticky, bittersweet hoop of desiccated coffee at the bottom. He exhales. Nirvana. And pure hell. Desperate, he extends his tongue into the mug, hoping to lick the dry ring, but his tongue isn't long enough and the mug is too deep. He gives up.

The phone numbers for Caring Health, his neurologist, and Bill's cell are written on a piece of paper and held by a magnet to the refrigerator. Next to this is a photograph of Grace and Karina at Grace's high school graduation. They're both wearing black, both beaming. Grace has her mother's smile.

There are no other photographs. No other smiling children on what used to be his refrigerator. The son he always wanted. A sister for Grace. All those years trying to get Karina pregnant, believing in her doctor's appointments, jerking off into plastic cups, hoping. None of it was real. Maybe this is why he can't remember loving her.

All that time wasted.

It's 9:06.

With nothing more to explore, he's walking back to the den when he's struck with the sudden, out-of-body, slow-motion realization that he's falling. He went to step right, but his leg never responded. Something in the interplay between neurons and muscles broke off. Something didn't fire or listen or land. Something let go, unplugged, and the command to walk fizzled out, the connection severed. In the split second before he hits the floor, he's aware that he cannot break his fall and thinks to turn his head, but not soon enough. His chin and nose take the brunt of the impact.

Warm blood drains down his right nostril. He can taste its metallic saltiness in his mouth. He registers the pain, throbbing and sharp, mostly at the bridge of his nose, between his eyes. Internally, he scans his limbs, trying to discern if anything is broken. He can't seem to find his right leg. A realization sinks in like liquid concrete funneling into his body, transforming him into immovable stone. Nothing is broken, but he's not getting up. His right leg is gone, consumed by ALS. As he lies facedown on the kitchen floor, he knows he'll never walk again.

He tries to yell for Grace, but he can barely get enough air into his lungs in this position to breathe, never mind produce loud sound. He lifts his head and tries again.

"Graaa."

He lowers his head, resting his right cheek on the cold tile floor. A puddle of drool mingled with blood pools beneath his chin. He's not sure he has the strength to lift his head again. He finds the only part of his body still available to him. His left foot. He lifts and drops it over and over, banging his wool-slippered foot against the floor like a foreboding, muffled drumbeat.

Several minutes pass. Tired, he stops tapping his foot. Panic wants him now. It forms a fist in his stomach, its claw reaching for his throat. He won't be able to breathe if panic takes him. Grace. She comes down every night at ten for his last feeding and to hook him up to the BiPAP machine. What time is it? It won't be long now. He has to fight against the panic and keep breathing.

He's lost in the feeble yet steady rhythm of his inhales and has no sense of how much time has passed when he hears Grace's footsteps.

"Oh my God!"

He opens his eyes, and Grace appears over him like an angel.

"What happened?"

He doesn't expend his limited energy to state the obvious.

"Okay, I'm calling 911."

"No," he whispers. "Please-don."

"Why? I'll call Bill or someone at Caring Health."

She looks over at the refrigerator, at the phone numbers on the door.

"No. Is-late."

"What if you broke something?"

"I-din."

"Your face is all bloody. I think you broke your nose."

"There-goes-my mo-de-ling ca-reer."

"I have to roll you over then."

His head is turned to the left. She places a hand on his left shoulder and hip and pulls on him carefully but with great effort. He assists as much as he can with his left foot, and she finally manages to turn him onto his back. She grabs a dish towel from the counter, runs it under the tap, crouches over him, and wipes his mouth, cheek, and neck. As she scrubs the cloth too roughly against his skin, working to loosen the blood that has dried and crusted on his face, cold water drips down his neck, soaking his back. She's gentler around his nose.

She stands up and studies him now. He studies her, too, and can't tell if she's worried, disgusted, or scared. Probably all of the above.

"I'm not strong enough to get you into bed."

"Thas o-kay. I-ca slee-here."

She folds her arms over her chest.

"I'll be right back."

He sees the light flick on in the den, and a few moments later, he hears the wheels of the BiPAP cart rolling toward him. She wiggles three pillows under his head, adjusts his arms to match their position on either side of his body, and drapes his bed comforter over him. She leaves again. This time, he hears her footsteps running up the stairs. She returns with her pillow, a blanket, and her blue-and-white gingham comforter.

"I'll sleep next to you. In case something happens."

She plugs in the humidifier and the Bi-PAP, turns them on, and checks the settings. He doesn't bother to mention that she's forgotten to feed him. He's not hungry. She holds the mask in her hand, and he's afraid of how much it's going to hurt when pressed against the bridge of his nose.

"I'm sorry I didn't hear you right away."

"Don-be-sor-ry. I'm-the-one who-sor-ry."

"For what?"

He's sorry he didn't give enough of his time to her. He's sorry he's running out of it. He's afraid he doesn't have much left. He's sorry he wasn't a better father to her. He's sorry she didn't feel loved by him.

It's now or never.

"Ev-er-y thin. I-love-you-Grace. I'm-so sor-ry."

She closes her eyes, and a gentle close-lipped smile settles on her mouth. She opens her eyes, and tears stream down her beautiful face. She doesn't wipe them.

"I love you, too, Dad."

She fits the BiPAP mask over his face, and

he endures the screaming pain between his eyes as air flows in and out of his lungs. For the first time in as long as he can remember, he feels peace when he breathes.

CHAPTER TWENTY-SIX

Karina, Elise, and her students are early, sitting at a cluster of four round tables, three chairs at each huddled in a half-moon facing the stage. They're at Snug Harbor Jazz Bistro on Frenchmen Street, just outside the French Quarter, tucked away in a windowless, candlelit, cozy room behind the dive bar out front, waiting for the show to start. Tonight features up-and-coming jazz pianist Alexander Lynch, accompanied by drums and a bass, a simple trio. With a background in classical piano and then Broadway, Alexander is new to the jazz scene. Elise saw him in New York at Blue Note in October and can't stop raving about him, says he reminds her of Oscar Peterson.

The room hasn't filled in yet. Karina counts fifteen tables plus a balcony above them. Their seats are right up front, inches from the stage, which feels intimidating, threatening even, as if she were sitting too close to an open flame, as if being here could be dangerous.

She pulls at her lavender silk scarf, spreading it across her front like a bib, covering her cleavage as much as possible. After much angst, she decided to wear her best black dress, spaghetti strapped and tight around the bust, flaring and flowy from the waist to the knees, probably too short and too revealing for her age. She bought it over a decade ago. It fit her better then. She fears she looks like ten pounds of potatoes in a five-pound bag. Elise is in jeans and black suede ankle boots, a black velvet blazer over a graphic T-shirt, laughing and chatting with her students, totally at ease, as if she were a regular, as if this were her seat and the club was expecting her. She fits into everything.

The students are also in black and jeans, edgy and casual and cool. They belong here, too. They're all in their early twenties, about where Karina left off before giving up, still believing it's all possible.

Karina slides the bottom olive off the plastic skewer in her martini and chews on it while Elise leans over to the table to their right. As Elise's back is now to her, Karina can't hear the conversation and feels excluded, out of place, conspicuous. She doesn't deserve to be on this field trip. She's not a teacher at Berklee. She's not a student. She's not even a real musician.

She's Elise's sad, pathetic neighbor. She's an old, suburban piano teacher, a has-been, a never-was. Once upon a time, an almost-was.

She wants to be home, in her flannel pajamas, reading a book in her living room. But as soon as she imagines being on her couch, she hears Richard calling her from the den. She drags a long sip from her martini and pulls another olive into her mouth with her teeth. It's an enormous relief to be away from him, to have a break from the distressing sound of his struggling to clear a cough, from having to tend to him all day and night. She blinked her eyes open this morning in her hotel bed and felt almost giddy, realizing that she had just slept through the night undisturbed.

And then Guilt came marching in, stomping with its monster feet and pounding its drum, scaring any nascent feelings of relief and lightness back into their holes. She shouldn't have stuck Grace with him for four days. Grace shouldn't have to clean up her father's piss and be up all hours of the night while Karina is well rested and wearing a poorly fitting black dress, drinking a dirty martini, and listening to jazz with a bunch of kids. What if something goes wrong?

"I can't wait for you to hear this guy," says Elise, leaning back over to Karina. "Abby just called him the Mozart of jazz."

Karina nods. It's been so long since she's been to any kind of live musical performance, years since she's been to Symphony Hall, the Hatch Shell, Jordan Hall. The last time might've been to see Richard at Tanglewood. He played *The Marriage of Figaro* overture. Eight years ago? Can it really be that long?

She wouldn't feel so uneasy if they were at a concert hall, if she were tucked somewhere safe and civilized in the orchestra or mezzanine section, waiting to hear a recital or concerto. Classical music has always been her home base, her comfort food, her security blanket. At Curtis, she started as a classical pianist, and by third year, her career looked more promising than Richard's. They never acknowledged this aloud, but they both knew it. Her teachers praised her and gave her opportunities normally reserved for seniors or graduates. They did not offer these opportunities to Richard.

He congratulated her whenever this happened, but his words were rigid and cold, spoken through his teeth, and would leave her feeling insulted instead of championed. Whenever she privately or publically surpassed his playing, he'd grow distant and critical of her in other ways. He didn't like her hair. He ridiculed her grammar. He withheld affection, refused sex, and pouted. She craved nothing more than to be loved by him when he felt self-confident and admired in the spotlight. Ironically, the biggest obstacle to his center-stage bravado seemed to be her.

When they were students, their technical skills were similarly matched, but her playing was emotionally connected and far more mature. While Richard could master the technical complexity of any piece, listening to him play often made her picture the notes on the page, the chords, the key, intellectually appreciating his athleticism, hearing the music as dissected elements rather than a whole. Not until after graduation, when they lived in New York, did something click in him, and he began to play the emotion of a piece and not simply the notes.

She remembers Professor Cohen and the Test. Each student was asked to play a piece but not until Professor Cohen left the classroom. The Test was simple. Could the student make the teacher cry in the hallway?

The first time Karina took the Test, she

played Schumann's *Fantasiestücke,* op. 12, no. 1. She played the closing gesture, tender and quiet, and waited, breath held, for Professor Cohen to return. The door opened, and Professor Cohen was smiling with clasped hands and wet eyes. She made him cry several times that semester. Richard never did.

She discovered jazz first semester of her senior year. She breezed into the campus coffeehouse for a quick espresso, on her way to something else, and stayed for two hours, mesmerized by three of her classmates, a trio of piano, drums, and trumpet playing Miles Davis. This music was so different from the sacred, rigid exactness of Mozart or Chopin. It had an exhilarating freedom, a playful exploration outside the structure of the melody. She watched the three improvise, detour, collaborate, creating something original, discovering the music as they played it, following a free association, a harmony, an embellishment, wherever it led them. They generated a momentum, a magical chemistry, a river that flowed through everyone there. Her heart was captivated, dizzy, spellbound.

She doesn't think her relationship with Richard would've lasted beyond graduation if she hadn't discovered jazz. In abandoning classical piano for jazz, she ensured that they would never compete, that the classical spotlight would be his to shine in. But switching from classical piano to jazz wasn't an easy transition. Jazz is complex and in many ways technically more difficult than classical piano. And her decision was at best frowned upon, more often snubbed and mocked. Although neither genres are mainstream music, the world of classical piano is privileged and white, played in grand symphony halls to audiences who sip champagne. The jazz world is historically poor and black, played in hole-in-the-wall nightclubs for patrons drunk on bourbon.

Alexander, the drummer, and the bassist take the stage, and the audience applauds while the musicians ready themselves at their instruments. Alexander is slender, about Karina's age, with a mop of glossy black hair and fingers that extend for miles, poised on the keys like a sprinter in the blocks, ready to explode into action, holding for the gun to fire. Alexander nods, and the three begin.

The melody is a simple repetition, a catchy, easy-breezy tune, but soon breaks into improvised solos. As Alexander plays, Karina closes her eyes, and the notes become a summer-evening stroll down a country road drenched in moonlight, more of a mood than a melody, sultry and slow, in no hurry at all. Softened by vodka, she rides the notes, allowing herself to be carried, and her blood is flowing hotter. She's turned on.

Karina remembers living on East Sixth Street in New York City, hanging around the Village Vanguard, listening to Branford Marsalis, Herbie Hancock, Sonny Rollins, and Brad Mehldau, learning through listening, watching, asking, performing, and improvising. Learning jazz was a three-dimensional experience of unique expressive discovery, lived and breathed on the fly in spontaneous jam sessions. Learning classical piano had been an academic exercise in practiced techniques, adherence to strict rules, memorizing the notes on the page, practicing alone. She never felt more challenged, more alive, than when she was playing jazz.

The next two pieces are high energy, a call to action and a celebration. Alexander's fingers are a fiddler crab running from a seagull's pursuing shadow; a hummingbird drinking nectar from the keys, trilling arpeggios inhabited by God.

He's traveling low to high on the keyboard, coloring outside the lines, hitting notes that land just shy of displeasing. This is renegade music, exciting, provocative.

"Holy shit, right?" says Elise.

Karina nods. She closes her eyes again during the fourth piece, entranced by Alexander's riffs, the way his chord extensions wander from the head. He's playing outside now, and the song becomes about the journey, not the destination, about getting lost along the way and what he might discover, an embellished grace note, an ascending harmonic progression, a meandering Sunday drive. He varies the phrasing, changing the shape and texture, inserting blue notes and trills that sound like children laughing. He dances across the keys, courting the notes, loving them, and the music is a gentle morning rain playing on a windowpane, delicate, lonely, longing for a lover, a childhood friend, a mother.

The song ends, and the audience applauds. Karina opens her eyes and tears spill down her face. She is enraptured, changed, remembering who she is.

She is a jazz pianist.

With stunning clarity, she suddenly sees the role she's been playing, the costume and mask she chose and has been wearing for twenty years. She's been hiding, an impostor, unable to give herself permission to do this, to play jazz, to be who she is, shackled inside a prison of blame and excuses.

At first it was all Richard's fault for moving them to Boston. Jazz pianists live in New York, not Boston. Then Richard started traveling. He was hardly ever home. They rarely had sex anymore. She needed to refill her birth control pill prescription, but it was February and so cold outside, and she didn't feel like walking to the pharmacy.

She was lazy. She was stupid. She was pregnant.

Her excuse then chasséd over to Grace and motherhood. Now she couldn't be a jazz pianist because her baby needed her. Richard still spent much of the year touring. She was essentially a single mother. She was consumed and devastatingly lonely in the demands of young motherhood. There was often no room for a shower, never mind for getting back to playing jazz. So she tended to Grace full-time, creating a safe nest where Karina could hide. She promised herself it would be a temporary shelter.

Karina remembers her mother, born in an oppressed country, stuck in an economically depressed town by her husband's meager coal-mining wages, trapped in a bad marriage by her religion, confined within the dirty beige walls of her small home, raising five children. Every day, she wore a dingy white apron, her prematurely gray hair pulled into a bun, resignation in her eyes, and her arthritic hands to the bone cooking and cleaning and tending to the needs of her children, whose singular dreams were to leave that house, that town, that country, as soon as they could. They all left her.

Karina swore she wouldn't repeat her mother's life. As much as Karina loved being Grace's mother, she would not bear child after child, adding brick after brick to the wall of her maternal prison. Grace would be her only child. One and done. But Richard wanted many children, a big family.

Her carefully buried deception peeks out from its hiding space for the briefest moment, long enough for shame to seep through the walls of her stomach, sickening her. She drains her martini, distracting her tortured, guilty mind with the cozy warmth of booze.

When Grace turned five and went to kindergarten, Karina would have the time to pursue jazz. That was the plan. But then Grace went to school, and Karina's excuse migrated back to Richard. She discovered charges for an expensive dinner and drinks for two on his credit-card bill; salacious text messages from some woman named Rosa on his phone; a pair of black lace panties in his suitcase, not a gift for her. At first, these betrayals shattered Karina's heart. She felt stunned, gutted, humiliated, dishonored. She wept and raged and threatened divorce. And then, after a few days of wild emotion, she would feel wrung out, calm and strangely satisfied. Over time, her heart hardened to it all. She almost craved the detective work, the thrill of finding the next damning text message, the momentary drama it awakened in her and ultimately, the narrative it supplied.

Grace was in first grade, eighth grade, a sophomore in high school, and Karina painted herself the victim, trapped in a bad marriage by the rules of a church she no longer believed in but still obeyed and the barbed-wire reasons of her own making. She carefully constructed her life, creating a predictable stability in her safe career as a teacher, teaching students to play classical piano in the private confines of her suburban living room, where her students have always been too young, unformed, and musically naïve to question her, stretch her, or push her outside her comfort zone.

And she could blame Richard and his affairs for holding her back. He was wrong and bad, and she was right and good, and she could resent him for her unfulfilled dreams of playing jazz, and this was the perfect excuse, the brilliant smoke screen deflecting anyone who might inspect the situation for the truth. The truth is, she was terrified of failing, of not making it, of never being as recognized and loved as an artist as Richard is.

But then she got divorced and Grace went to college, her excuses literally out the door. With seemingly no one left to blame, she pointed her finger at the hands of time. Too much had passed. Her chance had passed. It was too late.

She watches Alexander on the stage, new to the jazz scene, about her age, and that last pin falls. She can now see that every collapsed excuse she abided to like God's commandments existed only in her mind. Her unfulfilled life has always been a prison of her own making, the thoughts she chose and believed, the fear and blame, paralyzing her in her unhappiness, telling her that her dreams were too big, too impractical, too unlikely, too hard to achieve, that she didn't deserve them, that she shouldn't want them, that she didn't need them. These dreams of playing jazz piano were for someone else, someone like Alexander Lynch. Not for her.

As she listens to Alexander play, she steps out of the carefully constructed, now-unlocked cage in her mind. She hears him messing with the melody, accenting the ascending chords and varying the phrasing, and she feels the exuberant curiosity in his improvisation, searching for something new, unafraid, and his freedom becomes hers. She sees what's possible for her if she dares to claim it.

The trio finish their final piece of the night, stand, and bow. The audience is on its feet, applauding, begging for more as the musicians humbly exit the stage. Karina wipes the tears from her eyes in between claps, feeling breathless, cracked open, pulsing with desire, and, although she's not quite sure how, ready to live.

CHAPTER TWENTY-SEVEN

Richard wakes from having dozed off, parked upright in his wheelchair in front of the TV, wishing he could be reclined. Although the TV has been on since this morning when Bill set him up here, he stopped watching it at least a couple of hours ago. His heavy head has tipped down, chin to chest, and rolled right, and he doesn't have the neck-muscle strength to correct it. His towel bib has fallen off his chest, and the front of his shirt is soaked with drool. His eyeballs are still tired from straining to look up and left to see the TV. So he stares at the floor, where his eyes and head are pointed, and listens to *Judge Judy,* surrendering to what is.

He's in the Maserati of power wheelchairs. Frontwheel drive with two motors, it's tricked out with mag wheels, eight-inch casters, a tilt-in-space reclining feature, and a hand-operated joystick that comes standard with this model. But because he has no hands, he has no way to control it. He ordered it so long ago, when he still had the use of his left hand, when he could still play the piano, when he could still hope that he'd never actually need the chair. He's in the driver's seat of a sexy sports car, unable to place his hands on the steering wheel or step his foot on the gas, forever parked in the garage.

There are tech devices that would allow him to control the wheelchair with his chin or tongue or even his breath, but Karina and Richard haven't ordered anything. The activation energy is a mountain precipice — too many insurance forms, the astronomical cost despite any coverage, the wait to receive the device. It's probably hard for anyone associated with Richard to invest time or money in his ability to move his chin or tongue. How much longer will he be able to breathe? Ordering a wheelchair-operating device powered by breath begs an answer to that question, and Richard would rather not ask it. So he's trapped wherever someone parks him, mostly here in front of the TV or in the living room. He can't leave the house until the ramp is completed because his chair doesn't fit through the door to the garage.

For some absurd reason, the loss of his legs took him and Karina by surprise. It shouldn't have. Bill and the other home health aides from Caring Health, his physical therapist, Kathy DeVillo, and his neurologist all told them, warned them, practically begged them to build the ramp sooner rather than later. Don't wait. They both blew it off. Richard truly believed he might never need the damn chair. He'd been wearing the ankle foot orthotic on his right foot quite comfortably for so long, and his left leg seemed to be in good shape. He formulated his own highly unscientific, clinically unproven theory that the disease had arrested, rendered permanently dormant in his legs, and threw his faith into this theory like a religious zealot. He would never lose his legs. Amen and hallelujah.

Shortly after ALS severed his right leg from his control, his left leg threw up its white flag. Paralysis settled in rapidly, as if someone had pulled the stopper at his ankle and all the sand came pouring out. Sitting in his wheelchair, staring at the floor and unable to leave the house, it's clear now. No part of him is safe from this disease.

He hoped they wouldn't have to spend any money on an unwanted construction project, an ugly, utilitarian ramp extending from the front door to the driveway, announcing his handicap to the world. Thankfully, his condo finally sold last week, so he can afford the ramp. He'd much rather leave that money to Grace.

So here he sits, Mr. Potato Head without arms or legs, a bobblehead on a breathing torso. His neck is too weak to hold his head up reliably, especially later in the day — making use of the Head Mouse, even when he's wearing a neck collar, an exercise in frustrating madness, so he's disconnected from his computer until they get the Tobii eye-tracking-technology device. It's been ordered. He's down to 120 pounds from 170, physically disappearing, and yet he's taking up more and more space — this wheelchair, the hospital bed, the BiPAP machine, the shower chair, the Hoyer lift that should arrive any day now.

Transferring him from the bed into the chair in the morning and from the chair into bed in the evening is a massive chore that requires great strength and trained technique. Despite how slight and fragile his mass is, he's deadweight, like a sleeping child. Karina can't do it. Bill has been coming for two shifts since Richard lost his legs, morning and evening, using all his muscle and height and a gait belt to lift Richard's body safely from point A to point B. The Hoyer lift, which looks like a cross between an exercise machine and a hammock swing, will make it possible for anyone to safely move him in and out of bed.

He hears the doorbell ring. Just weeks ago, this might've been the sound of him stepping on the call button taped to the floor by his bed, but now, it can only be the actual doorbell at the front door. He hears men's voices and the sound of something being rolled into the living room. It must be the lift.

A few minutes later, Bill's legs and feet appear before Richard.

"Hey, Ricardo, let's get you out here. Karina has something for you." Bill says this with unbridled exuberance, like a parent about to present a small child with a special gift. *Oh, goody! A Hoyer lift! Just want I've always wanted!*

Bill rights Richard's head back into position against the headrest, and an enormous relief washes through Richard like warm water. Bill wheels him out into the living room. Richard stares at a grand piano in front of the bay windows facing the street where the couch should be. Karina is beaming.

"Wha?"

"I saved it," says Karina.

"Is-tha-mi?"

"I couldn't let someone else own your piano."

He can't believe she did this. It's incredibly thoughtful and sweet and well-intentioned, but seeing his piano again, after he'd already said good-bye and made peace with never seeing or touching or hearing it again, turns him inside out, as if he's just unexpectedly bumped into an ex-lover in the living room, still not over her. He's all emotion and no words, choked up.

Karina and Bill stare at him, expectant, hoping for joy. He wants to give it to them, searching for a way. He looks at his piano, his beloved, from across the room. He can't bear for them both to be paralyzed, still, silenced.

"Wi-you play-fo-me?"

"It'll need to be tuned."

"Tha-so-kay."

Karina hesitates. She's never played his piano. His piano was his. He smiles and sends her a long blink, his version of permission and please. She acquiesces, sits at the bench, hands poised over the keys, and pauses.

She twists around to face him. "What do you want me to play?"

322

He thinks, his favorites all raising their hands emphatically like eager students who know the answer. Mozart, Beethoven, Chopin, Debussy, Liszt. Pick me! Pick me! Too many choices crowd his head. Karina, sitting at his piano, waits for an answer. She's waiting to play. She's been waiting for twenty years.

"Play-me soh-jazz."

This time, Karina smiles and slow blinks, her version of a nod, a thank-you, and the energy in her gesture is passed between them, a moment of invisible yet palpable connection. She breaks the spell, thinking now, deciding what to play, her eyes scanning upward, as if reading her own mind.

She grins. "I'll do 'Somewhere over the Rainbow.' Bill, you want to sing?"

"Do happy little bluebirds fly? Hell yeah, I'm singing."

Bill scooches next to Karina on Richard's bench. Karina begins to play, setting the mood in a prelude before the lyrics begin. Richard expected her rendition to be loungy, predictably ragtime, upbeat and swingy, but she slows it all down instead, dwelling on the notes, adding interesting chords and embellishments, and he's genuinely surprised. Impressed. Enjoying it. She's into the melody now, and Bill is singing. Their rendition is restrained and romantic. It evokes a gentle sadness, a fond memory of a lost love. It's a dreamy lullaby, easily the most beautiful song Bill has ever sung.

Richard listens to Karina play and Bill sing, and instead of feeling grief stricken or jealous that he'll never play his piano again, he feels strangely happy. He's setting his piano free, letting it go, sending it off on its next journey without him. Then, as Karina plays the final phrasings and his heart moves with the notes, it occurs to him that it's not his piano he's letting go of, setting free.

It's Karina.

CHAPTER TWENTY-EIGHT

The Hoyer lift still hasn't been delivered, and until it gets here, Bill is the lift. He's singing Madonna's "Like a Prayer" while securing a gait belt around Richard's legs, just above the ankle. It's evening, and Bill has already brushed Richard's teeth and washed his face. Even though Richard won't go to sleep for another five hours, it's time to get him from the wheelchair to the bed. Richard is Bill's last patient of his shift, and Bill is Richard's last hired help of the day, and Karina can't get him out of the chair. So to bed he goes.

Bill weaves a second gait belt around Richard's torso and secures it snug around him while Karina looks on. Bill grabs the suction wand from the rolling cart next to him, flicks the machine on, and vacuums out the saliva pooled in Richard's mouth. Bill has learned through experience to do this prior to moving Richard, otherwise the puddle of saliva waiting in Richard's mouth tips forward when he's vertical, spilling out and onto Bill. His job is not for the squeamish. He then fits a soft cervical collar around Richard's reclined neck so his head won't flop forward. He arranges Richard's socked, belted feet parallel on the pivot disc, a human-size lazy Susan placed at the base of his chair, adjacent to his destination, the bed. It takes a grown man and all this time and equipment to move him a few inches. Bill squats in front of Richard like an Olympic skier.

"One, two, three."

Bill pulls on the gait belt around Richard's chest with his right hand while lifting him under the shoulder with his left, and in a forceful snap, Richard is standing on his paralyzed legs.

The extensor muscles in his legs are spastic and rigid, making it possible for him to bear his own weight. While completely unresponsive to any voluntary command, like a child's plastic action-hero figure, he can be stood up if balanced properly. Bill lifts and rests Richard's arms atop each of Bill's shoulders to keep them from hanging down and pulling painfully on Richard's shoulder sockets. Bill's biceps are positioned under Richard's armpits, his hands clasped around Richard's back. Richard stands slightly taller, but they're pretty much eye to eye.

"My friend David would be so jealy if he knew I got to slow dance with you like this every night. He has such a crush on you."

Richard raises his eyebrows, requesting more information.

"He saw you play at BSO three years ago. I almost went with him. Isn't that funny? I almost knew you before I knew you."

The belt around the bottom of Richard's legs keeps his ankles from rolling out. Without it, he'd be standing on top of his anklebones instead of the bottom of his feet. Bill keeps him balanced on his feet for at a least a minute before moving him along, somehow intuiting how delicious this feels, to be stretched out and vertical, his bones stacked and bearing weight, like finally standing after a transatlantic flight in a cramped plane seat. Richard's been sitting in this chair, in the same position, for eight hours. Richard sighs, enjoying the sweet relief of being an erect structure, visiting the memory of being an upright man.

Their slow dance ends when Bill spins Richard ninety degrees on the pivot disc, so that his butt is now up against the bed. Using the gait belt around Richard's middle,

Bill lowers him carefully onto the mattress. As always, Bill sticks the landing.

"I still think I could do that," says Karina.

"I've been doing this a long time, honey. I make it look a lot easier than it is. Believe me. You don't want to drop him. You could both get hurt. Wait for the Hoyer. It should be here any day."

Bill tugs on each side of the slide sheet, squaring Richard's body in the center of the bed, and arranges Richard's arms and legs like flowers in a vase. Reaching over to the bedside table, Bill grabs what looks like a one-liter clear-plastic water bottle. He reaches under Richard's boxer shorts, pulls out his penis, inserts it into the bottle, and waits a few seconds. As usual, nothing happens. The waiting was just a courtesy. Bill then pushes down on Richard's abdomen with the heel of his hand, pressing firmly on his bladder over and over, as if he were pumping water from a well. It works, and the bottle slowly fills with urine.

Karina looks away, trying to offer a sense of privacy, a strange and futile gesture. Richard's body parts are in varying states of nudity and being handled all day long. He is showered, toileted, wiped, washed, dressed, and undressed. His body is simply another task to complete, a job to do. His naked body is treated neutrally by every home health aide, every visiting nurse and physical therapist, a thin layer of a latex glove between his skin and actual contact with another human being. His is just another penis, just another saggy ass, just another patient's decrepit body. So Karina doesn't need to look away. He's just another ex-husband with ALS.

When his bladder is emptied, Bill tucks Richard's penis back into his boxers and leaves the den to wash the bottle in the bathroom. Now Karina takes over. She lifts Richard's T-shirt, attaches a syringe of water to his MIC-KEY button, and flushes the line. Normally refreshing, the water feels alarmingly cold in his belly. She then switches to a pouch of Liquid Gold.

"Okay you two." Bill is now wearing his hat and coat. "I'm off like a slutty prom dress." He gives Karina a one-armed hug and a kiss on the cheek. "Be good," he says to Richard. "See you tomorrow."

"Thank you, Bill," says Karina.

Richard slow-blinks. It's the end of the day. He's too tired to form words.

Karina presses slowly and steadily on the syringe plunger, delivering Richard's liquid dinner into this stomach. The entire meal takes about a half hour, and they usually have the TV on to keep them company, occupied, and safely distracted, but today, the TV is off. Bill's singing must've snagged a circuit in Karina's brain. She's humming "Like a Prayer" while she stares vaguely at the wall, a slight smile on her lips. He wonders what she's thinking about.

She's had a lightness about her since she returned from New Orleans. He hears her singing pop songs while cooking in the kitchen and noodling jazz riffs on her piano in the mornings. He's been catching her face enjoying distant daydreams. Her energy has changed. Her presence feels less heavy, less oppressive, happier, hopeful even, and while he can't put his paralyzed finger on the reason for it, this unexplained shift in her has provoked a corresponding shift in him. He watches her face, and he recognizes her again, the woman he fell in love with so long ago. She's feeding him, taking care of him, and what he'd been selfishly viewing as an act of martyrdom or duty, he suddenly sees as an act of love.

His heart swells, overwhelmed, and as she hums Madonna, he remembers the first time he heard Karina's voice, her Polish accent, how desperate he felt to hear her speak to him, his delight when she finally did. He stares at her green eyes, her amused mouth, and hopes she catches him looking at her.

Just like all those years ago, he aches for her to speak to him. He's never told her that he's sorry for cheating on her, for hurting her, for stealing that smile from her lips for so long. But he is sorry and hopes that she somehow knows this, that she can sense the regret and apology in him the way he can sense this new joy in her. He wants to hear her voice tell him that she's okay. He wants to be forgiven. He wants.

The syringe is emptied. Karina refills it with a second helping. As she's reattaching it, her warm, gloveless hands touch his bare, concave stomach, and although from her perspective, her hands are in the business of feeding her ex-husband through a PEG tube, for Richard, the touch feels intimate, personal, human.

At first, embarrassed, he hopes she doesn't notice that he's hard beneath the bedsheet and his boxers, but then he hopes she does. Every day he wakes to morning wood and can do nothing but wait it out. He hasn't masturbated since his left hand left him in October. He purposefully no longer imagines anything sexually desirable during this daily rise and fall. But now, as he's unexpectedly turned on, he imagines Karina touching it, touching him, and his desire is excruciatingly urgent, building in his penis, his heart, and his mind, silently begging for her to notice. He wants her to lie down next to him, to kiss him while stroking him. He wants to be a man and not a failing body in a bed. He wants to be touched, to be loved, to come. It's been so long. He wants.

She finishes the syringe, flushes the tubing with water, and caps the MIC-KEY button. She lowers his shirt, pulls the covers up to his chest, and stands.

"Okay, you're good until ten. You want the TV on?"

He stares at her, unblinking.

"You want anything?"

He smiles. If only he had the strength to tell her.

She hesitates, eyeing him quizzically. "Okay, I'll check on you in a bit."

She leaves the door to the den cracked open. He sits in bed and stares at the open door, listening to the sounds of her making her own dinner in the kitchen, wanting.

CHAPTER TWENTY-NINE

Richard sits in his wheelchair in the living room where Karina left him about a half hour ago, where he'll stay until Karina or the next home health aide moves him. She parked him in a rectangular patch of sunlight, angled toward the windows, as if a warm and sunny view of Walnut Street is supposed to make him feel more optimistic, less trapped. He knows she's well-intentioned. He watches the blithe movement of squirrels and birds. Everything alive moves.

He hears Karina sneeze three times. She's been fighting a cold for the past week, staying away from him as much as possible so as not to infect him. She's in the kitchen, cooking breakfast. Triggered by the torturously delicious smells of coffee and bacon, saliva pools in his mouth. He gurgles on it and swallows over and over, trying to push the gluey liquid down, struggling not to choke. A string of sticky drool descends over his bottom lip and lands on the cotton towel draped over his chest like a bib for this very reason. He turns his head left and right, but the spiderweb of drool won't break. He gives up.

He shifts his focus away from the sun and animated existence and instead looks upon his Steinway. Eighty-eight glossy black and white keys. God, what he wouldn't give to touch them.

Ten feet in front of him.

A million miles.

He stares at it with agonizing desire and apology, as if he's broken a sacred promise, a marriage vow. He imagines the action of each key, the blending colors of sound, music coming into existence, birthed through his body. He imagines a series of ascending arpeggios, and they become the sound of Karina's laugh.

His piano. The relationship is over. He's still working on letting it go. It's not you, it's me. Taking the blame doesn't change a thing. They are divorced, rejected and abandoned, reduced to pitiful statues collecting dust in the living room.

Careful not to tip his head even slightly downward else it flops forward, chin to chest, unable to right itself, he stares at his legs, his feet angled toward each other, pigeon-toed, and he suddenly resents Bill for arranging his feet in this unmanly way, a body position that speaks uncertainty, meekness, submission. Then he laughs at himself, as if anything about an emaciated man dying of ALS in a wheelchair could possibly communicate machismo, as if anyone but his piano were in the room to judge him. Bill dressed Richard's feet this morning in thin wool socks and black loafers. Shoes on a man whose feet will never again walk this earth. The irony and tragedy of wearing shoes make him want to cry. He can't stand to look at his feet. Literally.

Instead, he studies the rubber flesh of his flat right hand, limp and lifeless; his curled, distorted left hand, no longer possessed by him; both placed on pillows over the arms of his wheelchair in exactly this position by Bill over an hour ago. Richard's entire body is a costume discarded, the party over. He returns to what used to be his elegant left hand and commands the fingers to straighten, knowing they won't. He changes tack. *Please.* His limbs are petulant children, unreachable through begging, bribery, ultimatums, or sweet talk.

He tries to imagine the war beneath his skin; the invaded countries of his neurons and muscles overwhelmed, decimated; the neutral territories of bone, ligament, and tendon rendered useless by the horrific destruction surrounding them. His entire body is detaching, unzipping from his soul.

He turns his head ninety degrees left, then right, testing himself, relieved that he can still do this. Once his neck and voice are paralyzed, he'll be reduced to eye-gaze technology and a computer-generated voice for communicating. He opens his eyes wide and pinches them shut tight. Good. When he can no longer blink, he'll be locked in. He doesn't want to die, but he hopes he dies before that happens. Maybe that won't happen.

He can feel his tongue wriggling inside his mouth, undulating as if a family of earthworms were dancing within it, celebrating a rainstorm. When he speaks, his tongue feels thick, the volume thinned and barely audible. His words, once a finely detailed painting, are painfully slow to produce and almost impossible to comprehend, strangled and lacking consonants. A Pollock piece. Free jazz.

Already compromised to what Dr. Goldstein says is now 39 percent forced vital capacity, every single inhale is a struggle. Every exhale is incomplete. He's forced to sip air a teaspoon at a time when he's desperate to gulp it down by the gallon, each taste an agonizing disappointment, evidence of the withering muscles surrounding his ribs, his abdomen, his diaphragm. Pulling in enough air to simply sit motionless in the wheelchair is conscious, draining work.

He's probably close to needing the BiPAP 24-7 but won't admit this aloud or even request it for purposes of a temporary rest during the day. He won't let anyone advance his wheelchair one inch onto the handicapped ramp of that slippery slope. Even now, every single night, he still can't believe this is his reality. He's traded bed partners, beautiful women for a BiPAP. It's the worst monogamous relationship of his life. And they can never break up. Without the BiPAP at night, he might retain too much carbon dioxide in his sleep and suffer brain damage or suffocate and die.

He doesn't want to die.

He opens his mouth wide and closes it several times, regrettably sensing a new and unmistakable slackness in his jaw. And so it begins. Once the weakness ensues, there is no abortion, no retreating, only a relentless, insidious icy downward luge into paralysis. Soon, his jaw will hang open, ribbons of saliva will continually stream over his bottom lip, and he won't be able to talk. He frowns as he imagines this likely development, the impossible-to-mask spectrum from pity to disgust in Karina's and Bill's and every stranger's eyes when they look at him. He doesn't even want to face his piano like that.

When will this next irreversible insult be inflicted? Tomorrow? Next week? End of the month? This summer? The answer is yes.

He studies his hands that will never again look familiar to him, fingers that used to carry exquisite strength and agility, that a year and a half ago played eighty-seven pages of Brahms I without error. He misses playing Brahms, feeding himself lunch, scratching his nose, touching a woman, making Karina laugh. He apologizes to his beloved piano for abandoning it, to Karina for abandoning her, and he suddenly feels the cumulative weight of every single loss all at once like a concrete slab dropped onto his chest.

And he can't breath. Without the slab on his chest, every inhale was already an intended dive into open ocean, stopped dead in ankle-deep water. Now, suddenly, the tide has gone out. He's gasping, drowning on dry land. He can feel the adrenaline kick, the fight-or-flight animal instinct. This is life threatening. *More air now.* Yet, he can't run, and he can't fight, and he can't get more air now. He tries to use his next exhale to call for help, but he succeeds only in spitting. Karina's in the kitchen drinking coffee, and he's dying in the living room without notice.

Inhale. Exhale.

His body is seized, the tendons and muscles of his neck squeezing, shaking violently with effort. Each breath feels like drawing air through a thin, clogged straw. It feels like suffocating. Fear rises in his throat where oxygen should flow. He swallows, choking on it.

Breathe in. Breathe out.

Shallow sips. He's so hungry for air. His cells are literally starving for oxygen. Keep breathing.

He calls up what it took to master Rachmaninoff's Piano Concerto no. 3. Ten grueling hours every day, relentlessly focused, playing each movement over and over, fighting through excruciating physical pain and mental exhaustion until he could play the entire piece by memory and without error. Now his tenacity, his will, his purpose, is trained on breathing.

In. Out.

This is now his song to play. He is not this paralyzed body, these screaming lungs, this primal fear. He will be an instrument of breathing.

Breathe.

Again. Pull the air in. Push it out. Again. It's not enough. He's fatigued, strangled, starving for air, failing.

A few short and long months ago, playing piano was like breathing to him. Now breathing is breathing to him. His work. His purpose. His passion. His existence. He has to keep breathing.

He doesn't want to die.

CHAPTER THIRTY

Karina panicked and called 911. Richard was intubated in the ambulance by a woman with intensely focused blue eyes and a raised coffee-bean-brown mole above her right brow. He never lost consciousness and kept his eyes on hers while she worked on him. Insertion of the endotracheal tube was violently swift and invasive, and the gagging, discomforting pressure of the first few moments was quickly eclipsed by the massive relief of air moving in and out through his windpipe. Once in the ER at Mass General Hospital, someone drew blood, and he had a chest X-ray, which revealed pneumonia. A nurse ran an intravenous line of antibiotics, and he's now in the ICU with Karina, waiting for Kathy DeVillo.

Karina is standing next to him, over him, her arms crossed as if hugging herself, watching him intently, studying him, which worries him because he's not doing anything. He wonders what she's seeing. She looks scared.

The antibiotic fluid running through his veins is ice-cold. Despite staring at him like a specimen under a microscope, Karina doesn't seem to notice that his skin is covered in goose bumps. He wishes she'd lay a heavy blanket over him. His face itches where the tube is taped across his mouth, and he wants to ask Karina to scratch it for him. He tries to talk, but his effort is smothered, blotted out when it hits the impenetrable wall of hard plastic running the length of his throat. He cannot speak. He stares wide-eyed at Karina, sharing her fear.

With the BiPAP, he was still in charge of breathing. He initiated the inhales, and the machine assisted him, ensuring that the draws were deep, the exhales complete. As he watches his chest rise and fall, he realizes he's no longer involved. The ventilator is doing 100 percent of the work. He is being breathed. His fear dials up. His heart pounds as if running for its life. Yet his breathing is steady, untethered from his terrified heart and the blood accelerating through his cold veins.

Kathy DeVillo enters the room, wearing black yoga pants, a frumpy oversize gray sweater, a soft pink scarf, no jewelry, and no makeup. It's Sunday. He imagines her at home on her couch, watching a movie on Netflix when she was paged. He wishes he could apologize for bothering her like this. She stands on the other side of the bed, opposite Karina, and takes a noticeable moment before speaking. Her mouth is somber. Her eyes look into Richard's like peaceful warriors.

"Hi, Richard. Hi, Karina. So." Kathy sighs. "Here we are. I'm going to do a lot of talking. You ready?"

No one answers.

"Yes," says Karina.

Kathy gives Karina a close-lipped smile and then looks straight down into Richard's eyes, waiting a moment. He's afraid of what she's about to say. Although he's never heard the speech she's about to deliver, he knows what's coming. This train has been barreling toward him on a one-way track for fifteen months. And he's still not ready for it.

"So you know you've been emergently intubated, and you're in the ICU. My purpose today is to give you all the information I know. I'm your GPS, but you're still the driver of the bus, okay? I'm here to tell you, if you go right, this will happen. If you go

left, that will happen. You make the decision, but here are the consequences, okay?
Blink once for yes. Keep your eyes open for
no."

Richard blinks.

"If you hadn't been intubated and put on
a ventilator, you would've died. Falls,
significant weight loss, and pneumonia,
these are the three red flags of ALS. They
signify the disease escalating and failure to
thrive. When these happen, it tips you over
the cliff. About a month ago, your FVC was
around thirty-nine percent. The pneumonia
tipped you over. You weren't getting suf-
ficient oxygen, and you don't have enough
reserve. The choices now are to have the
tracheostomy surgery and stay on a vent or
to be extubated and terminally weaned."

She pauses. No one says anything. *Terminally weaned.* Does that mean what he
thinks it means? He can't ask.

"So let's look at the first choice. The
surgery. The general surgeon will say, 'Trach
surgery is no big deal,' and he's right. It's a
straightforward procedure. That's his tribe's
language, but it's not the language of ALS.
In terms of your psychological well-being,
this choice will change your life. It's a very
big deal. If you get the surgery, you will
need a *lot* of infrastructure to care for you."

She points her gaze at Karina, and Kathy's expression is high-definition clear. Karina would be the infrastructure.

"In theory, you can get trached and vented and live a normal life span. But you're going to need twenty-four-hour, seven-days-a-week, three-hundred-sixty-five-days-a-year ICU-level care. You either need to pay about four hundred thousand dollars a year for private nursing care, or you'll need at least two people willing to do this for you at home. This is required. You're in the ICU. Only certain specialized docs and nurses can care for you now. Unless a minimum of two people get extensive training to be your ICU nurses, we cannot let you go home because it wouldn't be safe. It's a 24-7-365, no-vacation job."

"What about long-term-care facilities? Could he go there?" asks Karina.

"There are three places in Massachusetts equipped to care for people with a tracheostomy on a ventilator, but there's about a one-year waiting list for a bed in any of these, and it's extremely expensive. Most insurances won't cover it. Yours doesn't cover it."

Richard watches Karina's face pale as she begins to absorb the dreadful ramifications of this choice.

"A trach is not a silver bullet. If you get this surgery and go on a vent, you are trading one can of worms for another. You're still getting a can of worms. This is not a cure, okay? It's important you understand this. The disease will continue to progress. You might eventually be locked in. All you're doing is protecting the airway."

"What happens if he doesn't get the surgery?"

Although Karina asked the question, Kathy delivers her answer to Richard. She never breaks eye contact.

"If you choose not to do the surgery, we'll either order a palliative-care consult here or you'll go home to Hospice. You'll be extubated to a BiPAP. They'll give you medication to keep you comfortable, and they'll slowly bring down the BiPAP machine. Your breathing will get shallower and shallower, and eventually you'll stop breathing on your own. You'll die of respiratory failure."

Death by suffocation. He's avoided imagining this in any detail, what the actual end of ALS might look like for him. Even with the need for the PEG tube and the BiPAP and the paralysis of his legs, despite every escalating loss in ability, thoughts of his death continued to be blurry and remote like a car racing by on a road in the distance, the make and model impossible to describe. Now the damn thing is parked right in front of him, and his heart is screaming, pounding, panicked. Again, his breathing remains calm, dictated by the ventilator, and the mismatch in physiology feels like a shattering earthquake in the foundation of his being. Like he's coming apart.

"Could the antibiotics clear the pneumonia and then he'd be like he was before this happened and breathe on his own?"

"This isn't a spinal-cord or lung injury. This is his diaphragm no longer working. It can't heal."

"But he was breathing earlier today. Couldn't this be just a momentary crisis and he could come off the vent and still breathe?"

"That's very unlikely. I see about three hundred people in your position every year. And in the twelve years I've been doing this, I've only seen that happen one time."

So there's a chance. But it's remote. And Kathy has had this horrific conversation over three thousand times. Richard wants to cry for both of them.

"If you were us, what would you do?"

"I'm not you, and even though I'm around it every day, I'll never know what it's like to have ALS. I don't know your finances or your relationship, so I really can't answer that. I will say this. If you choose the trach, every six months I'll ask you, 'When is enough enough for you?' In our experience, patients who go on the vent typically get pneumonia after pneumonia. The disease doesn't stop. Eye movements can be good for many years, but like I said, eventually he might be locked in."

"What do most people do?"

"About seven percent get vented."

"Why so few?"

"This is a very difficult, intimate decision. If Richard gets this surgery, assuming you're his caregiver, your quality of life is going to go way down. I don't care how kind or tough you are, you'll end up getting something called compassion fatigue. It's essentially PTSD."

Kathy waits, perhaps thinking that Karina will have another question. She's silenced. Kathy turns her attention back to Richard.

"In Massachusetts, if you decide to get the trach and later change your mind, you can elect to go off the ventilator in the hospital or at home with Hospice. How old is Grace again?"

"She's twenty," says Karina.

"She's in college, right?"

"Yes."

Richard blinks.

"If you wanted to see her graduate or get married, if you wanted to stick around a bit longer, some people choose to go on the vent for this one last thing and then elect to go off it."

Grace graduates in a little over two years. He'd like to see that. He'd like to see her get married. He'd like to meet his grand-children. He'd like to live.

Kathy sits on the edge of his bed so she's now closer to eye level and puts her hand on his. Her eyes are the color of deeply steeped black tea, tired and kind. Her hand is so blessedly warm and human.

"Are you afraid to die?"

He blinks.

"I'm sorry to be so blunt. Are you afraid of suffering at death?"

He blinks.

"What else are you afraid of?"

Letting go. Disappearing. Not existing. There is another fear, lurking in the shadows of his consciousness, but he can't identify it.

"I'm going to leave you and Karina with some information and a letter board. I know you haven't had to use one of these yet, and it'll be slow and frustrating, but it'll give you a way to express whatever you need to ask or say."

"How quickly do we have to make this decision?"

"I don't want you to make this decision today. Think on it and think of questions, and I'll be back tomorrow. He can't be intubated like this for very long. This decision can't happen over a week's time. It can't wait too long."

Kathy goes over how to use the letter board. Richard only half listens. He's more captured by the steady, rhythmic sounds of the ventilator, the push and pull of air forced in and out of him, the percussive music of his body being breathed. In. Out. In. Out. A clock ticking. Kathy finishes her tutorial.

"Okay, I'll be back tomorrow. So we're one hundred percent clear on the choices. Your choice is either to be extubated and most likely die, or you're getting the surgery and asking Karina to take care of you twenty-four/seven. You understand that these are your choices and the consequences of each?"

Richard blinks and doesn't look at Karina. He assumes she understands as well.

It's either his life or hers.

CHAPTER THIRTY-ONE

Standing at the end of a long line in the hospital cafeteria, Karina waits to pay for her second cup of coffee. She's in no hurry. The man in front of her is dressed in blue scrubs, carrying a tray of yogurt, granola, fruit, and orange juice. She's hungry, but the thought of food makes her nervous stomach turn. More coffee won't sit well in her either, but she needed something else to purchase, a reason to stay in the cafeteria, and coffee seemed like the simplest choice. She left Richard's room in the ICU yesterday evening and hasn't drummed up the nerve yet to return. She hasn't picked up that letter board. She doesn't know what he's thinking, what he wants to do. She hasn't asked him. She knows she has to. One more cup of coffee first.

If this were a movie, she'd have her hands over her eyes, her breath held, silently begging the woman waiting in line to pay for coffee not to go up to the ICU. If this were a book, she'd close it without turning the page. She doesn't want to know his decision.

She's such a coward. She didn't used to be. She used to be fearless. She left her family, her home, her country, when she was eighteen and never looked back. Where did that woman go? She wishes she could reclaim that courageous spirit who graduated with honors from a college in a foreign country and played piano in New York with the best jazz musicians in the city. Maybe she could start by being a woman who finishes her coffee, takes the elevator to the ICU, picks up that letter board, and finds out what happens next.

What if he wants the surgery?

She can't be his 24-7 caregiver. But there's no one else. His parents are dead. His brothers have jobs and wives and kids to raise. Private help is insanely expensive, and Richard's money is gone, already sunk into his care, the wheelchair, the lift, Grace's college. He can't ask Grace to do this for him. Karina won't let him.

He's not her husband anymore. She doesn't have to do this. He's not her burden to bear. She thinks of his affairs, of all the women he's slept with. Where are all these women now? Not in the hospital cafeteria. Not in the ICU. Not in her den every day for the rest of his life.

She thinks of the decade she spent lying to him, pretending to want more children, feigning disappointment every month, feeding him medically plausible reasons for her fictitious infertility, pretending to go to doctor appointments. The first coffee sours in her stomach, and she feels as if she could throw up.

He wanted more children. He especially wanted a son. Every month for years, he thought they were trying to conceive. She got an IUD when Grace was three and never told him. She was afraid to tell him the truth, that he wouldn't want her anymore, that he'd divorce her. And then where would she be? Disgraced and alone, a single mother to a preschooler, divorced and unemployed in a foreign country.

When Grace was thirteen, Karina went to her ob-gyn to have the IUD replaced. But it wouldn't come out. It had embedded in the wall of her uterus, and she needed surgery to remove it. Petrified of surgery, she confessed everything to Richard. Her decade of deception.

When she allows herself to remember that day, she's still haunted by the reaction on his face, his expression evolving from shock to grief to rage. The rage remained, burned into his features and probably his heart. It took them a year to separate and another two to get officially divorced, but their marriage was over the day she told him what she'd done.

He's never forgiven her. She doesn't blame him. Whatever his sins were, this one was entirely hers. Maybe caring for him on a vent for the next decade is what she deserves, penance for this unforgivable sin. Maybe that would finally absolve her.

If he says he wants the surgery, can she refuse to be his caregiver? She'd essentially be sentencing him to death. If he wants to live, who is she to say that he should die? Should she shut up and do whatever he wants, whatever it takes to keep him alive? An old but familiar resentment flares. Twenty years ago, he accepted that teaching position at New England Conservatory, made the decision to move them from New York to Boston without regard for her happiness, her freedom, her career. He stole the life she wanted from her. And here she is, all these years later, considering the real possibility of playing jazz again, and Richard still has the power to stop her.

She doesn't want to be sentenced to life

as his caregiver, a prisoner chained to his paralyzed body. What will he do? It's going to be a death sentence for one of them.

"Is that it?"

"Huh?" Karina looks up, baffled.

"Is it just the coffee?" asks the cashier.

"Oh, yeah. Sorry."

Karina pays and finds an empty seat at a table for two. She wraps her hands around the paper cup and brings her nose to the lip, inhaling the smell instead of drinking. She checks her phone, hoping for a text or email that will keep her busy. She has nothing.

She tries to imagine where Richard's head is at, to gamble on his decision. While his body is useless and essentially dead already, his mind, his intellect, his personality, are still perfectly intact. What would she do? She takes a sip of the coffee she doesn't want and knows her answer before she swallows. She wouldn't get the surgery. She wouldn't go on a vent. She wouldn't want anyone giving up his or her life to keep her alive. She wouldn't want to linger on like that, locked in, totally dependent on others for everything.

But Grace. She wouldn't want to leave her yet. What will Grace do after college? Who will she marry? What will her life look like?

Who is she going to be? Karina wants to know, to be here to see it all.

What if it's not forever? What if he chooses the surgery so he can see Grace graduate in two years, or he only needs caregiving for one more year until a bed becomes available in a facility? Could she do that? She stayed married to him, trapped in their broken relationship, persevering for at least ten years for the sake of Grace, appearances, her religion, and security. So she could do this for one or two years. But what if it's more? What if he wants to go on living at any cost?

She closes her eyes and prays, searching for the right thing to do. She opens her eyes and stares into her coffee, at the doctor reading his phone at the table across from her, at the cashier ringing up the next customer. No one and nothing have an answer for her.

Even Kathy couldn't tell them what to do. *The trach surgery is a horrible choice. I would never do that. I recommend extubation and death by suffocation at home with Hospice. That's the only way to go.* Karina wishes the decision were black-and-white like this. Instead, she and Richard have been thrown into the deep end of a gray ocean. There is no horizon, no North Star visible in the gray sky, only these impossible choices before them.

She sits until her coffee is stone cold, the cup still full. It's almost eleven o'clock. Time to face the music. She tosses her cup in the trash, rides the elevator to the ICU, and takes a deep breath before entering Richard's room.

The back of his bed is partially reclined, so he's sitting up. He's awake, looking at her with round, alert eyes. He looks smaller than he did yesterday, his emaciated body disappearing beneath the hospital sheets like a magic trick, the breathing tube and ventilation machine overwhelming his modest mass. The machine clicks and whirs, and Richard's chest forcefully rises and falls about every three seconds. She eyes the letter board on the table next to his bed and then quickly returns her gaze to Richard's chest, pretending she didn't notice it.

She tries to smile. "Has Kathy been here yet?"

He does nothing but stare wide-eyed back at her, and she wonders whether his lack of response means no, he didn't hear her, or he's ignoring her.

"Are you still waiting for Kathy?"

He blinks.

"Okay."

She could wait for Kathy to find out if he's made a decision. She doesn't have to ask him. Kathy can do it. That's Karina's plan. She sits in the visitor's chair next to his bed and intends to stay busy on her phone until Kathy appears. Karina scrolls through her newsfeed on Facebook without interest. She's sitting to his right, and Richard can't turn his head, but she can feel his eyes on her. She glances up, and his eyes lock onto hers, desperate, begging for communication.

"We're going to wait for Kathy, okay?"

He stares at her, unblinking.

"Do you want to tell me something before she gets here?"

He blinks.

Shit.

"Do you know what you want to do?"

He blinks.

Her stomach hollows out, and her heart beats in her throat. Reluctantly, slowly, she picks up the letter board. She turns back toward the door, trying to will Kathy's appearance. No one is there. She turns back to face Richard and holds up the letter board.

"Is the first letter in the first row?"

She waits. Nothing.

"Second row?"

He blinks.

"Is it *E*?"

"*F*?"

"*G*?"

"*H*?"

He blinks.

"*H.*"

"Is the second letter in the first row? . . . Second? . . . Third? . . . Fourth?"

He blinks.

"Fourth?"

He blinks.

"Is it *O*?"

He blinks.

"Okay, *H-O.* Is the third letter in the first row? . . . Second? . . . Third?"

He blinks.

"*M*?"

He blinks.

"*Home*?"

He blinks. A tear falls from his right eye. She pulls a tissue from her coat pocket and blots his face.

"You want to go home?"

He blinks.

But does that mean he wants to have the surgery and go home on a vent or be extubated and go home?

"Do you want the surgery?" she hears herself ask.

He stares at her, eyes wide, tears welling out of both now. He doesn't blink them away.

"You want them to take the tube out and go home?"

He blinks through wet eyes.

"My God, Richard. You understand what that means, right?"

He blinks, and she is simultaneously relieved and devastated. She bursts into tears, crying hard, alternately mopping his face and hers with the same pathetic tissue.

"I'm so sorry, Richard." She searches her pockets for another tissue, not finding one. "I'm so sorry. Do you want me to call Grace?"

He blinks.

"Okay. She'll be here. Who else? Your brothers?"

His eyes remain steady.

"Bill?"

He blinks.

"Trevor?"

He doesn't blink.

"Okay. Me, Grace, and Bill. Anyone else?"

He stares through his shiny, wet eyes straight into hers. She wipes her nose with the damp tissue and sniffs.

"Are you scared?"

He blinks.

"I am, too."

She sits on the edge of his bed and holds his bony, lifeless hand in hers. She pulls out her shirtsleeve and gently wipes the tears from his eyes and cheeks and then does the same to hers.

"Thank you," she whispers.

He blinks.

CHAPTER THIRTY-TWO

Grace still hasn't taken her coat off. She's standing at a remove from the end of his bed, her suitcase by her side. She arrived about an hour ago, coming straight from the airport. Her face is drawn, her eyes steeled, her expression flat and unfamiliar to him. She feels so far away. This is not her normal face. He wants to tell her to come closer and smile, an absurd request even if he could make it given the circumstances, but he wants to see her face the way he loves it most — bright eyes, rosy cheekbones perched high atop each side of an easy smile, happy. He supposes his face, unshaven with a tube inserted into his mouth and taped to his cheek, looks unfamiliar to her, as well.

Karina asked her many questions about classes and her boyfriend when Grace first arrived, but they've run out of conversation. Everyone in the room is quiet. Karina is sitting in the chair next to him, her arms crossed tight in front of her chest as if she's cold. She looks tired, serious, vaguely alert. Kathy is standing by the ventilator, reading something on her phone. Bill sits at the foot of the bed, rubbing Richard's feet and calves with his warm, strong hands. God bless Bill.

The sense of waiting is fog-thick, ominous, surreal. The moment feels important, urgent, yet absolutely nothing is happening. It's absurdly mundane.

A slender woman with a boyish haircut and many silver-studded earrings enters the room.

"Hello. Is this Richard?"

"Hi, Ginny," says Kathy. "Yes, this is Richard Evans. And this is his ex-wife, Karina; their daughter, Grace; and home health aide extraordinaire Bill. This is Ginny from Hospice."

Instead of shaking hands, she hugs everyone. She stands over Richard and places a hand on his shoulder. Her eyes are brown and without makeup, clear and calmly confident. She smiles in a way that feels natural and not at all inappropriate for the situation. There is no joy, no pity, no forced falseness in her gesture, and without words she communicates, *I'm here with you.* Richard wishes he could thank her.

"I'll let the doctor know that you're here," says Kathy, excusing herself from the room.

"Let's talk about a few things before the doctor comes. Our goal today is to get you comfortably home. The doctor is going to remove the endotracheal tube and switch you over to a BiPAP. We won't know until he does this, but if your breathing muscles are totally gone, the BiPAP won't be able to sustain your breathing. If that should happen, I'll administer morphine and a sedative through the IV line, so they'll take effect immediately. I'll be here to make sure that you feel calm. You won't struggle, and you won't feel like you're suffocating. And everyone will be right here with you. Does that sound okay?"

The mechanical ventilator breathes air into Richard's lungs. Then it draws air out. Absolutely nothing about what she just said sounds okay. He blinks. Karina holds his hand in hers. Bill squeezes his foot. Ginny, whom Richard had never seen before a minute ago, keeps her hand on his shoulder, and he's grateful, reassured by her presence and touch. This isn't her first rodeo.

Kathy DeVillo returns with Dr. Connors, a blue tie peeking out from beneath his buttoned white lab coat, a pen and a phone tucked in the front pocket, a stethoscope around his neck. He was clean shaven when Richard was first admitted to the ICU but now has the beginnings of a beard. He's been in and out, checking on Richard many times over the past three days.

"How we doing?" asks Dr. Connors.

Richard's trachea feels bruised, dry, and brutalized. His lips are painfully chapped. He's fixated on an obsessive desire to clear his throat and struggling to ignore an intense itch on the top of his head that seems intent on burrowing into his brain. And if things go sideways, he's going to die today.

"Are we waiting on anyone else?" asks Kathy.

Everyone looks to Richard. He doesn't blink.

"No," says Karina.

"Yes," says Ginny. "I've called for a music therapist."

"A what?" asks Karina.

"Someone to come and play guitar, something relaxing to keep Richard calm."

Richard raises his eyebrows in alarm, hoping Karina sees him.

"God no," says Karina. "No. Call him off."

"Are you sure?" asks Ginny.

"Positive. He'd detest that."

Richard blinks several times.

"I'll play something from my iPhone." Karina looks to Richard. "Mozart?"

He thinks. *No. Keep going.*

"Bach?"

He stares, unblinking.

"Schumann?"

He blinks.

"Okay."

She doesn't ask him which piece. He trusts that she knows. He watches her search. Then the music begins.

Of course, she knew. It's Schumann's Fantasie in C Major, op. 17, his greatest masterpiece, and Richard's favorite piece to play. He listens to the first few measures of the first movement and wonders.

"Yes, this is you, playing at Carnegie Hall," says Karina.

His mouth is immobilized, but his eyes are smiling. He blinks.

The serious business of what awaits them pauses as everyone listens. The first movement of this fantasy is dense and dreamy, a passionate lamentation, Schumann expressing his longing for his beloved Clara, separated from him by her father. Richard locks his eyes with Karina's as they listen, knowing she knows the meaning behind the composition, and his heart aches for her to know how grateful he is to her and how sorry he is. Even if he didn't have a tube in his throat, even if he weren't too tired and scared to use the letter board, even if it weren't too late and he could speak, he's not sure he could find the words big and true enough to heal what he's done to her.

He keeps his eyes with hers alone, willing the notes to speak for him, and he's swaddled in her gaze. Tears spill down his face. Karina squeezes his hand and nods.

The second movement changes mood abruptly. It's a majestic march, powerful, extroverted, bombastic, fast, and extremely difficult to play. Richard's professional career passes through his consciousness. Curtis, New England Conservatory, the prestigious concert halls and symphonies, the world-renowned conductors, the orchestras, the festivals, the solo recitals, the audiences, the standing ovations, the press and accolades. It was a beautiful life. It all went by so fast.

Dr. Connors checks Richard's vitals and explains what he's about to do.

"Are you ready?"

Richard looks to Grace. Bill notices and extends an arm, inviting her closer, inside their circle. She edges next to her mother.

"I'm here, Dad." Grace looks terrified. "I

love you."

Richard blinks, loving her back. He prays this isn't the last time he hears her say those words.

Dr. Connors positions himself over Richard's face and peels back the tape.

"Okay, on three. One, two, three."

Dr. Connors yanks hard on the end of the tube, and it slides up from inside Richard for a surprising length, a procedure as brutishly physical and indelicate as the tube's insertion. The tube is out, and everyone looks at Richard, waiting. No one, including Richard, is breathing.

He's playing the third movement now. The melody is solemn, a reconciliation. The Bi-PAP mask is placed over his face, and still there is no air. The ventilator is quiet. There is no sound but for Richard playing Schumann. His head begins to tingle as the room narrows. He stays focused on Grace and Karina and Bill and the music, and suddenly there are no boundaries between the vibrations of the notes and the people in this room. He doesn't want to leave them. He wants to keep listening, vibrating, breathing, being.

He wants a few more notes. Another movement. Just a bit longer. He doesn't want to die in the ICU.

His lungs call out to his diaphragm and the muscles of his abdomen, searching, pleading. He plays the final notes of Schumann's Fantasie, slower, softer, hopeful, a whispered prayer to God. Everyone in the room and Richard's lungs wait in stillness for an answer.

CHAPTER THIRTY-THREE

They've been home for three days now. With Richard's consent, Ginny weaned him off the BiPAP two days ago. His breathing is extremely shallow, but he's still going. Despite the shortness of his breath, he doesn't seem to be agitated or struggling. Ginny has him on regularly scheduled doses of morphine for any discomfort and Ativan for anxiety. He's sedated, in and out of consciousness, sleeping most of the time. Karina knows it's not right to think this way, but she keeps wondering how long he can go on.

When they arrived safely home, she and Bill rolled Richard's hospital bed into the living room so he could be next to his piano. Grace is camped on the couch with her bedding and pillow, still in her pajamas at dinnertime, typing a paper for school on her laptop. She's been sleeping on the couch, watching over her father day and night, waiting for the end. They're all waiting.

The house is eerily quiet. They haven't turned on the TV. Karina canceled her piano lessons for the week. She hasn't left the house in three days. They're existing outside of time, cocooned in the living room, unaware of world events, ears tuned in to the faint, intermittent sound of Richard still breathing.

It's not that Karina's needed at home. There's not much to do now. She's got cabin fever and would love to go for a morning walk with Elise, but she can't risk leaving the house. He might not even be conscious when it happens, but she feels she should be here. She owes that much to him. To both of them, maybe.

Ginny comes for a couple of hours each day to oversee things, to monitor Richard and administer his meds while she's here. She just left a few minutes ago. Bill comes in the evenings. He tends to Richard's body and keeps Karina company. He should be here in a couple of hours.

She checks the time. She'd normally feed Richard now. Instead, she delivers a syringe of water through Richard's PEG tube, then caps the MIC-KEY button. Two days ago, Richard was awake when Ginny was here. She asked him if he wanted to discontinue nutrition. He blinked. She asked him if he wanted to discontinue the BiPAP. He blinked.

He has pneumonia and is no longer being treated for it. His 110-pound, paralyzed body is pumped full of morphine and Ativan. He hasn't eaten in two days. Yet, part of him is still holding on.

"I'm going to take a shower," says Grace.

"Okay, honey."

Karina sits in the wing chair positioned next to Richard's bed. She studies his face while he sleeps. His cheeks are sunken beneath his speckled beard. No one has shaved him since he was rushed to the hospital six days ago. His lips are cracked and scabbed. His hair and eyelashes are black and beautiful.

He exhales. She waits and waits. She wonders and leans in. He inhales. How does he still have the strength to keep breathing?

She puts her hand on top of his. His hand is bony and cold, unresponsive to her touch, the skin mottled, pooling with blood. This disease is hideous. No one should have to go through this.

"I'm so sorry, Richard. I'm so sorry." She starts crying. "I'm so sorry."

At first, her apology is purely about the unfairness and horror of having ALS, but as she keeps crying and repeating herself, the meaning of her apology changes. She moves to the edge of the wing chair and lowers her head closer to his ear.

"I'm sorry, Richard. I'm sorry I denied you the family you wanted. I'm sorry I deceived you. I should've had the courage to tell you the truth. I should've set you free to live the life you wanted with someone else. I'm sorry I stopped being the woman you fell in love with. I pushed you away. I know I did. I'm sorry."

She watches his face as she thinks, searching the darkened hallways of their history for any more boxed-up, unspoken words. She finds none. Her tears subside. She pulls a tissue from the box on the side table, wipes her eyes, and blows her nose. She takes a deep breath and sighs, and the unexpected noise that leaves her is low and anguished, a howl. She inhales again and feels twenty years lighter.

"We did the best we could, right?"

She waits, listening to him breathe. She returns her hand to his and scans his face for any sign of responsiveness. She can't know if he's asleep or knocked unconscious on high doses of Ativan or in a coma. He doesn't open his eyes. She searches for even an incidental, involuntary twitch in a facial muscle that she can interpret. He's still. He can't squeeze her hand. She can't know if he heard her.

"I wish I'd done better."

"Everything okay?" asks Grace.

Karina turns around. Grace is standing at the bottom of the stairs in a maroon University of Chicago sweatshirt, black leggings, and slippers, wet hair pulled up in a ponytail. Karina can't tell by her posture or expression if Grace heard any of Karina's confessions or crying.

"Everything's the same. You hungry?"

"No."

As if in solidarity with her father, Grace hasn't eaten anything since yesterday. Grace settles herself back on the couch. The day is fast turning to night, and darkness invades the living room. Grace's face is illuminated by her laptop screen like a flashlight. Karina stands, intending to turn on a lamp, but, once up, walks over to the piano instead.

She sits down and places her fingers on the keys. Without thinking, she begins playing Chopin's Nocturne in E-flat Major, op. 9, no. 2. The melody is gentle, relatively easy, and delicious to play, like comfort food. She loves the freedom the piece gives her with the tempo, the glassy trills, the decorative tones. The melody evokes sense memories of her mother's pierogi, a gentle rain outside her dorm window at Curtis, dancing a waltz with Richard in New York. The piece builds, its crescendo a passionate embrace, then tumbles into trickling water, thrown confetti, a return home, safe, held.

She plays the final tender note, and the sound floats throughout the room before disappearing, a sweet memory. She turns around and is surprised to see Grace up from the couch, sitting in the wing chair. Her eyes are glossy, wet with tears. At first, Karina assumes Grace was moved by Chopin's nocturne. But then Karina listens.

She keeps listening. She waits and holds her breath, straining to hear an inhale. The room remains quiet. She waits past the point of knowing, to be sure.

He's gone.

EPILOGUE

Karina's standing in the den, an empty cardboard box in her hands. It's been eight days since Richard died. She's been avoiding this room.

Bill brought boxes for Richard's clothes. She's donating them to Goodwill. She stands without moving, observing all the equipment that was part of her every day for months, now abandoned, historical relics. The hospital bed, the wheelchair, the Hoyer lift, the suction machine, the cough-assist machine, the BiPAP, the piss bottle, the pivot disc. She's offering those and anything she might be forgetting to Caring Health.

She places the box on the floor but doesn't know where to begin. The room feels strange without Richard in it. She supposes it will go back to being the den after she clears everything out, but she can't imagine that. He lived in this room for only four months, but it no longer feels like her den. Richard had ALS in this room. She looks at his empty bed, the wheelchair, his desk chair, and feels his energetic impression everywhere, this room still thick with intense memories of Richard and his ALS. Her eyes well, and she rubs the goose bumps on her arms. Or he's decided to haunt her.

She sits down at his desk and swivels in the chair. Maybe Grace will want his computer. She went back to school yesterday. She seems to be doing okay. It's good she has classes and her friends and a demanding schedule to give her life structure, to keep her moving forward.

The house is quiet again. No more whirring of the BiPAP, no alarms sounding when the mask goes askew, no more coughing, gagging, choking. Those sounds are done and gone. Richard is gone.

What will she do now? She feels the familiar void, like something heavy and queasy sinking in her stomach, as if she's eaten something gone bad. Should she resume her piano lessons? Or should she pack up the entire house and move to New York? Her heart races, nervous at the daring thought of it. She swivels in her chair, not settling on an answer.

Maybe packing up Richard's clothes is

enough for right now. She sighs and doesn't move off the chair. Instead, she checks her email on her phone. At the top of her inbox is an email from Dr. George. She opens it.

Dear Karina,
I'm so sorry about Richard. I enjoyed getting to know him, if only briefly. I know you said he decided on using a computer-synthesized voice when the time came instead of banking his own. Well, I double-checked the recorder I lent you before wiping it and giving it to another patient, and there was a single legacy message on it that you'll want. I've attached it for you here.

Be well,
Dr. George

She hesitates, then taps on the attached MP3 file.

"Hi, Ka-ri-na. I-like-tha Doc-to-Geor calls-thi-sa le-ga-cy me-ssa. I-been-thi-king a-lot a-bou wha-my le-ga-cy will-be. Will-i-be-my pi-a-no ca-reer? Or-Grace? Tha-sa-be-tter one.

"May-be-iss this. Wha-I-have to-say to-you.

"Ka-ri-na. I'm-sor-ry. I'm-sor-ry I-chea-ted o-nyou. I'm-sor-ry I'm-the-rea-son you-sto-pla-ying jazz. I-was-a te-rri-ble hus-ba to-you. You de-ser be-tter.

"If-I-ha-da wish fo-my-le-ga-cy, ih-wou-be this. You-are-so ta-len-ted. You-are-sti-young. You-are-hea-thy. You-have e-ve-ry-thing you-nee.

"Go-to New-York. Play-jazz. Live-your-life. Be-ha-ppy."

She sits still in the chair, amazed to be hearing Richard's voice again, stunned by his message, these words she's always wanted, needed. She plays it again, and the sick feeling in her stomach dissipates. Her heart is pounding, awake, excited. She plays it again, and his words release the last of her grip on twenty years of blame and resentment, of being right at any cost. The cost has been astronomical.

A plan for her future forms as she listens, determined thoughts that sound pitch-perfect in her mind's ear, a composition of notes she's been wanting to play her whole life. She's going to pack up this room, and then she's going to need more boxes. But first, she plays his message again, grateful to hear the sound of his voice, forgiving him, feeling his presence in this room and in his words, knowing she, too, is forgiven, free.

LISA'S CALL TO ACTION

Dear Reader,

Thank you for reading *Every Note Played*. Maybe prior to reading this book you read *Tuesdays with Morrie,* watched *The Theory of Everything,* or dumped a bucket of ice water over your head. You probably had some awareness of ALS. I hope you now have a deeper understanding of what it feels like to live with this disease.

I also hope you'll join me in putting that empathy into action. By making a donation to ALS care and research, *you* can be part of the progress that will lead to treatments and a cure and help provide proper care to the people who desperately need it now.

Please take a moment, go to www.Lisa Genova.com, and click on the "Readers in Action: ALS" button to make a donation to ALS ONE, an extraordinary organization determined to deliver a treatment or cure for ALS and dedicated to offering improved care now. For more information on ALS ONE, go to www .ALSONE.org.

Thank you for taking the time to get involved, for turning your compassionate awareness into action. Let's see how amazingly generous and powerful this readership can be!

With love,
Lisa Genova

ACKNOWLEDGMENTS

This book began with Richard Glatzer, who, along with his husband, Wash Westmoreland, wrote and directed the film *Still Alice.* Richard had bulbar ALS, which means that his symptoms began in the muscles of his head and neck. I never heard the sound of Richard's voice. He brilliantly codirected *Still Alice* by typing with one finger on an iPad.

Richard, I am forever grateful to you for all you gave to the creation of the film *Still Alice,* for sharing with me what it feels like to live with ALS, for showing us all what grace and courage look like, for not giving up on your dreams. Richard died on March 10, 2015, shortly after Julianne Moore won the Oscar for Best Actress for her role in the film.

I met Kevin Gosnell, his wife, Kathy, and his sons, Jake and Joey (and later Scott), shortly after Kevin was diagnosed with

ALS. Within minutes of knowing him, I knew three things:

1. Before ALS takes him, Kevin is going to change the world.
2. He's also going to change me.
3. I love this man and his family.

Right after Kevin's devastating diagnosis, he framed his terrifying situation in the most selfless way I can imagine. He thought, "How can what I'm about to go through serve others?" He then gathered the best people in medicine, science, and care and formed ALS ONE, an extraordinary collaboration determined to discover a treatment or cure for ALS while promising the best possible care to people living with ALS now. I invite you all to learn more about Kevin's important legacy at ALSONE.org and get involved. Kevin passed away on August 8, 2016.

Thank you, Kevin, for inviting me into your home, for sharing your life and family with me. I owe so much of my understanding of ALS to you. But beyond that, you were simply one of the best human beings I've ever known — your generosity and grace; your loving leadership; your unwavering sense of purpose, of contribution to the world beyond yourself; the life lessons you gave to your boys, which I now give to my children; the enormous love you shared with your family and everyone who came into your life. I always felt like part of your family in your home. I love and miss you. I hope I've made you proud.

I met Chris Connors at the ALS clinic at Massachusetts General Hospital six days after his ALS diagnosis. I was struck by how calm and laugh-out-loud funny he was given his situation. I adored him immediately and asked if we could stay in touch. We spent the next many months corresponding by email. His "ALS Diary" was intimate, vulnerable, heartbreaking, and hilarious. I laughed and cried through most of his emails.

Chris, thank you for sharing your humor, how much you loved Emily and your boys, your fears, your courage, and so many specifics of dealing with the losses that come with ALS. I feel incredibly lucky to have known and loved you. Chris died on December 9, 2016. I encourage you all to Google his obituary.

I met Chris Engstrom at his parents' house on Cape Cod. He was my age, handsome, scrawny, his strangled voice mostly unintelligible. He was an artist educated at

Yale and loved hiking in the woods, but he could no longer walk or hold a paintbrush in his hands. The hiking boots on his paralyzed feet broke my heart. But he could raise his eyebrows to say yes, and he could still communicate — at first using a rollerboard strapped to his arm, his hand placed by someone else onto a computer mouse, later with only his eyes using a Tobii. He had a beautiful smile and a twinkle in his eyes — I'm pretty sure he was flirting with me.

Chris became my dear friend. Thank you, Chris, for sharing your fears and frustrations and anger, your hopes and beliefs and love. I'm in awe of your artwork and poetry. I'm still envious of your writing! Thank you for reading the first many chapters of this book, for offering me insights and spot-on feedback, for not letting me get lazy with even one word. I love and miss you. Chris Engstrom died on May 7, 2017.

Enormous gratitude also goes to Bobby Forster, Steve Saling, Sue Wells, Janet Suydam, David Garber, Arthur Cohen, Chip Fanelli, and Lawrence Jamison Hudson. Thank you for your generosity and trust, for sharing your experiences and perspectives, for helping me understand ALS for this book, and for sharing wisdom beyond the pages of this story.

Thank you, Kathy Gosnell, Rebecca Brown George, Casey Forster, Ginny Gifford, Joyce Siberling, Jamie Heywood, Ben Heywood, and Sue Latimer, for so generously sharing your experiences with ALS. Your love and support for your husbands, brother, and friend are extraordinary and inspiring.

Thank you, Dr. Merit Cudkowicz, Dr. James Berry, and Darlene Sawicki, NP, for allowing me to shadow you at the ALS clinic at Massachusetts General Hospital, for answering every question I asked, for helping me understand the clinical picture of ALS. It would be easy to imagine a team such as yours needing to build emotional walls. There is no cure for this disease. You witness too much heartbreak, loss, and death. I'm utterly amazed by all of you, so grateful for the kindness, dignity, and humanity you give to every patient, every day, above and beyond the call of pure medical care. You are all heroes.

And then there is Ron Hoffman. Ron is the founder and executive director of Compassionate Care ALS, an organization that provides much-needed guidance, equipment, and comfort to overwhelmed families traveling this unfamiliar, complex, difficult journey. He is an angel and a hero, and I'm beyond grateful to call him my dear friend. He is also the author of *Sacred Bullet.* Everyone should read this important book. Ron, thank you for inviting me into your world, for the many road trips and house calls, for showing me this beautiful work that you do, for teaching me so much about ALS, living, and dying. You are a gift to every person who is lucky enough to know you, including me. For more information on Compassionate Care ALS, go to www.c-cals.org.

Thank you to Erin MacDonald Lajeunesse, Kristine Copley, and Julie Brown Yau of Compassionate Care ALS and Rob Goldstein of ALS TDI for sharing what you know about caring for people with ALS and for introducing me to people who have it. Thank you to John Costello for showing me all the fascinating, creative tools people with ALS can use to continue communicating as they become increasingly paralyzed. Thank you for all that you do to help people with ALS stay connected, for preserving their voices. Thank you to Kathy Bliss for helping me understand the important role of Hospice and palliative care.

Thank you, Abigail Field and Monica Rizzio for the wonderful piano lessons. For insights into classical piano, jazz piano, and life as a concert pianist, enormous thanks to Abigail Field, David Kuehn, Dianne Goolkasian Rahbee, Jesse Lynch, and Simon Tedeschi.

Thanks and love to Anabel Pandiella, John Genova, Louise Schneider, and Joe Deitch for taking me to piano concerts; to Gosia Mentzer and Anna O'Grady for answering many questions about Poland; to Jen Bergstrom, Alison Callahan, and Vicky Bijur for your insightful edits and for championing this story.

Love and gratitude to my team of early readers: Anne Carey, Laurel Daly, Mary MacGregor, Kim Howland, Kate Racette, and Danny Wallace. Thank you for reading the chapters as I wrote them, for going on this ALS journey with me, for your unwavering love and support.

Thanks and so much love to Sarah Swain, James Brown, Joe Deitch, Merit Cudkowicz, Ron Hoffman, and Kathy Gosnell for reading the manuscript and offering invaluable feedback.

AUTHOR'S NOTE

In May 2017, about the same time that I finished the final draft of this book, the FDA approved a new drug for the treatment of ALS. Radicava became available by prescription to patients in August 2017, as this book goes to press. Administration will be by intravenous infusion in twenty-eight-day cycles and cost $1,000 per infusion. We don't yet know whether insurance will cover this. In a trial in Japan, Radicava slowed a decline in physical symptoms by 33 percent.

ABOUT THE AUTHOR

Acclaimed as the Oliver Sacks of fiction and the Michael Crichton of brain science, **Lisa Genova** is the *New York Times* bestselling author of *Still Alice, Left Neglected, Love Anthony,* and *Inside the O'Briens. Still Alice* was adapted into an Oscar-winning film starring Julianne Moore, Alec Baldwin, and Kristen Stewart. Lisa graduated valedictorian from Bates College with a degree in biopsychology and holds a PhD in neuroscience from Harvard University. She travels worldwide speaking about the neurological diseases she writes about and has appeared on *The Dr. Oz Show, Today, PBS NewsHour,* CNN, and NPR. Her TED talk, What You Can Do To Prevent Alzheimer's, has been viewed over 2 million times.